52070

D0349696

OTHER GREAT EPISODES BY ANN RINALDI

A RIDE INTO MORNING
The Story of Tempe Wicke

A BREAK WITH CHARITY
A Story About the Salem Witch Trials

ANN RINALDI

GULLIVER BOOKS

HARCOURT BRACE & COMPANY

San Diego   New York   London

CHAPTER 2

the *Fifth of* MARCH

A   S T O R Y   O F   T H E   B O S T O N   M A S S A C R E

Requests for permission to make copies of any part of the work should be
mailed to Permissions Department, Harcourt Brace & Company,
8th Floor, Orlando, Florida 32887.

Library of Congress Cataloging-in-Publication Data
Rinaldi, Ann.
The Fifth of March: a story of the Boston Massacre/Ann Rinaldi.
p.   cm.
"Guilliver books."
Summary: Fourteen-year-old Rachel Marsh, an indentured servant in
the Boston household of John and Abigail Adams, is caught up in the
colonists' unrest that eventually escalates into the massacre of
March 5, 1770.
ISBN 0-15-200343-6 (hc) ISBN 0-15-227517-7 (pbk.)
1. Boston Massacre, 1770—Juvenile fiction. [1. Boston Massacre,
1770—Fiction. 2. Indentured servants—Fiction. 3. Adams family—
Fiction. 4. United States—History—Colonial period, ca.
1600–1775—Fiction.] I. Title.
PZ7.R459Fi   1993
[Fic]—dc20   93-17821

Designed by Lisa Peters
First edition
A B C D E
Printed in Hong Kong

For Phillip John,

my second grandson,

who has the world in his smile

and the stars in his eyes

Acknowledgments

NO HISTORICAL NOVELIST works alone. I owe a debt of thanks to the researchers and the writers of the many books I used to study Boston and its inhabitants in this exciting era. However, the books listed in the bibliography are only the most recent chapter of my education about the American Revolution.

I have been a student of Colonial America for years, and my education has been ongoing. My research includes all the historical reenactments I did with my family in the years of the Bicentennial, from 1976 through the 1980s. In these living history encampments, done with the Brigade of the American Revolution, I learned my history hands-on: I made the clothing, cooked the food, slept in the tents, and learned the dances, songs, philosophy, and lifestyle of the people of the times.

It goes without saying, then, that my first debt

is to my son, Ron, who introduced me to reenacting and to American history, who inspired me, and whose extensive library on American and military history is always at my disposal.

For this particular book, heartfelt appreciation goes to Vincent M. Kordack, supervisory parks ranger at Boston National Historical Park in Boston, Massachusetts, for his advice and for supplying me with additional reading material and maps pertaining to Boston in 1770.

Further appreciation goes to Ann Curran, from the Oakland Historical Society in Oakland, New Jersey, for her research of the clothing illustrated on the book cover. Ann, a dear friend, is clothing consultant for the Brigade of the American Revolution.

I am also grateful to my family, for nurturing the novelist in their midst: to my husband, Ron, for accompanying me on research visits and listening to my problems; and to my daughter, Marcella Loureiro, for the brightness and normalcy she brought into our lives by presenting us with our second grandson while I was writing this book.

Thanks, also, to my agent, Joanna Cole, who always listened, and to my editor at Harcourt Brace, Karen Grove, for being so receptive to my ideas and giving me so much leeway in my creativity.

—Ann Rinaldi

the Fifth of March

Chapter One

IN THE TERRIBLE hot days of that June, Jane and I went to see the lion they had on board the sloop *Phoenix* at Long Wharf. We took Nab with us. She was almost three, and that morning I'd dressed her all in white with a blue ribbon tied around the waist of her ruffled skirts.

"See 'ion," Nab kept saying as she clutched my hand with her little one. She couldn't say the letter "l" yet. She could say a lot of things, however, and was especially fond of nursery rhymes. She tripped along between us, chatting constantly.

"She's such a serious little baggage," I told Jane.

"We women have to be serious," Jane said. "Someday soon we're going to have as much say in matters as men. So we must practice."

Jane said things like that all the time, though she was the least serious person I'd met since coming to Boston in April. Jane loved good times. I'd met her in the fresh fruit stall in Faneuil Hall a week after we arrived. We got to talking about the price of lemons, and in the first five minutes I found out she was maidservant to Sarah Welsteed, who was sister to the Chief Justice of Massachusetts Bay Colony, Thomas Hutchinson.

Jane was seventeen and proud of her position. I was fourteen.

"Who are you bound to?" she'd asked, right out.

"John and Abigail Adams, from Braintree. He's a lawyer. Her husband says she's descended from many shining lights in the colony."

"But you're not proud of your position."

"Why would I be? I'm indentured, just like you."

She bit into an apple. "Be proud," she said. "The day is coming when all us common people will be."

Jane had a way about her. She was saucy and sure of herself, not like any indentured servant I'd known. She always acted like she was privy to some secret that the rest of the world didn't know about yet.

But after only two months in Boston, I realized that most everybody I met was like Jane. Not only the gentry, but the common folk, from the boys who ran with the street mobs to the men who drove the carts up from the ships to deliver their wares. They were different from common folk in Braintree.

"Be proud," Jane said again, "and be ready to take your opportunity when it comes."

"What opportunity?" I asked.

Her smile was knowing. "It will come one of these days," she said, "and we must all be ready for it."

I felt left out of the conversation. But that was my way. I always felt left out. Everyone else was ahead of me, always playing at some game, it seemed, the rules of which I still had to learn. But as soon as I learned the rules, they always seemed to change them.

But I'd caught on to this much. The common folk in Boston *were* different. It was as if they were waiting for something to happen. You could see it in their faces. Their eyes were bright and hard, their manner cocky. The most lowly scullery maid had that air about her, the roughest street urchin. They all scurried about as if on some important mission, acting as if they had a part in what was about to happen.

But what *was* about to happen? Was I getting fancy notions, living in Boston? Uncle Eb had warned me about that.

On our way to see the lion that morning, I

confided in Jane. "Nobody's humble in Boston," I said. "Why?"

We were on Long Wharf, which ran half a mile into the harbor. Jane stopped. People scurried by, talking, whistling, bargaining at the stalls.

"You don't know?" Jane asked.

I felt ashamed, like I'd missed something again, something that was right before my eyes. "Uncle Eb always said I was flighty. He was always on me to pay mind to things," I confessed.

"You said he doesn't like you, no matter what you do."

"He doesn't. He hasn't even bothered to ask after me since I've come here."

"Rebellion," she said.

"What?"

"Rebellion, that's what's on the minds of all these common folk."

Oh, that. "You mean the trouble because of the taxes on tea, glass, paper, and painters' colors?"

"Yes, that. The Townsend Acts. People are just as fired up as they were when they had the trouble with the stamps. You should have been here then! A mob wrecked Hutchinson's mansion that time. The Crown almost brought troops in."

We commenced walking. "Boston's like a keg of powder about to explode right now," Jane said. "Of course, Boston's always been that way. But now folks don't like the way the Crown has anchored that warship at our docks, without a by-your-leave. I tell you, it's not a good sign. It's trouble."

Jane saw trouble behind every bush. She was speaking of the *Romney*. It had slipped into the harbor the first week in June, with its big guns aimed right at the town. A British warship! Mr. Adams said that from his bed he could hear the boatswain's high whistle calling the sailors to life in the morning.

"You must pay more mind to things," Jane advised. "We're right in the middle of everything here in Boston. I keep my eyes and ears open and learn a lot working for my mistress. You should, too, living in *that* house."

"Keep my eyes and ears open for what?" I asked.

"So you can decide which side you'll favor."

I studied her haughty profile as we walked. Jane had taught me a lot of things: my way around the winding streets, how to bargain for things in Faneuil Hall, how to get down to the docks early to get the freshest fish. She'd even let me watch her fix her mistress's hair so that I could make Mrs. Adams fashionable when she went out.

I would have been lonely if not for Jane. She was the only friend I had, outside the house. But

I was becoming sensible of the fact that she had a secret life. I knew, by then, that on her days off she ran with a considerable rough crowd, nameless friends from Gray's Ropewalk Works.

I knew she frequented coffeehouses by the docks. And that one of her friends was Captain Ebenezer Mackintosh, who was twenty-eight and a shoemaker. But he was also leader of Boston's South End Gang.

Jane was becoming more and more brazen as the weeks went by. The words she was speaking that morning were not hers. She was parroting somebody, I decided. Most likely Mackintosh.

"Why should I choose sides?" I asked.

"You'll have to. Everyone will. The Crown or the Patriots."

"Oh, them."

"Yes, them."

"Gangs," I said. The Patriots wanted liberty. I'd heard Mr. Adams reading some letters to his wife from the *Boston Gazette* about this liberty. It sounded more like outright treason to me.

A few times Dr. Joseph Warren, the Adamses' family physician, had stopped by and asked Mr. Adams to go to meetings held by the Patriots and harangue the mob into action. Mr. Adams had said no. He would go to no meetings. He believed in the written word and the law. If the Patriots needed legal papers written, he'd write such papers, but he would go to no meetings.

Dr. Warren's handsome face had gone sad when Mr. Adams said that. I much admired Dr. Warren, not because he was the most handsome man in town, so much so that I went hot and cold every time I ushered him into the house. But because he seemed a man who knew what he was about and believed in it.

But I admired Mr. and Mrs. Adams, too. Their house on Brattle Street was calm and orderly. They would allow none of the fury on Boston's streets in that house, though it was in the middle of much activity and clients were always banging the door clapper.

I felt safe in that house. And when I brought clients into Mr. Adams's law office, I'd sense that whatever was wrong in the outside world could be made right in that office.

Never mind about mobs and meetings, acts that put taxes on tea, paper, glass. Something told me the rules for making things right were in that office. Inside Mr. Adams's many books that stood like soldiers on his shelves, all gussied up in good leather coats with gold trimmings.

So many books! All Mr. Adams had to do was look inside them and he could come up with an answer to anybody's problems.

It followed, then, that if a person read books, one didn't have to attend meetings where mobs screamed foul words. Neither did one have to threaten others. Or choose sides.

Mrs. Adams read books, too. She had her own. No woman I'd ever known had done that. And she had women friends who read. Like the beautiful and fancy Mrs. Mercy Otis Warren, no relation of the doctor, but wife of James, the representative from Plymouth and sister of James Otis, a famous young lawyer.

Mrs. Warren came to call wearing green taffeta and lace. Or crimson silk. She not only read books, she wrote plays. Never had I heard of a woman doing such a thing! And people listened to her so carefully when she spoke.

There must be some secret power to the words in books, I decided. But was it only for the highborn and well-bred? Or could I learn some of it, too?

It had been on my mind, of late, to ask Mrs. Adams that question. I'd decided that's where the real power was. And that was the side I wanted to favor.

But I could not tell Jane this. So I took the conversation the way she wanted it. "Which side will you favor, Jane?"

"Well, as I see it, the Crown's never done twopence for folks like us. And my mistress said the other day that her brother, Hutchinson, is going to break down the spirit of rebellion. I don't like that, I can tell you."

It was all she would say at the moment. So I didn't press her. I knew there were things she could not divulge, matters she was involved in that I honestly did not want to know about.

"Oh, Lordy," she said then. "Look at that line to get on the *Phoenix*. Well, we'll just have to wait. Would you like an ice, Nabby? There's a stall over there. How about you, Rachel?"

She went off to get us some ices. I stood holding Nabby's hand and pondering Jane's words. I must have looked melancholy when she returned, for she smiled.

"You don't have to take sides today," she teased.

"I don't care about sides," I told her.

"And why not?" She studied me. "What do you want out of life, Rachel Marsh? You've never said. You're fourteen. It's time you knew."

Nobody had ever asked me that before. So I'd never had to ponder it. But I did then. And I was surprised I was able to provide her with an answer.

"For the moment I want a proper dowry," I said. "The Adamses said they'd dower me."

"And after the moment?"

"To marry and find my place in the world. I

9

want a place of my own." The words seemed right, once I said them.

"You mean a house?"

"No." How could I explain? "I want a place. It has to do with the kind of person I want to be. And how I fit in to everything. I want people to listen when I open my mouth. And know I'm worth listening to."

She stared at me. "That's all?"

To me it was not all, it was everything. I wanted to have my place, like Abigail Adams and Mercy Warren. But I couldn't say that to Jane. She only understood things you could see and hold and own. I was not sure I understood myself.

"I want to be free of my uncle Eb. And never have anyone treat me the way he treated my mother," I finished.

She understood that. "There are people all around you who think England's treating us like your uncle Eb treated your mother," she said.

I nodded.

"That's what all these people in Boston want," she said. "To be free of the Uncle Eb in their lives. To most of them that Uncle Eb is the mother country."

I said nothing. Such words frightened me. They were treason, nothing less. And Jane should know better than to go about saying them.

We said no more about the subject. We saw the lion that day. We had to stay in line half an hour. Nabby loved it, although it was only sleeping in its cage and looked very old and lazy. The ship's master had brought it back from Africa.

Jane said it reminded her of the colonies. That they were a sleeping lion. I decided to be careful about telling her what went on in the Adams household. And not to mention at home anything she said. I didn't want to hurt my position.

When we parted she looked at me in that shrewd way of hers. "Go right home, this day," she said. "Don't loiter."

Her hand was on my arm. I met her eyes. They were unblinking. And it came to me then.

There is going to be some trouble this day, I told myself. *And Jane knows of it.*

I felt it in my bones.

I just stared at her. She withdrew her hand and smiled. "It's hot. You should get Nabby home. Don't loiter."

"Yes," I said. I took Nabby by the hand and drew away. Jane smiled at me, weakly. A chill went through me, and I began to rush in the direction of King Street. "Come along, Nabby. Your mama is waiting." My heart was beating fast.

11

Chapter Two

IT WAS CHRISTOPHER SNIDER who told me what the trouble was. Snider, who ran with the gangs of noisy boys always out for trouble on the streets, was fourteen and the son of a poor German immigrant.

I'd met him because, somehow, he knew Jane. I had never asked how. Mayhap I should have.

He darted in front of a fish vendor's cart on sighting us. At the same moment Boston's bells began to ring, those of Christ Church, New North, and King's Chapel, all at the same time.

"Ho! Rachel Marsh! Have you seen Jane?"

"I just left her at the wharf. Why are the bells ringing?"

Everyone in Boston knew the bells rang for fire, for funerals, and to announce the opening and closing of the markets. And they rang for riots. All the signals were different, and I was just starting to learn them.

Now they rang for a riot.

People were rushing past us, grabbing children by the arms. I saw a milk-and-butter vendor darting into an alley, heard doors slamming shut, locks bolted.

Chris wiped his nose with his sleeve. "Fight. Between the sailors from *Romney* an' our people."

"Why?" I asked.

"You mind, how last month John Hancock's *Liberty* came into port with all that wine?"

I knew the story. The Adamses had discussed it. John Hancock was one of New England's richest merchants, who had long since gone from the side of the Crown to the Patriots. He was so angry over the Townsend Acts that he said he would suffer no customs officers to board any of his incoming ships. Once he'd had his men carry such officials off one of them.

"Last month he locked the man from customs in a compartment below deck," I recited proudly, "and wouldn't let him out until the wine was unloaded. Then the man was warned to say nothing of the wine or what happened."

"You know a lot. For a girl," he allowed.

I felt pride. "What's happened?"

"Seems the customs man's tongue got loose. The Crown put out an order to seize the *Liberty*. Sailors from the *Romney* sent a boat with armed men. They cut *Liberty* from her moorings. Some of

13

our people got wind and were on the wharf. They threw stones. Hit some of the lobsterback sailors, but they pulled the *Liberty* anyways!"

Chris was out of breath. "They say Hancock's to be arrested for smuggling! Our people don't take kindly to that. Last I saw they wuz draggin' a customs boat up Fish Street. Gotta find Jane. She knows where Mackintosh is. We need him!" He stopped talking, wide-eyed with the possibilities of it all.

"You'd best get the little one home," he said. Then he ran off.

I didn't say anything to Mrs. Adams when I entered the house. I would not break the peace in that place. They treated me well. My job was to care for the children. I didn't have to cook. Sukey, the nigra girl, did that and the cleaning. A woman came to do the washing and ironing. Luke took care of the yard and stoop, hauled out the ashes, fetched wood, cared for Mr. Adams's horse, and polished his boots. I served guests tea or cider and helped Mrs. Adams dress when they went out.

I had the best position in the household. I'd been with them two years, since I was twelve, and was privy to what went on. They trusted me. I was often at the table with them, in charge of the children, when important matters were discussed.

I got the job back in Braintree, over Hannah Crane and Alice Brackett. Mr. Adams was a country lawyer then, riding circuit most of the time.

I had been living with Uncle Eb, who had a shop and small farm. He was my mother's older brother.

Mama had met my father on a visit to family in Worcester, sixty miles west of Boston. My father was one of thousands of French who were neutral in the French war. But the English were afraid they would take arms and fight with the French. And so they drove seven thousand of them out of Nova Scotia. They had scattered, but some lived near Worcester.

My father made fine farm implements. Mother married him in Worcester, against Uncle Eb's warnings, and brought him to Braintree. My father couldn't speak English well, but he made such wonderful farm implements, which Uncle Eb sold in his store, that Uncle Eb let them live in his house until they got settled.

They never got settled.

Mama said that Uncle Eb would insult my father at every turn, saying Frenchmen couldn't be trusted, that they were wicked Papists who burned Protestants alive. And that Massachusetts men must drive them out so they could take their fishing fleets to the Grand Banks again without being raided.

Never mind that Uncle Eb wasn't a fisherman and my father had never raided or burned anybody. Uncle Eb made his life so miserable that in 1756, when I was two, and England declared a new war on the French in North America, my father joined the first military expedition his countrymen mounted and left to fight.

We never saw him again. He was killed on the Plains of Abraham, fighting with Montcalm against Wolfe. I never found out where the Plains of Abraham were, but I always liked the name. It was like something out of the Old Testament.

After father died, Mama and I were under Uncle Eb's thumb. He was as sharp as a crab apple to Mama. The first thing he did was make her change our name, from Marceau to Marsh.

He never could pronounce our name, he said. Mama let him have his way with that, of course, like she suffered every other thing he did to her. All so we could have a home. And I was too young to protest. So I became Rachel Marsh, not Rachel Marceau.

Mama kept house for Uncle Eb and minded the shop when he went off on trips to Boston to establish himself there as a merchant.

To earn extra money, Mama also did sewing for the gentry. Then she took sick in the epidemic of 1763. There's an epidemic every few years in Massachusetts. She got the pip, bad. Her throat closed up, and in three days she died.

I was just nine years old. And I grieved for her something awful, in between working in Uncle Eb's store. I took Mama's place there. And in the house.

After she died, Uncle Eb started to talk real sweet to me. It turned out that my grandfather had left half the store to Mama. Uncle Eb said he wanted to transfer his establishment to Boston, and if he invested my part of the money, as a Boston merchant he could give me a fine dowry someday. But I must continue to keep house for him, there.

It took him three years to establish himself in Boston. And it took me that long to understand that whatever dowry money came from Uncle Eb wouldn't be worth it.

Just before we were to move, I heard that Mr. Adams was looking for a girl to help his wife in Braintree. I knew John Adams's mother, Susanna Adams. Mama had done sewing for her.

I knew that both Hannah Crane and Alice Brackett wanted the position. So I took myself over to Mrs. Adams's house. And there she was, down with an illness that would have killed three mules. She was a widow and her sons, John, Elihu, and Peter, were helpless. I offered to stay and help her sister nurse her.

By the time Susanna Adams recovered we were fast friends. And though I was only twelve and not fourteen like most girls who are bounded, she recommended me to John and Abigail as a clever girl and a neat one and one that wanted a Place.

I got that Place. I convinced Uncle Eb to bind

me out. I think he was glad to do it. He was taking his shop to Boston and would be moving in different circles. He would soon be wearing velvet waistcoats and going to the White Horse and Lion taverns, where meetings were held and politics spoken.

I didn't care about my share of the money. I knew I'd never see it. I set about proving Susanna Adams's words to be true. I promised myself I would never do anything to make me unworthy of my Place. No matter what.

I didn't care if I never saw Uncle Eb again. I didn't know it when I rushed into the Adamses' house in Boston that day with Nabby, but he was about to come back into my life.

Abigail was waiting for me, serene and smiling, with little Johnny. Nabby ran to her, skirts flying, to tell her about the " 'ion." Abigail listened, then said it was time for their noon meal, which was ready in the kitchen, and I should take it out to the table under the pear tree in the back garden.

"Then, Rachel, naps for them both. Oh, it's so hot. How was the wharf?"

"Busy."

"Why are the bells ringing?"

"I don't know. Could it be fire?"

"Oh, by the way, I've a message for you. Your uncle Eb sent word around earlier. He wants to see

18

you. At his shop. He suggested early tomorrow morning."

She smiled as she gave me the note. I didn't. Uncle Eb hadn't been in touch with me since I'd come to Boston.

"He wants something from me." I felt a sense of dread.

"No, I'm sure he just wants to see how you're faring."

Abigail Adams could never understand somebody like Uncle Eb. How could she, with all that loving family she had back in Braintree? I never saw so many people gathered around the table as when the Quincys and Smiths came to visit.

No, I couldn't explain about Uncle Eb. She'd think I was ungrateful. Like most people who were mean to their own kin, Uncle Eb put on a good face to the rest of the world.

"I can spare you for a while tomorrow," she said.

I nodded and was about to take the children out back for their noon meal when the front door knocker clapped. Out of habit I went to answer the summons.

John Hancock stood there, looking down at me.

Now I know trouble when it comes knocking on the door and stands there on the front stoop. I ought to. I've seen enough of it. Even if Chris hadn't told me of Hancock's trouble, I would have known it by the way he looked. He was in complete disarray. This was not like John Hancock. He was always garbed with care and style. His waistcoats were either silk brocade or velvet. He dressed in accordance with his social position.

And he was rich. But he was also generous. He'd given a fire engine to the town. And bells and deacons' benches and bibles to the churches. He was always giving firewood and casks of rum to the poor and having oxen roasted for them on the Common.

But standing on the stoop, he looked besieged. His thin, handsome face was covered with sweat and he was in shirtsleeves. He'd been running and his chest heaved with the exertion. I just stared.

"Hello, Rachel. Is Mr. Adams in?"

"No, sir, but my mistress is."

I stepped back to admit him. Then I closed the door against the sights and sounds of a mob running through Brattle Square.

The mob was "out" all night long. People knew what to do, of course: bolt the doors, shutter the windows, stay inside. When the mob was "out" all manner of things happened. They could burn, destroy, tar and feather, or pull down houses if they chose to. All night we heard them, blowing their conch shells or whistles, beating their drums, stamping their feet and shouting. The half of Boston that didn't barricade themselves inside that night ran out to join the frolic.

Ever since the trouble with the stamps, the North and South End mobs had buried the hatchet and agreed to work together in Boston. That night they did their work.

They attacked anyone connected with customs and broke the windows of their houses. I lay in my bed listening to the distant sound of breaking glass. I heard Mr. Adams out in the hall. I got out of bed and peeked. He was in his nightshirt. Abigail was with him. "They're a trained mob," he said. "They have leadership; they could be soldiers. But a trained mob is still a mob."

There was a dead coldness in his voice. He hated violence. And he knew that his cousin Sam Adams was at the root of this night's violence, if not out there marching, disguised with the revelers.

In the morning I took breakfast at the table with the Adamses, so I could oversee the feeding of the children. We found out that last night's riot already had a name. Bostonians were fond of naming their violent acts. They called it the Liberty Riot.

21

"Don't go out today," John Adams told us.

"I must go see my uncle Eb. He's sent for me," I told him.

He nodded. "Well, the worst is over. They've broken some windows, burned a customs official's boat, and driven the customs men and their families to Castle Island. Just be careful, Rachel. I should ask Luke to accompany you."

"Thank you," I said, "but Sukey was to market already. And she said the streets are deserted."

"They usually are the morning after the mob is out," he said.

He agreed to let me go alone. I liked Luke, but he lingered too much on errands. He knew too many young people and always wanted to stop and talk with them. I didn't want to talk with anyone that morning. I needed the time alone, to think. And to prepare myself. I always had to prepare myself for a row with Uncle Eb. And I sensed this would be a row.

The streets were all but deserted. I hurried along, worrying. Not about the mob, but about Mr. Adams.

When John Hancock had come to call yesterday he had asked Mr. Adams to be his counsel against the Crown. Mr. Adams had agreed. Later I heard him tell Abigail that the business with Hancock was serious, that the Crown was going to sue the rich young merchant for all he was worth.

I didn't want John Adams to get into trouble. I didn't want anything to happen that would change our life on Brattle Square.

Look at what had happened to the lawyer James Otis, brother of Mercy Warren. He'd had a high position with the Crown but resigned to argue cases against it. He went about ranting and raving about power and kings. People said he was demented.

Would John Adams get like that? No, I reminded myself, he was doing legal work for his friends. He wasn't running to meetings at the Salutation on Ship Street, where people like Sam Adams met and drank and talked treason.

A fancy carriage was parked on the cobblestones in front of Uncle Eb's shop. Sleek horses and a nigra driver in velvet waited. The shop door opened and two elegant ladies came out.

"I knew that Ebenezer Drake signed the non-importation agreement with all the other merchants," one said, "but who would have guessed he'd have such fabric? Right from London!"

Uncle Eb was a Tory. You didn't rise so quickly in the Boston merchant community not being one. Any paper he signed, agreeing not to import English goods, was a sham.

The ladies swept past me like I was a piece of

dung. I caught a scent of lilac perfume, saw a blur of pale blue and yellow gowns. I stared after them, struck dumb by what they were and what they stood for.

Everything I admired. Yet at the same time I despised them, for reasons I could not name.

EBENEZER DRAKE, the gold-lettered sign over the door said. FINE FABRICS AND FURS.

A clerk showed me the way to the warehouse in back. It was large, dark, cavernous, and echoing. Piles of goods lay all over and a wagon load was being unloaded. Uncle Eb stood there with a work-man. I heard something about a shipment of pelts. Uncle Eb looked dandified in good gray broadcloth with lace at his throat. *So,* I thought, looking at him. *Fabric from London.*

"How have you been, Rachel?"

"I'm faring well."

A clerk brought tea. There were even little cakes. Never in my life had I eaten with Uncle Eb. Always I had done the serving.

"Are you staying out of trouble?" he inquired.

"I'm keeping."

He eyed me over his spectacles. He had always been an innocent-looking man. No one who met him, who looked on his round face, his balding head, his rotund body, and stubby hands, would

24

ever think him capable of evil. But I knew better.

"Just because I haven't come to see you at the Adamses, doesn't mean I haven't kept an eye on you, Rachel," he said.

There it was. Something coming. I nibbled a cake.

His eyes went over me. "That's a good grade of fabric in your short gown. The print is straight from France."

"Mrs. Adams had clothes made for me."

"Ah yes, it wouldn't do to have the housemaid not dressed proper."

"I'm not the housemaid. I care for the children."

"Your hair looks better like that, too."

"What do you want from me, Uncle Eb?"

He laughed. "Same old Rachel. Can't make a silk purse out of a sow's ear. Aren't you proud of your uncle Eb?" He waved an arm to take in his surroundings. "Never dreamed I'd do this well, did you?"

"You've done well," I agreed.

"A person minds his own business and applies himself, he can do well in Boston. Providing he keeps away from the influence of the rabble."

His eyes met mine, as if I should take his meaning.

"If you'll just say plain what you want," I said.

He set his teacup down. "I have many customers who are high-placed with the Crown. Would you believe that, Rachel?"

I said yes, I would believe it.

"Lieutenant Governor Hutchinson told me yesterday that Governor Bernard is worried because too many influential people are defecting from the Crown."

"I don't know any influential people."

"Come, Rachel. You can say such? Living in that house?"

That house. It was the second time within twenty-four hours that someone had reminded me of the house I was living in. I held my breath.

"Word came to the governor yesterday that John Adams is going to defend Mr. Hancock."

I held my breath.

"The governor knows he's lost Mr. Hancock to the Crown. He likes to think he hasn't yet lost John Adams."

"Your note, fetching me, came before Mr. Hancock yesterday," I said. "Which means you already knew of the trouble on the wharf. And you expected Mr. Hancock to run to John Adams. And because I live in that house . . ." I stood up.

"Dear child, I simply wanted to see you."

"You lie. You expected to learn things from me today so you could tell Hutchinson. Only news travels faster than fire in Boston, so everybody knew

26

last night that Mr. Adams is going to defend Hancock. There is nothing I can tell you, Uncle Eb."

"Ah, but there is! Governor Bernard is sending Attorney General Mr. Johnathan Sewall to call on Mr. Adams."

"All this means nothing to me."

"Mr. Adams is going to be offered the position of Advocate General of Admiralty for Massachusetts. A valued position with the Crown."

We glared at each other.

"Mr. Adams will be given time to think on the offer. Perhaps two weeks. All I want," he said, "is for you to let me know, beforehand, what Mr. Adams is thinking."

"I won't be your spy, Uncle Eb."

"Dear child, I'm your uncle. A simple conversation between us does not a spy make."

"It does, and I won't do it."

"Very well." He sighed. "I'm gratified that you're so fond of the Adamses."

"I am."

"Do they feel about you in kind?"

"Yes."

"Then wouldn't they be disturbed to know you are mixing with bad company these days?"

My ears were buzzing. My mouth went dry. This man was truly evil. More than I'd heretofore realized. "Bad company?"

He folded his hands across his ample belly. "I

know the people you've been running with, Rachel."

"I don't run with anybody."

"Let me see now," he reflected. "Jane Washburn, that's her name, isn't it?"

"She's a maid in a respectable Tory household."

"I know where she works. I know everything about her. Including the fact that she's fast friends with Mackintosh. You know how Mr. Adams feels about mobs. Would you want him to know you're friends with her?"

I sank back in the chair, beaten. I liked to think that I was like my mother, brave and saucy. Only cast in an even sharper mold. But right then I thought of my father. And knew what he must have felt like living under this man's roof.

I felt trapped. I had vowed never to do anything to hurt my place with the Adamses. But what did that mean now? Did it mean doing what Uncle Eb wanted? Or refusing him?

I did not know. But I knew I needed time to mull it over. Mama had once told me that when I found myself in a dolorous situation, I should give it time. I would do that, yes.

I stood up again. "If you can tell Mr. Hutchinson what John Adams is thinking before anyone else knows, it will be in your favor, won't it," I said sweetly.

28

He beamed. "Dear girl! You are clever! I always knew you took after me."

"I'll think on it," I said.

He blinked. "Think?"

"Yes. You must give me time. You said Mr. Adams is to be given two weeks. I will let you know within a week of Mr. Sewall's visit." I flung him my best smile, but I was trembling inside.

He nodded, and I walked out. No, I did not walk out. I escaped.

Chapter Three

HOME AGAIN. To the two-story white brick house on the cobblestoned Brattle Square. Inside the entry hall I just stood, listening. From the street came sounds of horses clop-clopping by, the wheels of a cart. But the world was sealed off. The quiet ticking of a tall clock in the parlor welcomed me. I looked around at the graceful staircase, the wainscotting on the walls. I went into the parlor.

Nine chairs were set along its walls. Straight-backed. Cherry. Their clean lines were so certain. They comforted me. I allowed my eyes to go over the familiar things: the marble top of a small table, so smooth; the spotlessness of the near-white carpeting; the graceful lines of the draperies.

I felt my own edges softening. Everything was just as I'd left it. I peeked into the smaller room behind the parlor. It was Mr. Adams's office. It was empty, so I ventured in. There were the hunting scenes on the walls, his large desk, his many books, the copper fire screen in front of the hearth. Nothing had changed in my absence.

The only change was in me.

I stood breathing in the very air of the place, making it part of me. I had always thought that if I could stay close to John and Abigail Adams long enough, if I could just move in and around the rooms they occupied, I would become like them.

This morning had proven that I had not yet accomplished that. Uncle Eb had me all in fragments. I would have to do better, I decided. I would have to get to a place in my life where Uncle Eb could no longer hurt me.

How to do that? By learning to think without my head getting muddled. By knowing what I was about and not allowing people to make me doubt it. I moved back into the parlor. Surely, living amongst such lovely things helped one, didn't it?

Why, Abigail Adams was soft as the draperies yet strong and straight inside as the nine chairs. She shone like the copper candleholders. And something ticked quietly inside her, like the tall clock, never missing a beat.

How did one get to be like that? Was one born to it? Or could you get that way if you tried hard enough?

It was then that I heard her voice, coming from

an upstairs bedroom. I becalmed myself. She would need me. I had no right lollygagging about now.

But I would, this day, open my heart to her. Many times she had smiled sweetly at me as I brought in tea. Many times she had inquired after my personal well-being. Always I had held back, hesitating to let her know about my life, shamed by its shabbiness, afraid she would not understand.

No more, I decided. I was tired of being a sow's ear, as Uncle Eb had called me. But more than that I sensed, somehow, that Abigail Adams could help me out of my present predicament. Whether I would confide to her what Uncle Eb wanted this day, I had not yet decided. I would see how matters progressed between us. Perhaps I would not have to.

"So you want to know about books," Abigail Adams said.

"Yes, ma'am." It was more than books I wanted to know about, but I did not know how to put my yearnings into words. If I started with books, I thought, there was no telling what turn the conversation might take.

She was in her bedroom doing needlework. Sukey had given the children their noon meal and put them down for their naps.

Now Abigail Adams furrowed her pretty brow, picking her words carefully. She always did that, I noticed. Before she commenced to speak she gave deep thought. I must remember that.

"You've had schooling, I've been told."

"Yes. Dame school. No Latin. But I can write a good hand."

"That's more than most girls your age can do. Most Boston children finish their education with dame school. One thing that shocked me when I came here was how little schooling most children in Boston receive."

She smiled and looked up from her needlework. "Girls receive no formal education at all. Not much has changed since I was your age."

"Where did you go to school, Mrs. Adams?"

"I didn't." She smiled again. "I so desperately wanted an education. But my mother frowned on it. Said I was not strong enough. Then my father came to my rescue."

"What did he do?"

"Without letting Mother know what we were about, he sent me, from the age of eight on, for extended visits to my uncle Isaac and my grandfather Quincy. Both had wonderful libraries. Both helped me become educated."

"How wonderful to have such a father!" I thought of my own father, unable to do anything

33

for me. Silence came between us, thick with unsaid words.

"Can a person become educated if they are not born to it?" I asked.

She smiled and stitched. "We are all born to education. I like to think it is a right. The question is, however, can our society tolerate a woman becoming educated? This is supposed to be the age of enlightenment. But ofttimes I think that only men are to be enlightened. And we women will be regarded, forever, as domestic beings."

She spoke without bitterness and smiled.

"So then, I have two faults," I said dismally. "Being a woman and not being gentry."

She was kindness in itself. "I have always thought that gentry is found in the way one conducts one's self, Rachel. I know many who are highborn and do not act like gentry. As for books, what is in them is there for everyone who wishes to learn."

"I would learn," I said, "but I don't know how to start."

"I can tell you." She set her needlework down. "But a better idea would be to send you to young Henry Knox, the bookseller."

"Henry Knox?"

"Yes. He's twenty years old. Very active and amiable. He is not highborn, as you would put it, but he is self-educated. Just meeting him would give you encouragement. His shop is patronized by young and old. And a great gathering place. You might even make friends there. I know you haven't had many friends since you came to Boston."

She looked at me gravely, and I blushed. I had not told her how I'd learned to fix her hair in the new fashion, so she did not know of my friendship with Jane. Did she have suspicions? Well, I would not confirm them. But I owed her something.

"Mrs. Adams, I would confide in you."

"Do. Yes, if it helps you. I know how alone you are. If I didn't have my sisters to confide in when I was young, I don't know what I would have done."

So I told her about Uncle Eb then, and what he wanted me to do. Though I did not tell her of his threat to me. She listened quietly, never missing a stitch in her work. "And so, you have decided not to give away any secrets from this house. I always knew you were trustworthy, Rachel."

I stared. "But how do you know what I have decided? I don't even know myself."

"Yes, you do, dear. Or you wouldn't have asked to have this conversation with me, in which you volunteered information about your uncle Eb."

She was right. Relief flooded my veins. She had helped form my mind for me. How could I have ever dreamed of being anything but trustworthy?

But what to do about Uncle Eb? Would he follow through with his threat and ruin things for me here? Oh, I did not know. I must think. I smiled at her. "You see why I want to be educated, now, don't you?"

"No. Tell me."

"So I can think things through clearly. Like you."

"Oh, my dear, life confuses most of us most of the time. But education does help, yes. Is there something worrying you, then?"

"No, ma'am," I lied. I had to lie, much as I hated to do it.

"So," she mused, "they are sending Mr. Sewall to us. To offer Mr. Adams a position with the Crown. I'm flattered. I know my husband will be, too."

"Do you think he'll take the position?" I asked.

"I leave it to him."

"You won't advise him?"

"No." She cast me a careful look. "One of the things you must learn, if you intend to become educated, Rachel, is that as a woman you must ofttimes keep your opinions to yourself in the company of men. Or you will be considered a shrew."

"But I hear you discussing important things with Mr. Adams all the time!"

"We have rousing discussions, yes. But I do not advise him. There is a difference. I trust him to do the right thing. And he will."

"How will I learn all this?" I asked.

"You will. I will help you. You've already learned much about trust and loyalty. And I shall tell Mr. Adams how faithful you are, Rachel. We always knew you would be, or we would not trust our children to you."

She was pleased with me, then. I flooded with joy and got to my feet. She sent me for paper and pen, and when I brought them out to her she wrote a note to Henry Knox. "I shall ask him to send home with you *Aesop's Fables* for the children," she said. "I'm sure you can read it to them at bedtime, can't you?"

She had never asked me to read to the children before. As she handed the note to me, her large brown eyes met mine. And I saw a warmth in them, a trust. No, she would not teach me herself, but she would do as her father had done for her. She would send me to those who could open the way for me to help myself.

"Thank you, ma'am," I said. "Yes, I can read to the children." There was a catch in my voice as I said it. I would do anything for this woman. She made me feel as if I could do anything. No one else had ever done that for me.

The first thing I would do for her, I decided, was to see no more of Jane Washburn.

On my next day off, which was Wednesday, I took myself to Mr. Knox's bookshop. It was a few doors down from Province House, on Marlborough Street, across from the Old South Church. Province House was a fine three-story brick building where the governor lived. I was getting to know the streets of Boston, if not its twisting lanes and back alleys. They said only the children and cats really knew the twisting lanes and back alleys, and, since I was not in either category, I did not attempt to navigate them.

Mr. Knox's shop was as wonderful as Mrs. Adams had said. And I saw, the moment I entered, why she had sent me. It had more to do with the way the place made a person feel than anything else. I could never describe it. You would have to be a person who loves books to understand, who loves the way they look and smell. And the quiet that surrounds them. And the way it seeps into your soul.

A little bell tinkled as I opened the door. The walls were lined with books of all kinds, some with gold lettering on them, some with the bindings almost falling off or carefully stitched back on. Some had the look of ages about them.

I wandered for a few moments in the aisles, just looking, not paying mind to the people. No one bothered me. No one asked if I had a right to be there. A clock ticked serenely in a corner. A table was in a clearing in the back, on a Persian carpet by a window with small panes. Two men were seated at the table, studying. In another chair, by the window, sat a very pretty young lady, dressed in blue. She was reading. A cat dozed on the window seat in the sun. I could live here, I decided. I felt at home.

"Can I help you, Miss?"

I looked up into the round, youthful, and kind face of a very large man. I supposed one could say he was fat, but he was not slovenly. He was big of bone yet graceful and dressed most neatly in the manner of the day. His linen was spotless, his hair tied back in a queue. The word to describe Henry Knox, I would soon learn, was *majestic*. It described not only his size, but his heart, mind, and vision. How could the frame that housed him be anything less?

"Are you Mr. Knox?"

"That I am, Miss. At your service. Welcome to the London Book Store. A primitive commerce in books, which I hope to improve upon. Look around you." He waved a hand. "There is something here for everyone. Some of it is literary pap, I know, but the rest of it should satisfy the taste of Boston's intellectual elite."

I looked around me. "I'm not one of them," I said.

This did not matter to Mr. Knox. He went on with his greeting, as if I were the president of Harvard. "There are books on law, medicine, and politics. There is a sprinkling of works on divinity. I have twelve copies of Dodd's *Sermons to Young Men*, one of *The Vicar of Wakefield*, and twenty-five copies of Armstrong's *Economy of Love*. There are twelve Bibles. I also have novels: *Pamela, Joseph Andrews, Tom Jones, Clarissa*, and *Sir Charles Grandison*. Do you read novels? Most young girls do. I also have *Robinson Crusoe* and *Peregrine Pickle*."

He stopped. I stared. Never had I heard such a speech. He was beaming. I liked him.

"And I have books on artillery."

"Artillery?"

"Yes." He glowed with pride. "Welcome to the London Book Store."

"Thank you." Silence followed as we looked each other over. I was glad I'd worn my best short gown and new shoes with the silver buckles. *I'll wager he knows where the Plains of Abraham are,* I thought.

He clasped his hands behind him, rocked on his heels, and blushed. "I get feverish," he confided, "whenever a new client comes through the door. Forgive me. Do you like books?"

I raised my eyes to him, helplessly. "I feel about books the way some girls my age feel about frocks and fabric. And the way others feel about flour and lard and bacon frying in the skillet."

He gestured to one section of the shop. "Frocks and fabric," he said. Then to another section. "Bacon frying in the skillet. Can you smell it?"

"Yes, I can. I'm afraid there's something wrong with me, Mr. Knox. I'm not like most girls my age."

"Thank heaven." He sighed.

"I need to learn."

His brown eyes went wide with pleasure. "So do we all."

"No, I mean it truly, Mr. Knox. I'm ignorant."

"Dear child,"—and he bent his large frame to me—"the only truly ignorant are those who think they know all. How much schooling have you had?"

"Dame school, back in Braintree. No Latin. But I can write a good hand."

He nodded. "So you have as much schooling as most young people in Boston. And you seek to improve yourself. Well, this is the place. I have many clients who come to do just that." He nodded at the two gentlemen at the table.

"And that pretty lady over there? Is she improving herself, also?"

"Ah, that is Miss Lucy Flucker. She is most fond of books."

"She dresses so elegantly. Is she highborn?"

"Her father is royal secretary of the province."

"That's what frightens me."

"What?"

"That you must be highborn to have to do with books," I said dismally.

He smiled. "The lady is also fond of me, if I may be so bold. She comes here to see me. Her parents don't approve."

"Oh!" I understood. He was blushing.

"What makes you think you must be highborn to have to do with books?" he asked. "I am not. I am the seventh of ten sons. My father died six years ago after suffering financial misfortune. I was left fatherless just as I was to be graduated from the Boston grammar school. I am now the sole support and stay of my mother and younger brother."

"Mrs. Adams said you could help me." I gave him her note.

He read it and beamed. "Ah yes," he said, "ah yes. I much admire the Adamses. He has an account here. Come, I will help you select some books. I have a special sale of the story-telling sort. And yes, I do have *Aesop's Fables*."

I followed him. There were shelves of quality stationery, which he also sold. He showed me his small shop in back, where he did bookbinding and printing.

He was most gallant, most cheerful. He selected some books on grammar for me and some of the story-telling sort. And some essays on the history of Massachusetts Bay Colony. He put them on Mr. Adams's account, as the note directed.

And in between his waiting on other customers who came and went, we talked. He told me how he loved hunting on Noddle's Island, how he had taught himself from the pages of Plutarch and from reading about famous generals and warriors, how he belonged to a group of colonial militia from the South End.

Mention of the South End brought up the name of Mackintosh. I looked uncomfortable. "Do you know him?" he asked.

"I know someone who does."

"Who?"

So I told him of Jane. There was silence between us for a moment. A town meeting had been called the day before, as a result of the riots.

He was taking some books from a crate and putting them neatly on a shelf. He lowered his voice. "A petition was framed," he told me, "asking the governor to remove the warship *Romney*. John Adams did a first-rate job writing instructions for the four Boston representatives in the Legislature, telling them the town's wishes in this crisis."

I nodded. "He stayed up all night writing it."

"Boston is in a ferment of anger." He shook his head and sighed. "The commissioners of customs want Governor Gates of New York to send troops to keep order."

He turned from the shelf. Our eyes met. "Troops. I would not like to see troops in my beloved Boston," he reflected quietly. "I don't like any of this. I study the art of war, but I'm a man of peace. I'm not like my ancestor, John Knox the Reformer. He took it upon himself, personally, to destroy Mary Queen of Scots."

I looked at him, wide-eyed. "Your family goes that far back?"

He laughed. "Everyone's does. I simply know who my rogue ancestors were. I take nothing from them, however. I prefer to make my way in my own sphere, head of my own house."

I listened. I liked to hear him talk. I was learning already. He took more books from a nearby crate and set them on the shelf.

I told him about my predicament with Uncle Eb then.

"What will you do?"

"I haven't decided yet."

"You've already made a decision not to give information out from the Adamses' house. A wise one, indeed."

I glowed at his praise. "But I don't know what to do about Uncle Eb telling them about my friendship with Jane. The only thing I can think to do is give up the friendship."

"Do you value this friendship?"

I thought of Jane, of all she'd taught me, of the good times we'd had. "I'm fond of her," I said. "But I don't want anything to ruin my place with the Adamses."

"So you'd sacrifice your friendship?"

"I might have to."

He straightened up from his exertions. "Would you take some advice?"

"Oh, yes. I've so needed to speak of this with someone."

"Of course, I don't like the Townsend Acts. Or all these displays of power by the Crown. I have enough of John the Reformer's blood in my veins for it to make me angry. Where does it end? Why not tax Georgia's pines, Virginia's tobacco fields, Pennsylvania's farms?"

I waited for what was coming next.

"But I am a man of peace. Both Whig and Tory come into this shop and enjoy it. Friendships are important. Do everything to keep them intact. If someone causes you to give up a friend, that person can't be worth your esteem."

"You mean the Adamses?" I gaped.

"No. I mean your uncle Eb. The Adamses haven't asked you to give up anything, yet. And I doubt if they shall. They're too intelligent for that."

"But John Adams doesn't like the mob," I reminded him.

He laughed. It was deep and hearty. "His own cousin Sam Adams is the leader of it. Has he broken off with him?"

"No. Sam Adams was just over yesterday, bringing sweet buns his wife, Betsy, had baked."

"And he'll continue to bring those sweet buns, though Sam ignites the mob to action and John Adams prefers the written word and the law. Do you know why?"

"No."

"Because that's how intelligent people conduct themselves. They allow for each other's differences."

I beamed at him. "Thank you, Mr. Knox." I could have hugged him. As it was, I stayed longer than I should have. He made tea, brewing it himself over a small hearth in his shop. He introduced me to Lucy, who was nice and didn't make me feel like a piece of dung, as had the ladies who came out of Uncle Eb's shop. And her dress was even prettier than theirs, too.

"Do you like my young swain?" she asked.

I liked them both and told them so.

"Her family hates my plebeian background," he said, "but we shall wed. We shall grow old together."

I felt a glow of warmth from them. I stayed until dusk. It was a lovely summer evening, but I had to hurry home. Though it was my day off, Mr. Sewall was coming to sup and I'd promised to help Mrs. Adams dress.

"Come back," Henry Knox said. "And read. This is the age of enlightenment, remember. You don't have to be highborn to be learned. Look at me!" And he laughed. "Who would think someone of Lucy's station would love me?"

"Uncle Eb says you can't make a silk purse out of a sow's ear," I told him.

"You are no sow's ear, Rachel Marsh. But you will soon be a silk purse," he told me.

I felt better than I had in a long time as I walked home. Dusk bathed Boston's streets. It was a sweet time. Candles were just being lighted in houses. I clutched my books close to me and made a vow.

I would, from this day on, try to better myself. It was possible. Look at Henry Knox. He was self-educated, wasn't he? And Lucy Flucker was highborn, and she adored him. Perhaps someday someone highborn would adore me, too.

Chapter Four

"WOULD YOU LIKE ME to fix your hair the way I do when you go to the concerts?" I asked Mrs. Adams.

"Yes, that would be lovely, Rachel."

I helped her into her rose-colored silk gown. It had short sleeves and a square neck, low enough to be fetching. She slipped it over her head, and I drew it in at the waist and fluffed the lace trimming. Then she sat, and I draped a large piece of flannel over her shoulders. By now I was practiced at doing her hair. I did it every Tuesday evening when they went to Deblois's Concert Hall on Queen Street.

"I'm glad for the breeze from the bay," she said. "It will make dining in the garden pleasant. I hope the roast mutton is done to John's liking."

"I was just in the kitchen. Sukey says it's perfect. She's been fussing over the salmon and says the new potatoes sent from Braintree are browning nicely."

"Mr. Sewall and Mr. Adams are fast friends since Mr. Adams was studying law in Worcester. Of course, for the past two years they've been publishing opposing essays in the *Gazette* about the trouble with the Crown. I hope that doesn't cast gloom on this evening's visit."

It was not like Mrs. Adams to worry. She took life as it came. Her husband, on the other hand, considered worry a duty. About twice a year he worked himself up to such a pitch about his health that he took to his bed, thinking he was dying.

"Silly that I should be nervous about a visit from Mr. Sewall." She gave a little laugh.

"Is his wife coming?" I did not care twopence, but I wanted to let Mrs. Adams talk. Clearly she had something on her mind.

"Heavens, no. Esther stays in Falmouth for the summer. She's very beautiful, you know. And cousin to Hannah Quincy, who was one of the girls my husband gallanted before he met me."

"In Massachusetts it seems like almost everybody is related to a Quincy," I said.

"Not Mr. Sewall. He's descended from Judge Sam Sewall, who condemned the witches in Salem." She smiled at me in the mirror. "Have you ever seen me so agitated, Rachel? You'd think Mr. Sewall is coming to pass judgment on us."

Tears glistened in her eyes. I fussed with her curls. Her chestnut-colored hair was alive and shining. "Is there anything I can do for you, ma'am? Can I fetch you some cool cider?"

"No." She fell silent while I arranged the curls. "I can confide in you, Rachel, can't I? After all, were it not for you, we wouldn't know what Mr. Sewall was coming for tonight, would we?"

I nodded and kept working.

She took a deep breath. "I feel tonight is a turning point in our lives, Rachel," she said. "If my husband refuses this offer, we will be out of favor with the Crown." She smiled at me in the mirror. "I know how hard he has worked and how ambitious he is. If he accepts, he will become rich and powerful. But then he will have to prosecute our friends."

Was she worried that he might accept? I tied a bit of lace in her hair.

"We've tried to be loyal to the Crown, tried not to draw lines. But sooner or later, it seems, one must declare one's self. If one is to be true to one's self at all."

Our eyes met in the mirror. Was I to take some meaning from those words? They sounded like a knell in my bones. Jane had said the same thing.

"I don't know why everyone feels they have to run around declaring themselves these days," I said. "Why can't things stay as they are?"

"Because they are not good, Rachel. Much as

50

we'd like to keep our heads in the sand and pretend they are. Everyone is taking sides. A man of my husband's importance cannot remain neutral."

Well, I decided, I would never take sides. I had better things to think of. All very well and good when you were well placed, but I would be like Henry Knox. He wasn't about to take sides. People like us couldn't afford to. We had to better ourselves. And the only way to do that was to mind our own business.

I took her ivory-backed hand mirror out of its silk case and handed it to her. She turned on the chair to admire my handiwork. "Lovely, Rachel. You are becoming more and more valuable to me." She got up and walked to the door. "Do I look presentable?"

"You look beautiful."

She nodded. "John loves this gown. But I'm not doing it justice tonight, Rachel. I've gained weight."

I minded that I'd not been able to cinch it in as tightly as before. "You look as good as ever," I said.

"No," she shook her head. "I would confide in you again, Rachel. I'm in circumstances."

"Oh." I did not know what to say. So I said nothing.

"I haven't told my husband yet. He has too

much on his mind. And I wanted to be sure. I'm not pleased. Johnnie's only a year and I'd hoped to wait longer." She smiled. "I suppose it's why I've been so edgy. It'll be our secret, Rachel, for a while, all right?"

"Oh, yes, ma'am!" I was so proud she'd confided in me. "I'll tell no one. And if there's anything I can do for you . . ."

She sighed wistfully. "Rachel, there is one thing I want more than anything at the moment. A good cup of tea. But you can't help me there. Since the nonimportation agreement we haven't purchased any. And we ran out of the last of our old supply last week. I'm afraid this is going to be difficult going without my tea."

I nodded. I'd missed the tea, also.

"You will walk the children a bit while we're dining, won't you? They may have a bit of maple sugar if they're good. But not too much. Johnnie is inordinately fond of it."

"Yes, ma'am. And I'll read to them at bedtime."

She went downstairs.

Just then I heard the door clapper. I went to the front window of the bedroom and looked out. The man who stood there was from the Crown, all right. You could tell by the way he bore himself. Like a bantam rooster. I never set much store by fancy clothes, but I did stare at Mr. Sewall's silk cinnamon-colored coat and shoes dyed to match. The shoes had heels on them. He carried a gold-headed cane. As he waited, I saw him take a small gold snuffbox from his pocket, open it, and sniff. Then he waved an elaborate lace handkerchief under his nose and sneezed.

The door opened and he went in. I felt a shiver. So, I thought, now Mr. Adams is to be made the offer from the Crown. And, as his wife had said, this night would be a turning point for them.

What would John Adams do? Did his wife know? Who ever knew anyone, really, or what they would do in a given circumstance?

Never mind what John Adams would do, I told myself, turning from the window. What would Uncle Eb do when I didn't run over there within the week with the information he wanted?

Would he tell the Adamses about my friendship with Jane? Could I believe what Henry Knox had told me? That it would not matter to them? Sam Adams was Mr. Adams's cousin. There was blood there. They had to endure one another.

The Adamses did not have to endure my friendship with someone like Jane, who was close to the mob. Oh, I was so confused! It had all seemed so simple when Henry Knox had explained it. But here, in this house, amongst the people and things I so dearly loved, it was not simple anymore.

Perhaps, just to be cautious, I could just avoid Jane for a while. That wouldn't be giving her up, would it? Perhaps I should just stay away from her until this crisis passed.

Then, if Uncle Eb did carry out his threat, I could say I hadn't seen her in a fortnight. Yes, that's what I would do. I went about the bedroom picking up things and setting them straight. I was good at neatening up. Mrs. Adams always said so. Too bad I couldn't set things straight in my own head.

When you're young, the world can still look good to you, in spite of the turmoil all around, my mother had once told me. You can lie to yourself and believe your own lies. Plenty of time to grow up, you think, I'm still young. Just let me stay like this a little longer.

What a terrible blow it is to find out, at sixteen, or eighteen, or twenty, that you are still doing it. And that it wasn't something you just got away with in childhood, but something you did in childhood that you could never get away from, she'd said sadly. Is that what had happened to her? Had she lied to herself when she married my father? Would I be the same way?

That evening was so lovely that as soon as I left the house, with Johnnie holding one hand and Nabby the other, I found my spirits lifting.

54

A breeze was coming off the bay and the air was like silk. You could drink it. Brattle Square itself was peaceful, its cobblestones shining clean. The big wooden church across the street had its doors open and people were sitting on its lawn in front and the whole scene was bathed in a yellowish reddish purple haze from the sunset.

Other people were strolling around, some with children. An occasional chaise went by, the horse clip-clopping, but at this time of day the carts with the fish and produce and firewood were all gone. I breathed in the sweet air, becalming myself and ready to believe my own lies.

"Where shall we go?" I asked the children.

"See 'ion," Nabby said.

"No. The lion's sleeping." She had never forgotten that lion. She had the memory of an elephant. I never saw such a child for fixing something in her head and refusing to let go.

"See 'ion!" she demanded. And she stood there, refusing to move. Her little face quivered. She looked the image of her father.

"Come on," I told her. "I'll get you some maple sugar. Your mama said you might have some if you are good. We'll go to the apothecary shop. Mr. Hollis will have maple sugar for us. *But only if you are good.*"

She relented, took my hand, and we walked on

down to the Old Feather Store. Nobody knows why it was called that. The man who had built it in 1680 had mixed fragments of colorful glass in with the plaster, and the bits of glass shone in the sunlight. All the children loved it.

In the apothecary shop you could buy headache powders, herbal remedies, and sweets. "Well." Mr. Hollis beamed down. "What can I do for these two young people?"

"Maple sugar!" Nabby shouted.

"Pease?" little Johnnie said. It was one of the few words he could say.

Mr. Hollis put the maple sugar in a small sack. I paid him. "Is there anything else? Is everyone well at the Adamses'?"

I told him we were all well. "Nothing else," I said. "Unless you have some pre-nonimportation tea. My mistress sorely misses it."

He shook his head no. "But I know somebody who might be able to get you some."

It was only then that I was aware of someone else in the shop. She came from the other end of the counter.

"Rachel? I didn't see you come in. How are you? I missed you on your last day off."

It was Jane. "I'm well," I said.

"You said you're out of tea? I can get some."

"It's all right," I said. I all but pushed Johnnie

and Nabby out of the shop. Thank heaven they were peering into the sack of maple sugar. They liked Jane. But I got them out before they were aware of her presence.

On the street again I took them both by the hand. "Come, children, let's get home."

"I want maple sugar!" Nabby demanded.

"Yes, of course, but let's walk along now. Come, it's getting on to dusk."

The shop door opened and Jane stood there. "Rachel? Is something wrong?"

"Nothing. No." My voice cracked. "I must get the children home."

"Will we meet on your next day off?"

We'd been spending all our days off together. "I can't," I said. "I'm going to be busy." I was very short with her.

"I heard! Patronizing Mr. Knox's shop. My, we're getting on in the world, aren't we?"

"Don't be silly." The children were pulling at me, begging for their sweets.

"Have you heard? The Crown's still got Hancock's sloop tied up and Sam Adams has written a circular letter to all the colonies, asking for a convention in Boston in September. So everyone can work together against the British. Old Hutchinson is talking about having troops sent down from Halifax."

57

Jane knew everything. But what would she say if she knew that Mr. Sewall was dining with the Adamses this very minute. "I must go, Jane," I said.

"Yes, I suppose you must." She sensed by then that something was amiss with me. The children and I commenced to walk away from her. But I must admit the act was not accomplished without a certain wrenching of my heart.

I always ate breakfast with the family in the dining room. Mr. Adams liked the children with him at breakfast, though they ate their noon meal and supper alone with me.

Next morning Mrs. Adams looked a little peaked and I noticed dark circles under her eyes. "Keep the children as quiet as you can," she directed. "My husband has been up most of the night over his law books."

"Yes, ma'am."

Sam Adams saved it from being a dreary meal. He came, bearing more sugar buns. The children squealed when he came into the room, and he kissed them both. Then Mrs. Adams nodded to me and I went to the sideboard and filled a plate with fresh broiled fish, eggs, ham, and biscuits. "We have no tea, Mr. Adams," I told him. "Would you like chocolate? Or this mixture Sukey made of raspberry leaves and sage?"

"Tea is a baneful weed, dear child," he said, accepting his plate. "I'll take the chocolate."

John Adams had barely given his cousin a civil nod when the man sat at the table. But I was glad to see him. I liked Sam Adams, ever since Abigail had told me how his father's fortunes had been suddenly reversed while he was at Harvard. And that the young Sam, within twenty-four hours, had gone from his private elegant eating arrangements to being a waiter, carrying food from the kitchen to the students in the common dining hall.

You only had to know this older cousin of John Adams briefly to realize that money did not matter to him. He could just never seem to take it seriously. His clothes all looked as if they'd been tailored for someone else. His hair was thinning and graying. And he had a palsy. Sometimes his hands shook. Sometimes his voice quavered as he spoke.

To me there was something tender in those frailties. Life had tried to beat Sam Adams, yet he went on, thinning hair, palsy, debts, and all. And he *was* in debt. Because he wasn't doing well in his job as tax collector. The reason being that if people couldn't come up with their tax money, he chose to accept any heartrending story they told him. And he would come away with no collections.

It was widely believed that he was about fifteen hundred pounds short in his collections. This did not seem to bother him, however. The common people all loved him. And this, to him, meant more.

I'd heard Mr. Adams tell his wife once that tax collecting was a shield for what his cousin was all about.

"He's a plotter," John Adams had said. "A spinner of webs, a setter of traps. And into these webs and traps he is wooing the best and brightest men in Boston."

Only recently had I started to understand. It was an accepted fact in Boston that Sam Adams was the mover and shaker behind the rebellion.

As I watched him innocently sipping his chocolate with a shaking hand and talking with the children, I found this difficult to believe. But you could never tell these days. The most unimportant-looking person in Boston could be working for what was vaguely referred to as "the mob." I was starting to understand that it had many levels.

Jane had told me about the Whig Clubs. She'd described them as smoke-blackened rooms above taverns. There, she'd said, both the rich and the poor met. People said it was to plot to overthrow the Crown. How she knew, I hadn't asked. Sometimes I thought that even Jane had a role in the mob.

It seemed, sometimes, as if everyone did but me. One more example of everyone else being part of something, while I was left out.

60

Then there were the Sons of Liberty, who went about smashing windows when something didn't please them. On the lowest level were the street urchins, like Chris Snider, who were paid to throw rocks at merchants still importing from England.

Sam Adams now looked across the table to his cousin. "Congratulations," he said.

"For what?" John Adams's voice was clipped and tight.

"For turning down the Crown offer."

"I haven't turned it down yet," John Adams said.

"You will, cousin, so allow me to congratulate you beforehand."

John Adams smiled then. But wryly. Abigail spoke. "How nice of you to visit us for breakfast. Is Betsy well?"

"Thriving. But I'm not just visiting, cousin. I was sent for by your husband. You see he wants to admonish me."

"John's been at his law books all night. He couldn't admonish a sleeping cat."

"You underestimate his legal powers," Sam said. "Go ahead, cousin, why don't you?"

The two men glared at each other across the table. I waited to be told by Mrs. Adams to take the children and leave the room. But no one said anything, so I stayed.

"I only want, Samuel," John Adams said, "for

you to keep your hotheads in line at your upcoming convention. I have Mr. Hancock's case to try. I don't want the Crown officials inflamed when I go into court because of any acts of your firebrands that can be construed as treason."

"The people have a right to convene," Sam Adams said. "And to throw out the laws if they don't like them. As one would throw out dirty bathwater."

"Just don't throw out the baby with the bathwater, Sam," Mr. Adams advised. "The Townsend Acts will be upheld or repealed, depending on the outcome of Hancock's case. I'm going to argue that they are unconstitutional, against the Magna Carta. Keep your mob under control, Sam. I don't need any more glass breaking in the night."

Nabby spilled milk on herself then, and I jumped to wipe it up. The children were finished. Mrs. Adams suggested I take them out back to play. So I wasn't privy to the rest of the conversation.

But from the garden, a moment or two later, I heard the two men laughing. So it is as Henry Knox says then, I minded. Intelligent people conduct themselves differently. They respect each other's differences. Instead of ending friendships over them, as I'd done with Jane.

———

The whole next week it was as if a pall lay over the house. What did lie over it was the heat, white and unrelenting, with scarcely a breeze from the bay. Mrs. Adams was feeling poorly. She didn't take her early morning trips to market, which she loved so much. She sat under the pear tree in the garden, doing needlework. Mr. Adams stayed hunkered over his books in his law office. On Wednesday of that week, while Mrs. Adams sat under the pear tree and I was playing with the children in the garden, he came out, unexpectedly.

"I don't know what to do, Abby," he said. "Should I ask to have the *Liberty* trial immediately? Or wait until business suffers in Britain because of our nonimportation agreement?"

My ears perked up. He was asking his wife what to do!

"You must go to court immediately and argue against the Townsend Acts," she said, "or Mr. Hancock and all Boston's merchants will be out of business."

He kissed her on the forehead. "Do you realize," he said, "that if I'd accepted the Crown's offer the other night, I would now have to prosecute John Hancock instead of defending him?"

They said something I couldn't hear then, and he went back into the house.

Now there is what I want, I told myself,

watching Mrs. Adams again pick up her sewing. I want to be married to a fine man someday and have him come to me and ask my opinion on a very important matter.

As it turned out, Mr. Adams got the *Liberty* trial put off until November. But it didn't matter that he hadn't taken his wife's advice. What mattered was that he looked to her to talk matters over with.

How I wished I had someone to talk things over with. I stayed close to the house all week, even on my day off, which I spent reading and studying. I was afraid that if I went out I would meet Jane. How would I face her?

Worse, I half expected to hear Uncle Eb's footsteps coming up the front stoop at any moment. I lived in fear of it. Time seemed not only to stand still but to sit on me. I had the information Uncle Eb wanted. I knew, before anyone else in Boston, except perhaps Sam Adams, who only *speculated* about the matter, that John Adams had made up his mind to turn down the Crown offer. I'd overheard him telling his wife such. Uncle Eb would probably kill for that information. But I made no move to go near him.

I thought I would lose my senses trying to get through that week. And then, toward Thursday, two things happened.

Mr. Hancock's *Liberty* was sold at a government auction.

"They plan to convert it into a coastal raider!" I heard John Adams saying loudly from his law office. I was in the kitchen with the children.

"By what right?" he demanded. "Don't they understand that an Englishman's property is sacred? That they can't confiscate and seize it without a proper trial and prosecution?"

I heard Abigail murmur something in reply. I wondered what words of consolation she could give.

The second thing that happened was that Mr. Adams left to ride circuit. He needed to get away to the country, I heard him tell Abigail, where law was practiced in the proper way. There was a case he was needed on in Salem. A young woman had died, giving birth in her mother-in-law's house. Neighbors were saying the mother-in-law had murdered her. They had exhumed the woman's body from the grave and had ordered the mother-in-law to touch the dead woman.

"The touch test," I heard Mr. Adams saying to Abigail as he mounted his horse in the backyard. "If the flesh shows color under the woman's finger, they will name her as guilty. Witchcraft still has a hold on them in Salem. I must defend the poor woman."

He leaned down from the saddle to kiss his

wife, while I stood there with Nabby on one side of me and Johnnie on the other.

"Still," he said, "even witchcraft sounds easier than what I have to put up with here in Boston."

That evening Mrs. Adams retired early. The children were abed and I was in my own room, studying the history of Massachusetts Bay Colony, with the window open, enjoying the breeze from the bay. Sukey appeared in the doorway. "Someone in the yard to see you," she said.

"Who?" My heart began racing. *Uncle Eb!* I thought.

"Chris Snider. He say he got somethin' for you."

I went downstairs and out to the back garden. Sure enough, there was Chris Snider, looking dirtier and more unkempt than ever.

"Is Jane all right?" I asked. I felt a hand gripping my heart. I'd been thinking dire thoughts all day, about my father and the woman in Salem accused of witchcraft. Mrs. Adams had looked especially pale and I was worried for her. I felt fear in the air all around me.

"Yes," he said. And he came forward and handed me a canister.

"What's this?"

"Jane sent it. Said to tell you it's legal. Pre-nonimportation."

Tea! "Where did she get it?"

He grinned his impudent grin and wiped his nose with the sleeve of his shirt. "We know where, don't worry. We know who's importin' illegally and who ain't."

"Tell Jane thank you!"

He sobered. "We got our ducks all lined up right," he said.

"Ducks?" I looked at him.

He hitched up his loose breeches. "Thing is, you ain't," he offered hesitantly. "Gotta know who your friends are today."

I nodded yes.

"Jane, she's your friend. Sooner you get sensible of it, better you'll be."

I ran my tongue along my lips. "Yes," I said again.

He nodded, satisfied, and turned. But before he slipped into the shadows of the garden he said something else. "That uncle of yours. He ain't legal," he said. "We got our eye on 'im. You see him, you better tell him that."

"I don't expect to see him," I said. "I hope I never see him again."

His grin was broad. "He'll be gettin' his one of these days, don't worry."

Then he was gone.

I stood in the gathering dark, clutching the

canister of tea to my chest. Then I ran into the house. "Sukey," I called, "put up some water! We have tea! Real tea!"

Thin as a rail and black as ebony, Sukey loved her tea, too. Her eyes went wide. "I doan allow none o' that stuff in my kitchen," she said.

With the exception of Mrs. Adams, everyone in the house acknowledged the kitchen as Sukey's domain. You didn't so much as heat water over the hearth without her permission.

"This is legal, Sukey," I told her.

I opened the top of the canister and we both whiffed it. I thought I would die, standing there, inhaling the fragrance.

"What make it legal?" she asked.

"Chris said it was. And *he* knows which merchants are importing illegally and which have merchandise from before the nonimportation agreement."

"Tha's different," she said. And she swung the copper kettle over the fire. "Chris and them boys been throwin' enough rocks at the merchants who ain't legal, sure 'nuf."

I thought of Uncle Eb and what Chris had said. But I promptly dismissed it from my mind. "I'm going to take a tray up to Mrs. Adams, Sukey," I said. "She didn't eat supper. How about

68

some bread and sweet butter and cooked fruit?"

She helped me. We even brought out the best dishes, and Sukey put a linen napkin on the tray. *Tea,* I thought, carrying the tray up the stairs. *We'll all feel better now. Tea will fix everything.*

Chapter Five

MR. ADAMS STAYED AWAY, riding circuit all week. So he wasn't there when Uncle Eb came.

He came on Friday. I had taken the children out for a walk, and he was sitting in one of the straight-backed cherry chairs in the Adamses' parlor when we got back.

Mrs. Adams sat across from him in the wing chair. I stood in the entranceway with the children, rooted to the spot, just staring at him.

I felt the blood pounding in the top of my head and rushing from my face at the same time. Mrs. Adams got up from the chair, turned to see me, and the children ran to her. She kissed them both, took them by the hands, and prepared to leave the room.

Every movement she made seemed to take an eternity. And her voice came as from a distance, working its way through the buzzing in my ears.

"Your uncle has paid a call, dear. I'll have Sukey give the children their noon meal."

Her face was very white. Dark circles under the eyes. What had he said to her? She was in circumstances! How dare he come to the house like this and upset her?

She closed the door behind us. I took the chair Mrs. Adams had vacated.

"Hello, Rachel," he said.

I saw no reason to answer.

"I was waiting to hear from you." He was sipping a mug of cold cider. "I was expecting a visit from you this week. Forgot your old uncle Eb, did you?" The voice was quiet, smoothed over with honey.

I recognized the tone. It was the voice he used back in Braintree when he was about to harangue my mother about giving someone credit at the store against his wishes. Or not recording something properly in his precious ledger books. Always, he made Mother cry.

Not me. I had never allowed him to make me cry.

"I didn't visit because I had nothing to tell you," I said.

"Ah, but you do, Rachel, you do. Of course, I know how forgetful young people are. So I thought to come here myself. And save you the trouble."

"You've no right to come here," I said.

"No right?" He smiled. "I am your uncle, Rachel, your only living relative, your guardian. I have bound you out to these good people. It is customary to inquire if they are satisfied with your services."

"And are they?"

He leaned forward in the chair. "Has Mr. Adams taken the offer from the Crown?"

"I don't know."

"Ah, Rachel, Rachel," he said sadly. "It is not nice to lie to your uncle Ebenezer, your only living relative."

I ran my tongue along my lips, which were dry. "Mr. Adams doesn't tell me his personal decisions," I said angrily.

"But you have ears, child. The walls in this house are not that thick. I know you take breakfast with the family. Mrs. Adams herself told me that. Breakfast . . ." He leaned back in the chair and stretched his stubby legs out. "What a wonderful time of the day. Everyone is perky and bright-eyed. The mistakes of the day have not yet disciplined us to silence our tongues."

"I don't know anything, Uncle Eb. And if I did, I wouldn't tell you!"

That brought him up short. Might as well get it over with, I decided. He drew in his breath, ran his hand over his balding head, and stared into his cider. "All my life I have taken care of you," he said sadly.

"Oh, Uncle Eb, please don't let's start talking like that now."

"All my life!" He did not raise his voice. It was not his way. He could do more damage to a person's mind with a harsh whisper. "You and your mother. After that Protestant-burning father of yours ran off and left you."

"My father never burned anybody. And he didn't run off. He went to fight."

"Do you think you and your mother would have had a home if not for me?"

"Mama worked and paid our way."

He grunted. "You'd have been charity cases, both of you."

"Part of that money you put into the shop was Mama's," I reminded him.

"Yes, but would she have been able to make the shop pay as I did? She was always giving people credit. Women don't know how to run a business. I built the business up. I now compete with the best merchants in Boston. And for what reason? Why do you think I have done all this, Rachel?"

"I don't know," I said wearily.

"For you!" He shook a warning finger at me. "Everything I do is for you. You are my only heir."

"I don't want any of your money, Uncle Eb," I said, "if it means I have to make such choices to get it."

"We all have to make choices these days," he said. "I've had to make mine and they haven't been easy. The best people are making agonizing choices. Even your precious John Adams has to make one now, eh? No more straddling the fence and cozying up to both sides. They've made him choose, haven't they?"

"He isn't my precious John Adams," I said. "I work for the man and I respect him. And I'll thank you not to speak ill of him, please."

He got red in the face then, something he seldom did. And his hand started to shake so he had to set his mug of cider down. "Chit," he said. "Disrespectful chit. You may say that now because you live here"—he made a wide gesture with his arm, taking in the sedate parlor—"but this is not your home, Rachel. These are not your people. They may buy you clothes, give you money for books at Mr. Knox's store, even allow you to sit at their breakfast table with them. *But that does not make them family!*"

His words shook my very bones. I clutched the arms of the chair to steady myself.

"Family!" he whispered urgently. "There can be no replacement for family. These people never will be that to you, no matter how good they appear. They come from old and venerable and monied clans in this commonwealth. The kind of people who got their money by keeping the rest of us in our place. You are a servant to them, no more!"

Silence in the room. Terrible silence. Except for the ticking of the tall clock in the corner.

"Don't speak ill of them, Uncle Eb." It was all I could think of to say. My mind was so muddled.

"I am saying the truth. Only you don't wish to hear it. Your head is full of foolish notions. How do you think the Adamses and the Quincys and the Smiths got their money? By looking out for each other. By riding roughshod over people like us. It's about time you learned that, girl. And you won't learn it from those books you get at Mr. Knox's."

"I'm going to Mr. Knox's for books to better myself, Uncle Eb. Is there anything wrong with that? You bettered yourself, didn't you, moving from Braintree to Boston?"

His eyes, always pale, seemed to take on a milky glaze as he looked at me. "Do you know what I have had to do here in Boston to rise in the merchant community, Rachel?" he asked.

I shook my head no.

"I have had to lick the boots of every highborn mother's son. I have had to use every means to ingratiate myself. Why do you think I needed this information about Mr. Adams's decision on the Crown offer?"

"I don't know," I said.

"So I can prove myself loyal to those who would grant me favors."

"Loyal, Uncle Eb?"

"Yes, loyal. Trustworthy to those who count on me for certain things."

I stood up. Some wellspring of strength restored me. "That is what I am about, too, Uncle Eb," I told him, "proving myself trustworthy to the people who count on me for certain things."

He got to his feet. "You made your decision, then."

"Yes."

"Where is Mrs. Adams?" He walked past me to the hall and stood framed in the sunlight.

"Mrs. Adams knows about my friendship with Jane, Uncle Eb. I had occasion to tell her last evening. She's a bit peaked and I feel responsible for her until her husband returns. I would take it kindly if you didn't disturb her."

His eyes met mine. They bore into me, into my very soul. He was angry. And for a moment he looked like he might explode. I held my breath. I had outwitted him! But he could never stand to be outwitted. What would he do now?

"Very well," he said coldly. "I will not bother

76

you anymore, Rachel. Consider our kinship at an end."

I just stared at him. Could he do that? I felt confused, slapped, bereft. *He was disowning me.* I stood there struck dumb.

My mother's brother, the only living relative I had. And he was disowning me! Because I wouldn't tell tales on the people I worked for! No, I didn't *love* Uncle Eb. Most times I hated him. And I'd seen him only once since coming to Boston. But always, in back of my mind, was the thought that he was there.

Now he wouldn't be there anymore.

So then, this was my punishment for not doing his will. Now there would be no one I could turn to, if need be, who shared a common past, no matter how unhappy that past might have been. When he walked out that door, he took my past with him.

"Uncle Eb?" I said.

He was at the door. "Yes?"

I must have looked stricken enough to frighten the dead.

"Oh, don't worry, Rachel. I'll make arrangements to set up a trust for you when you come of age. Of no greater or lesser amount than was your mother's original share. It isn't to keep your money that I sever our ties."

A trust? Was that all he thought I cared about?

"Don't you understand, Uncle Eb? *I couldn't do it!*"

That was the worst part. He didn't understand.

He turned and went out the door, into the sunlight.

Mama always held with saying that we are given revelations with every bad experience. I never asked her what revelation she learned when my father left. But as I was crying myself to sleep that night in bed, my mind kept pondering how you don't have to hold someone in high esteem to be grievous hurt when they put you out of their life forever.

I suppose that was the nearest thing to a revelation I was about to get. And what good it did me I cannot say. All I knew was that I was alone in the world now. Like one of the street urchins who ran around after curfew with no one to care if they ever went home.

I said nothing to Mrs. Adams of Uncle Eb's disowning me. I felt comforted about one thing, though. She *knew* about my friendship with Jane. Because the night before, when I'd served her the tea, I'd told her who had sent it around.

"How sweet of her. I must send a thank-you note," she said.

This I took to mean that she was giving her blessing on our friendship. And then I thought about something else. Because I'd told Mrs. Adams about

Jane first, Uncle Eb hadn't been able to sneak up on her like a barnyard cat on a mouse in the feed bin. So then I felt comforted about that, too. Because nobody can play the barnyard cat better than Uncle Eb can. And more often than I liked to recollect, I'd been the mouse.

"Thank you for the tea, Rachel. Just set it down. And stay a moment, will you?"

"Yes, sir."

Mr. Adams was home from riding circuit, one day, spending all his time over his law books again. I'd brought afternoon tea and was about to leave when he detained me.

"Sit, Rachel, sit." And he himself cleared some law books off a chair. I sat.

John Adams was not a tall man, like John Hancock or Dr. Warren. *Stocky* was more the word for him, with his round, pleasant face. But what he lacked in height, he made up in presence. When you were in the room with him, everyone else paled by comparison. He gave off strength, confidence. And when he spoke, everyone else fell quiet.

"I would speak with you, Rachel. Reason first, I want to thank you for sharing your knowledge about Mr. Sewall's visit. It gave us time to prepare ourselves."

I nodded mutely.

"Reason second, I would thank you for your loyalty, in general. May I take a guess at what your uncle wanted from you the other day?"

I lowered my head and fussed with my apron in my lap.

"He wanted to know my decision, concerning the Crown offer. Am I correct?"

"I'm so ashamed of him, Mr. Adams."

"The shame is not yours, dear girl. But I know you suffer his anger now."

I looked up. "He's disowned me, Mr. Adams."

He raised his eyebrows. "Love cannot be disavowed. It cannot be put on and taken off like a coat."

"But he's done just that, sir."

He shook his head. "Then there was no real love to begin with. Perhaps a sense of duty toward you, yes. But do not mistake it for love, or you will cause yourself unneeded grief at its loss."

"I have no one now," I whispered.

He smiled and poured two cups of tea. Then he offered me one. I sipped. "I've been having the same thoughts lately, Rachel."

"You, sir?"

"Yes. As you may know, I've decided to turn down the Crown offer. I must tell Mr. Sewall when he next calls. This will sever me from all favors, honors, security, and protection. As well as from many friends. I have made a choice, Rachel, just like you. So I, too, now feel very alone."

I ran my tongue along my lips, listening.

"You are feeling what many important people in Boston are suffering these days, Rachel. People whose ideas of right and justice conflict with what our parent, the mother country, tells us we must do."

"I didn't mean to make a choice," I said. "I just wouldn't tell Uncle Eb what he wanted to know."

He leaned forward and smiled. "Sometimes not making a choice constitutes making one."

I stared at him.

"Yes, Rachel. An act of omission is ofttimes a choice. By doing nothing you made your choice. Do you understand?"

"I think so."

"You have done something very honorable, Rachel."

"Then why do I have a mortification of the spirit?"

Again he smiled. "A little secret, I'll share with you. Doing good does not always make us feel good inside."

"Then what's the virtue of it?"

"Ah, Rachel, you have to ask that?"

I shook my head sadly. "No, sir."

"You did right and we are proud of you. And we are your friends, Rachel. Hear what I say now. The next few years are going to be difficult. Many old ties are going to be severed. Friends are going to replace family, on many levels. New ties will be formed. But they will be stronger and more free of corruption than ever before."

I met his eyes. What was he saying? "I'm not sure I understand, sir."

"You will, Rachel, you will. Be of good heart now. Since I made my decision to break with the Crown I feel more serene than I have in years. My heart is at ease, though I have given up much. Take heart from that, child, if you can."

I thanked him, curtsied, and left. I was not unappreciative. In all the years I'd known Uncle Eb, he'd never taken the time to speak to me like that or to be concerned with what I was feeling.

Mr. Adams's words warmed me. And I took them to heart. Though in all honesty, I did not understand them. And as much as I appreciated his sentiments, I decided it was all well and good for him to say he was lonely, when he had a wife and two children and another one on the way. Not to mention his cousin Sam and family back in Braintree.

So if I were pushed to tell the truth of the matter, I would have to say no, I did not understand

Mr. Adams's words to me that day. Although I tried.

It was a full three months later before those words of his started to make any sense at all to me. It was the first day of October, a bright blue day that made one happy at the fact of being alive. John Adams was away again, trying a case in Springfield. Mrs. Adams was writing letters that morning.

Jane and I and Nabby and little Johnnie, along with half the town, it seemed, stood on Long Wharf and watched in disbelief as a fleet of ships arrived in Boston Harbor.

British ships. Down from Halifax. Since Tuesday, the twenty-eighth, everyone in town had known that the squadron of ships was off Boston. Sam Adams's convention was still in session. Governor Bernard had himself taken by a small boat out to Castle Island to meet them.

And so, by the morning of the first of October, the British men-of-war, one after another, floated majestically into the harbor and dropped anchor at every wharf in town.

We would learn their names later. Street urchins would chant them. *Beaver, Senegal, Martin, Glasgow, Mermaid, Launceston*, and *Bonetta*. Their flags whipped in the brisk breeze.

At noon the troops and artillery started coming

ashore. At least a thousand soldiers disembarked on Long Wharf alone. The people pressed back as the soldiers formed up under the barking orders of their commanders. For the number of souls present, the quiet was almost eerie.

Then, with a shrieking sound of fifes and drums that caused little Johnnie and Nabby to cover their ears and hide against our skirts, the soldiers commenced to march.

Each regiment had two banners on long poles, the King's colors and their own. I thought their own colors were prettier than the Union Jack. Their flags had yellow borders with their regiment numbers embroidered on a red shield encircled with roses and thistles.

The soldiers' coats were red. The drummers were nigras with yellow jackets. Some of the other soldiers wore black coats with white laces. Still others had tall bearskin caps with badges in front and something written in Latin on them. I heard someone say they were grenadiers. The officers wore crimson sashes.

Never had I seen such a sight! It was both thrilling and frightening at the same time. As they commenced marching, every movement was in unison. They were like puppets we'd seen on Long Wharf, moving as if someone were pulling their strings.

Straight ahead they stared, looking neither to the left nor the right, eyes glazed, unheedful of the crowd.

That crowd and the vendors on Long Wharf just stood there, white-faced and staring, as the soldiers marched by, looking so smart in those bright red coats with the white straps crossed in front and their shining boots and all their other equipment hanging from their persons.

"What are they for?" I mouthed the words to Jane.

We were fast friends again, ever since she'd sent the tea. I thought it generous of her to overlook my brief lapse of friendship.

"What are soldiers always for?" she answered. "To make war."

"Against whom?" I knew enough now to say "whom" and not "who." I had faithfully studied the books I'd gotten from Mr. Knox. But at that moment it didn't seem to matter how you said it. And I minded, suddenly, that all the book learning in the world wouldn't help any of us then. Because I knew the answer to my question even before Jane said it.

"Against us," she said.

Troops! Troops in Boston! The dreaded word was on everyone's lips. We followed as they marched. Past the Custom House, past the Town

House, and the new courthouse, which was not completed yet. On Queen Street, for some reason, they halted.

We stopped, too. "Look." Jane poked me in the ribs and pointed.

On a second-story balcony of a house across the street was a young girl, my age, no older. She was wearing a blue dress and cape. Her auburn hair tumbled to her shoulders. She waved at the troops and smiled.

Jane nudged me again. Just up ahead of us a young officer had stepped out of line and was leaning against a fence, looking up at her. "By God," we heard him say, "that girl seals my fate. My spirits are lifted. Dammy, it might be worth the trip, after all."

"Oh, we're going to have a fine time, aren't we?" Jane mimicked his British accent as we continued. "Who is she? Do you know, Rachel?"

"That's Mr. Sheaffe's house. I know he has a daughter. I don't know her name."

Jane accompanied us home. To our dismay, some of the troops broke off and marched in our direction. A whole regiment of them set up right outside our house in Brattle Square. I bade Jane good-bye and got the children into the house. All afternoon Johnnie and Nabby stared out the windows as the soldiers set up their tents and drilled.

Abigail Adams refused to be ruffled. "Those are General Gage's troops, down from Halifax, come to keep peace in Boston," she told the children.

But over their heads she looked at me. I saw the question in her eyes. And I knew we were in trouble. For if Abigail Adams, with all her serenity and her book learning had questions, what was to become of the rest of us?

I wished Mr. Adams would come home. Somehow I was starting to understand the words he had told me in his office that day. About how things were going to become difficult. And old ties would be severed. And new ones formed.

By the time he did come home, in the middle of the week, everyone in Boston knew the name of the young girl on the balcony. It was Susanna Sheaffe. Within the week she was being courted by Captain Ponsonby Molesworth, the young man who had been so struck by her beauty at first sight.

Chapter Six

A NIGHTMARE STARTED that day in Boston when the troops came to us. Yet the people did not seem in the paralyzing grip of fear that nightmares bring. They seemed even more possessed by their desire to rebel. And determined to act upon that desire.

In our house we tried to keep matters calm. If that could be accomplished with troops fifing and drumming right outside the windows. Part of General Small's regiment, the Twenty-ninth, was camped on the green of Brattle Square. And the good general considered it his patriotic duty to drill his troops at five every morning.

He was especially fond of the Yankee Doodle tune, which mocked the Patriots.

Within the first two weeks of their arrival it became apparent that the one goal of the troops was to beleaguer us.

If the music weren't bad enough, all the British

bands seemed especially intent upon playing it in a very rousing manner on the Sabbath when most Bostonians were at Meeting. Gay airs they would play. Like "Fair Rosamund." His Majesty's ships would boom their guns in the harbor.

And the soldiers, too, started their mischief. They were rude to any women who passed their way, sometimes jostling them in alleys. They insulted the inhabitants who came to stand and watch them drill. They became drunk and offensive. They took over the Royal Coffee House, once the favorite meeting place of the Whigs, who had to move to the Bunch of Grapes. The officers had money to spend and soon they attracted camp women, who went about ordering fripperies from the shops and flaunting themselves in front of ordinary citizens. The Main Guard of the army set up opposite the General Court and aimed their cannon right at it. There were brawls, nightly, in taverns.

The Sons of Liberty seemed to disappear. Nobody knew where they were meeting. But we began to hear new names. Will Molineaux. Crispus Attucks. Names spoken in whispers, even when nobody was in earshot.

And within days of the troops' arrival there was word that the Sons would now fight back with a very powerful tool: influence.

Soon we saw the results. The people of Boston

refused to quarter the soldiers. It was, they said, against the Magna Carta. And winter was coming. The troops could not live in their tents in winter. There was no cold like the cold of Boston.

Within two weeks the British soldiers started deserting. The Sons were getting word to them of the wonders of this America. Thirty regulars deserted in the first two weeks.

When caught, they were shot on the Common. Such public as cared to was invited to attend. For lesser infractions soldiers were whipped, and the public was also invited.

Another thing happened, too, in those first two weeks after the troops came amongst us. A new word seemed to be bandied about, first by the British officers, then by their underlings.

American.

It was said with sneers when the soldiers referred to the people of Boston. Oh, it wasn't as if the people hadn't heard the word before. But they had always referred to themselves as British Americans.

Now they were Americans. But the soldiers said it as if the citizens were something lowly. They said it with contempt, as if Americans were a plague to be wiped out. And the soldiers said it with laughter, as if the people were dunces performing for their amusement.

But they said it. And before long, the people in the streets were starting to say it about themselves. But with a measure of pride. And to mark the differences between themselves and the soldiers.

I was confused by it. The word *American* did not seem right without the word *British* in front of it. *What did it mean,* I wondered. *And where would it lead us?*

I went to see Henry Knox. It was October fifteenth, my day off; Jane was busy getting her mistress ready for a large soiree at Hutchinson's house. General Gage had come to town to see to the quartering of the troops. A seventeen-gun salute at five that morning from the artillery had welcomed Gage. Both Nabby and Johnnie woke up screaming and remained fretful.

Mrs. Adams was heavy with child. Mr. Adams was daily going to court to argue John Hancock's case and was grumpy because of it.

It was a brisk but pleasant day. In an alley, a short way from Knox's store, I came upon a crowd. Many of Boston's alleys were covered over, making them good places to hide.

The crowd was not large as Boston crowds went. About ten people milled around a large man, who looked to be part Negro and part white and part Indian.

His height placed him in the category of a giant. His arms were muscled and bare.

"They want to put soldiers in the Manufactory House!" he shouted.

The men and urchins around him booed and hissed.

"They say clear out the poor! They call them the scum of the town!"

More rumbling from the assembled. I stared. I recognized none of them. I knew I should go on, but never had I been this close to a brewing fracas, and I was enthralled.

"The governor has sent Sheriff Greenleaf with deputies to clear out the building, but the poor have agreed not to move!" The mulatto lowered his voice, bewitching the crowd. "Tonight"—and he chuckled—"we'll see to it that a soldier accidentally falls off a bridge into the water."

Murmurs of approval.

"Tonight, a sentry will have his face cut with an oyster shell."

"I'll do it!" Someone with an Irish accent spoke up.

"You're a damned incendiary, Billy," said another with the same accent. "Sure'n I'll be seein' you hangin' in your shoes one of these days."

"Who will have his face cut?" someone asked. "How about Captain Wilson of the Fifty-ninth. He was in his cups t'other night and told a group of nigra slaves to go home and cut their masters' throats."

"I name who it is and I name who does it," the mulatto said. They fell silent.

"Tomorrow morning," he went on, "they shoot one of their own on the Common. At seven. This army is not a good thing. Armies are evil. Tomorrow morning when people are busy with the execution, here is what we do." He lowered his voice to a whisper.

I trembled. My mouth went dry. I ran.

"He's Crispus Attucks," Henry Knox told me.

He and Lucy were sitting at a small table in the back room of his shop, having sweet buns and hot chocolate.

"Shouldn't we do something? Tell somebody?" I asked.

"Sit down and join us, Rachel." They cleared a place for me at the table. Paperwork and books were all over it. I sat down and accepted some hot chocolate and a bun.

"Tell whom?" Henry Knox asked. "Colonel Dalrymple, who has somehow got the doors open to Faneuil Hall and the State House? And is even now housing his men there? And taking possession of the town's four hundred muskets?"

I shook my head no. "I thought you were neutral," I said.

"I am, Rachel. But there isn't much neutral ground to stand on anymore. It is shrinking."

"My head is muddled," I said. "Why do the soldiers call us American? I've always thought of myself as a loyal British subject, when I've thought of the matter at all."

He mused for a moment. "So have we all, Rachel," he said sadly, "but perhaps it is time for some new thoughts, then."

"I wouldn't know where to start," I said. "What is a plain American, without the British in front of it?"

"Perhaps," he said, "it is time to find out."

That was a frightening thought. And we all stared at each other for the moment. Then Henry started to talk of Crispus Attucks.

"His real name is Michael Johnson. Some say he's from Framingham, others say he's a crewman off a Nantucket whaler."

"I heard he just came to town," Lucy put in, "and that the Sons sent for him."

"It's possible." Henry chuckled. "The Sons of Perdition know he's an agitator."

"Do you think Gage will get the poor out of the Manufactory House?" I asked.

Henry sipped his chocolate. "They may be poor, but lawyers have advised them of their rights. I think Gage doesn't understand what he's become enmeshed in here. I mind that the occupying army thinks we citizens are dunderheads."

"They are going to shoot one of their own tomorrow," I said.

"This army is behaving disgracefully," Henry said. "Sad, because they have a fine history. The predecessors of those in the Fourteenth and Twenty-ninth regiments, who now are here, fought valiantly in the days of William the Third."

"I hear that the soldiers are underpaid," Lucy said, "and may seek work in town."

"The townsfolk will not take kindly to this," Henry said.

"I also hear that many will have no lodging come winter, and they haven't enough to eat," she added.

"You hear right, my dear," Henry agreed.

"Do you think there will be trouble?" Lucy asked.

Henry's sigh came from the depths of his ample frame. "You cannot quarter troops in a town against the residents' wishes and not have a fracas. Sooner or later some woman will cry rape, some mother's son will throw a rock at a sentry."

"And then?" Lucy asked.

"And then," Henry said, "they will find that a fowling piece is as good as a grenadier's musket. And then we will each have to search our soul and ask if we are American or British."

I purchased more books, then left. I had to stop at Mr. Piermont's before returning home. He was the French barber who came to the house to do Mr. Adams's white wig. As I approached the door of his shop I almost collided with three British officers.

"Ho, you American girls are a cheeky sort. And always in such a hurry!" one said.

There it was again. They saw me as American.

"I have business." I said it by way of apology.

"Business! A little chit like you? Hear that, Wilson? She has *business*. My sainted aunt, these Americans do give themselves airs."

Wilson. Was this the man they had been discussing in the alley? He held the door open for me and gave a mock bow.

"Far be it from me to detain you," Wilson said.

Inside the shop, Mr. Piermont scarcely gave me a nod. "Can I help you gentlemen?" he said to the officers.

"Wigs, we wish new wigs," Wilson said.

"Certainly." Mr. Piermont brought one forward. "This is what most of your officers seem to be wearing, with the hair on either side arranged in two or three horizontal rolls, placed close together."

They discussed price. Then each ordered a wig. Mr. Piermont fussed and bristled with pleasure. I watched them leave. I felt so pushed aside! So humiliated! Mr. Piermont had not even paid mind to me. He made me feel like dirt under the feet of the British officers.

Is this how they wanted us to feel?

They had called me an American. They had said I gave myself airs.

I kept staring in the direction in which they had gone. *They will push us into being Americans,* I decided, *even if we don't want to be.*

"May I help you, Rachel?"

I whirled around to face Mr. Piermont. "Mr. Adams requires you to come to the house and powder his wig." I said it angrily.

"Dear child, I simply haven't time. You can see how busy I am. Can't you bring the wig in?"

"He wears it to court every day. Mr. Adams was your customer long before the British officers, Mr. Piermont. And he'll be your customer after they are gone."

He shook his head sadly. "Will they ever be gone, Rachel?" he asked. "We may wish them gone, but will they be? I did not mean to slight you before. But they are here now, and they make things most unpleasant for us merchants if we don't pay them instant attention."

I understood then that he had not been catering to their whims, but that he feared them.

"Of course, some merchants are glad they are here. I hear your uncle is importing pelts for the winter like never before."

This news about Uncle Eb did nothing to cheer me. But I looked kindlier on Mr. Piermont, nevertheless. "Mr. Adams would be most gratified if you could find time to come and powder his wig," I said.

"Very well, Rachel. Tell Mr. Adams to make do with the wig one more day. I'll be there tomorrow evening."

My next stop was Mr. Hill's, the baker. I wanted fresh cinnamon buns to bring home for Mrs. Adams for tea. Anger had made me hungry.

"We've some pastries today," Mr. Hill said.

I selected some pastry. "I hear the troops are hungry," he said. "What do you know of it, Rachel? You've a regiment right in front of the house."

"No more than you, Mr. Hill."

"I'd like to bake some bread for them. I have my own children. And some of the soldiers seem no more than children. But I don't know. Would the Sons of Liberty consider this sedition?"

I liked Mr. Hill. He always managed to slip an extra bun into my package "to eat on the way home" at no charge. And when I came round with the children he gave them samples.

"What's sedition?" I asked.

He smiled. "You'll know it when you do it, Rachel. And I suspect that in the days to come most of us will be asking ourselves that question."

"If you mean doing business with the British, Mr. Hill, others are," I said.

He nodded. "What does Mr. Adams think of the troops?"

"He's plagued by the fifes and drums in the morning. But he's been too busy with Mr. Hancock's trial to say much of anything these days."

"He's a good man, fighting for the merchants of Boston in this trial. Here, Rachel, a cinnamon bun. To eat on the way home. Give my regards to Mrs. Adams."

I said I would and left. When I got home I found a sentry at our very door. He challenged me.

"Who goes there?"

I stared. Was he joking? He wasn't. He was young and serious and looked to be no older than sixteen. He held his musket crossways, in front of him. His hair was fair and his blue eyes had fear in them. This seemed odd to me.

"Who indeed," I said. "I live here."

"Your name?"

"I don't have to answer that!"

"Your name!" He said it with more firmness.

"It's none of your business. And I'll thank you to take your attentions elsewhere. Heavens, haven't you soldiers anything better to do than plague the public?"

He scowled. But it had no bite. His blue eyes slid sideways. I looked in the same direction. A superior officer was standing in Brattle Square, hands clasped behind his back, very dashing, watching him steadily.

"Give me your name, Miss," the sentry whispered, "or I'll be doing guard duty tonight, and I haven't slept in forty-eight hours. That's Major Small over there."

I looked at the young man before me. He was so different in manner and bearing from the officers. His eyes were pleading. But I was not ready to relent yet.

"Why should I?" I whispered back. "I've just met some of your officers and they were insolent and overbearing."

"They're officers, Miss. I'm not. Please."

In a moment I relented.

"I'm Rachel Marsh," I said loudly and clearly. "And I work for the Adamses, who live here. Now may I pass, please?"

"What's in the packages?"

"Books. And cinnamon buns, fresh from the baker's." The buns gave off the most delicious aroma. And I minded that his face looked pinched and half-starved. He sighed, lowered his musket, and stepped aside. He had been blocking my way up the steps. "Thank you, Miss Rachel Marsh," he said. "I'm ever so grateful."

Grateful? I went into the house. But not before I noticed that his hands were red with cold. And with that look of a hungry street urchin about him, I felt almost sorry that I hadn't offered him a cinnamon bun.

That evening Mr. Adams came in, angry and indignant. "Who is that insolent pup, challenging me at my own front door?"

I went to take his wig from him. "He's a sentry. He begged me to answer his challenge, that he would be punished if I didn't."

He sighed. "A man can't come through his own front door without answering questions? What are we coming to? Trouble will come of all this. The Crown is stupid for sending these troops."

"Yessir." I set the wig aside and took his black coat. Underneath he wore a black vest and a white shirt with a lace collar. These, with his black breeches and hose and shoes, comprised his court outfit.

"Did Mr. Piermont say he'd come tonight, Rachel?"

"No, sir. He said he can't come. He's too busy filling orders for British officers. He suggested to-morrow evening."

He frowned. "Have the children settled down

since being dongled awake by those tyrannical cannons?"

"Yes, they have."

"Good." He rubbed his hands. "The house is cold. Doesn't Luke have the fires going?"

"Mrs. Adams sent him out for more wood, sir. She said the house has many drafts. Wood is difficult to find. The British are . . ."

He held up his hand. "Don't tell me, I know. The British are buying up, or taking, all the wood. What's for supper and where is my wife?"

"Sukey's got stew bubbling. Mrs. Adams is dressing for supper."

"I have a hankering for greens, Rachel. Broccoli. Or artichokes. What I would give to be back in Braintree and making use of what's in our root cellar."

I smiled at him. "Perhaps I can grow some greens out back next summer, sir."

Mrs. Adams came into the parlor. "John, you look frozen. I've sent Luke for more wood. Rachel, get my husband some Madeira from the cupboard."

She eased herself into a chair, moving clumsily. I saw him eyeing her with concern as I fetched the wine.

"Things aren't going well, Abby," he told her. "The Townsend Acts don't allow Hancock to be tried by jury, and that's against the Magna Carta."

"Everything seems to be against the Magna

Carta these days," she said sadly. "How goes the trial?"

"Johnathan Sewall seems bent upon summoning all of Boston as witnesses. Do you know he's even called the tradesmen from whom Hancock buys his groceries? And Hancock's ancient aunt?"

"To what end, John? No one will testify against Hancock."

I gave Mr. Adams the wine. Sukey announced supper. "We'll have the children with us at the table tonight, Rachel," Mr. Adams said. "Their lives are so disrupted these days. And it's warmer in the dining room."

Next morning, the rumble of drums and marching feet outside our window announced the execution. The children were still sleeping. Mr. Adams had left for court. I came into the parlor to find Mrs. Adams with a cup of tea at the window.

"Ma'am? Come have breakfast."

"They're going to execute that young man, Rachel," she said. "His name is Private Richard Ames. He's from the Twenty-ninth camped outside. Hear the drums? They're marching him to the Commons now."

She looked pale. I heard the drums, deliberate and mournful and unyielding. "You should come have breakfast in the dining room," I said.

She would not leave the window. Something

103

held her there. The regiment marched out of Brattle Square. She stood, sipping her tea. In a little while we heard the barking of orders, the sound of guns echoing through Boston's streets in the bright cold.

Mrs. Adams swayed, gripped the window sash with one hand and, before I could reach her, fainted. The teacup clattered to the floor.

"Sukey!" I called, "Sukey?" We got her to bed. Luke put more wood on the fire in her bedroom. "Someone's stolen the wood I brought in last night," he said, kneeling in front of the hearth.

Mrs. Adams bade him not to report the theft. "No more shootings," she said. "We need no more shootings."

I sat with her. "I am more and more convinced that man is a dangerous creature, Rachel," she said, "and that power, whether vested in many or a few, is ever grasping and like the grave, cries 'give, give.'"

I didn't like this talk about the grave. "Shall I send for Mr. Adams?" I asked.

"No. I'll sleep." And she did. But just before she dropped off I heard her murmur, "The great fish swallow the small."

Chapter Seven

"DID YOU STEAL our wood?" In the autumn dark of that evening, after the children were in bed, I stepped out front and faced the young sentry.

"No, Miss. I'd not steal. There's no profit in it. Captain John Wilson of the Fifty-ninth found himself before Justice Richard Dana for haranguing the nigras to cut their masters' throats."

"Good. He deserves it. He's insolent and he needs to be brought down."

His blue eyes widened. "You know Wilson?"

"I met him by accident. He was most rude to me."

"Well, I've no fancy for your courts. Or for the whipping my superiors would order. So I didn't steal your wood."

"What did Ames do?"

"Who, Miss?"

"The one you people shot this morning."

105

"Deserter, Miss. Felt sorry for the poor bloke. He's a wife back home."

"Then why did he desert?"

"Cold and hungry, Miss. They got to him, they did, your people. Told him this country is a good place, that a man can own his own land here and do whatever he takes a mind to do if he works hard. Ames was always daft to own land."

"They told him no lies."

"Aye." He nodded.

I clutched my shawl about me. It was cold. In the distance on Brattle Square the camp fires flickered in the night, casting eerie shadows. Faceless forms moved between the tents. I heard some soldiers singing softly. The song drifted on the night air.

"I apologize for yesterday, Miss," he said.

I stared at him.

"My commanding officer was watching. I had to do my duty."

"Well, you did it." I started back up the steps.

"Miss?"

I turned.

"They say a soldier can get work at Gray's Ropewalk Works in his leisure time. Is that true?"

"How would I know?"

He spoke plain. "You live here and you look like a bright sort. Smarter than most maidservants."

I shrugged. "Why would you want to work there? Doesn't the army pay you?"

"The pay's meager, Miss."

Something in the way he said it caught at my mind. "You mean you're hungry?"

"We've no bread. The townsfolk won't provide us with anything."

"Some do. I've heard business is brisk since you people came."

"For officers' personal needs, Miss. There's always some who will provide. But we need things to dress up our basic provisions. For the most part the town won't sell us anything in large quantity."

"Well, I suppose you could try Gray's."

"Where is it, Miss?"

"Across from Commissioner Paxton's house. Down near Griffin's Wharf."

"Thank you, Miss. And, who made those cinnamon buns you brought home yesterday? I told my friends how just a whiff of them reminded me of home. My own mum made them. Soon's I get some money I'd like to buy some."

The darkness wasn't the only thing getting thick between us, I minded. I felt something in the moment, some kindred feeling take hold. "They come from Hill's bakery," I said. "He asked me about the troops. And if they were hungry."

He didn't answer.

"Look here, *are* you hungry?"

He took a moment, turning away, shifting the musket to the other shoulder. Finally, the answer came, muffled, for his face was still turned. "We're not supposed to complain to the townsfolk. Or bother them for anything. Strict orders."

I went into the house. Sukey was in her little room in back. In the kitchen I found two leftover cinnamon buns and wrapped them in a napkin. *Don't be a fool, Rachel Marsh*, I told myself. *Don't start anything you can't finish.* My mama had always said that. But what had *she* started when she married my father?

I thought of what Mrs. Adams had said earlier this day, about the big fish swallowing the small. If anybody looked like a small fish, it was that sentry. Matter of fact, he looked like he was already swallowed. And spit back up.

I hurried through the house before my good sense could get the best of me. Mrs. Adams was in bed, Mr. Adams in his office.

Sedition, Mr. Hill had said. *You will know it when you do it, Rachel.* Well, if this was sedition, I minded, it felt good.

Outside, I thrust the wrapped buns into the surprised sentry's benumbed hand. The blue eyes widened. "Thank you kindly, Miss," he said.

"My name's Rachel."

"And mine's Kilroy. Private Matthew Kilroy."

I wished he hadn't told me his name. It made him a person instead of just a sentry. It put a different light on things. I slammed the door shut, bolted it, and was about to run upstairs when Mr. Adams came out of his office and through the parlor.

"What is it, Rachel?"

I stared at him but did not answer. He was holding a heavy book in his hands and regarded me over it.

"Was someone at the door?"

"No, sir." My mouth was dry. There were tears in my eyes and he saw them. He came closer.

"What's troubling you, Rachel? You look as if you've just seen the Devil himself, child."

"I've just done sedition, Mr. Adams," I blurted out.

His eyes widened. "Have you now? That's a serious charge you're admitting to. May I ask how?"

"I've just gone and given two cinnamon buns to that poor, hungry, cold sentry out there," I wailed. "I know you don't like him. I couldn't help it!"

He nodded slowly. "I submit to you, Rachel, that it is difficult for us to shake off all our prejudices and habits."

What did that mean? That he approved or disapproved? He was ofttimes long-winded with his lawyer's talk. Even Mrs. Adams said so.

"Right now those soldiers, as a body, represent everything we fear and have come to hate," he went on, "but they are still our countrymen."

I thought of Wilson and the ones I'd met at Mr. Piermont's. My countrymen? Those fops? Not while I had breath in me.

Then I brought my mind back to what Mr. Adams had just said. "Does that mean you approve of my giving the buns to the sentry?"

"It means that if anyone accuses you of doing sedition with cinnamon buns, I shall defend you in court, gladly."

For a lawyer, that was a fine answer. I felt comforted by it as I went to my room.

It was cold in my room. Though Luke had found wood that day, he hadn't yet brought any to my hearth. No matter. I put on my warmest nightdress, got into bed, and started reading one of the books I'd gotten from Henry Knox's yesterday: *Clarissa; or The History of a Young Lady,* by Samuel Richardson.

I started reading, but my mind wandered. I thought of the young sentry out in the cold. Was he my countryman, as Mr. Adams had said? Or was he British and I American? I decided *he,* cold and hungry, was my countryman but not the officers and would ponder it no more. And that is how it started with me and Private Matthew Kilroy.

Many times that winter, I found myself doing sedition. Sometimes with a piece of smoked turkey or some stale cake or bread.

Matthew Kilroy continued to be grateful. And I became better than ever at lying to myself.

I told myself I was feeding him because he was my countryman. Or because he was young and away from home. And near starving.

In November Mr. Hill became the official baker of the Fourteenth and Twenty-ninth regiments, so the soldiers weren't starving for long. But I kept bringing Matthew buns and bits of food and bread.

"What you bring is better than anything Mr. Hill supplies us with," he told me one dark night. "Mr. Hill brings for two regiments. You bring just for me."

I blushed at that. And I kept right on lying to myself.

I did not admit to myself that it was because Matthew's blue eyes pleasured me that I kept sneaking food to him. Or because, when he smiled, it was like he was sharing a secret with me. Or because he had a dimple on one side of his face. Or because he waited for me at our front steps.

One night our hands touched, accidentally, as I gave him the food. He blushed and asked forgiveness. That tore at me. So did his pleasant and respectful manner. Such things tore at places inside where I had not, heretofore, known that I had places.

Oh, I was becoming sensible of my feelings.

But I did not understand them. In my jumbled and lying mind I understood that they had to do, in a roundabout way, with the fact that no man had ever waited at the front steps for me before in my life.

One especially windy night my mobcap blew off my head. He ran to fetch it, brought it back, and stared at me.

"Your hair is beautiful," he said.

It had come undone and tumbled about my shoulders.

"It's so dark and shining."

"I got it from my 'Protestant-burning' French father." And I found myself telling him about my father. I'd not told anyone about him before.

"I've no more love for the Frenchies than any proper Englishman. My own father was killed in one of your French wars. You may be part French, but you're bonny, Rachel Marsh. The wives and sweethearts of the men of the Fourteenth and Twenty-ninth and Fifty-ninth just landed, and I've seen some of them. And you're more bonny than any."

"Has your sweetheart come?" I asked.

"I've no sweetheart." He sighed. "Who would have me?"

The unanswered question hung in the sparkling night. Clear as a star in front of the eyes of both of us.

I was sure that no one in the house except Sukey knew what I was about in those cold November days. Every night, Sukey left a plate of leftovers on the kitchen table. And said nothing in the morning when it was gone.

Sukey. How like her to know and say nothing, to leave the food. Sukey knew better than any of us what it was to be hungry, I minded. I remembered the Adamses speaking of her past. Why hadn't I paid attention? All I knew was that it had not been good.

One night I came into the kitchen as she was cleaning up. And there was the plate, covered with a napkin. "Sukey, thank you," I said.

She turned. "You liked the roast? Mr. Adams said it was the best I'd ever cooked."

"Thank you for the food you leave every night. You know who I give it to, don't you?"

She scowled and shrugged. "Doan matter to me."

"I give it to that sentry, Sukey. He's cold and hungry."

"You be careful," was all she would say.

"I will. I know his superiors wouldn't like it."

"Ain't talkin' 'bout him," she said contemptuously. "Talkin' 'bout you. Be careful."

"Of what, Sukey?"

The whites of her eyes grew larger. "You doan know, maybe you better stop givin' the food," was

113

all she would say. But she still left it on the table every night.

By mid-November and the first snowfall, all the troops were quartered, finally, in distilleries, warehouses, and sail lofts all over town. Two companies of the Twenty-ninth, one of them Matthew's, were put in the sugar warehouse on Brattle Street. But he still came, every night at dusk, to do sentry duty in front of our house.

"I'm so glad they've found quarters," Mrs. Adams said as the house settled the first night Brattle Square was empty of troops. "Those poor things were freezing out there. I know quartering them is against the Magna Carta, but somehow that all seemed unimportant the worse the wind blew." She sighed. "There is much I have yet to know. Americans are supposed to be a very religious people. Would to heaven they were in earnest. Sometimes I fear they are only a less vicious people than others."

She sat in the easy chair. I brought her tea. Mr. Adams had gone to a meeting at Henderson Inches's house. "But that young sentry is still out there, Rachel."

"It's his nightly duty. All the sentries in Boston are from the Twenty-ninth," I said.

She accepted the teacup and looked at me with

innocent brown eyes. "You've become friends with him, haven't you?"

I could not lie to her. "Yes, ma'am."

"Be careful, Rachel," was all she would say. In the next moment she asked me about my reading.

"I'm reading *Rollin's Ancient History*," I told her. "Mr. Knox suggested it."

She told me how fond she'd always been of that book. Then we talked of other books. It was almost as if she was trying to remind me of my vow to better myself.

By the time December came, with its howling winds and snow and fat icicles dripping from the eaves and from the masts of the British ships in the harbor, Dr. Joseph Warren had advised Mr. Adams to send for Dr. James Lloyd. He was an obstetrician. And the first doctor in America ever to deliver babies. It was unheard of!

Sukey shook her head. "Midwives bring babies! Not doctors! Much less he be a man."

"But Dr. Warren recommended him highly, Sukey," I told her. "And Mr. Adams wants the best for his wife. And Lloyd was trained in England. And Dr. Warren said he was *scientific!*"

"Doan care what he be," Sukey grumbled. "He be a man! That ain't men's business. Doan care how scientized he be."

"Mrs. Adams is educated and far-reaching in her thinking," I told her.

She grunted. "Sooner or later all that book readin' will get a woman into trouble." And she gave me a meaningful glance.

But I admired Mrs. Adams for her courage. Lloyd was duly sent for, and soon he was making regular visits to the house. He had the biggest nose I had ever seen on a man and the kindest face.

As December progressed, the household was in a flurry of activity. There was the borning room to be made ready. Mrs. Adams would use a spare bedroom. The cradle must be cleaned and polished and lined with the softest of fleecy flannel. Sukey prepared special dishes for Mrs. Adams. I felt strangely removed from all the fuss, though I helped. Mrs. Adams had difficulty sleeping nights and was uncomfortable most of the time. She would sit in the easy chair in the parlor, days, with an open book in her lap. But most of the time she just stared into space.

I worried about her. And I longed for someone to talk to about Matthew. I know it was selfish of me to think of him when I should have been thinking of my mistress. But I thought about him all the time. I hoped he was warm enough at night in the sugar warehouse. I minded those blue eyes and how they smiled at me. I looked at myself in my bedroom mirror with a *good* look for the first time. Was I pretty, like Matthew said? My waist was slim, my bosom respectable, my chin pert, my eyes large and blue. But my skin tended to freckle and, except for my hair, I had always considered myself plain. I had never concerned myself with appearance before. Now it was all I thought about, when I wasn't thinking of Matthew.

And it seems I thought of Matthew all the time. I daydreamed about him. I went over and over in my head things he had said to me. And how he had laughed, how he tilted his head, how his voice came to me across the dark and moved things around in my soul.

I looked forward to his arrival in front of the house every night with an eagerness that surprised me.

Nabby and Johnnie would watch for him, too. It became a game with them. They would stand at the front windows every evening as dusk fell and the candles were lighted and one or the other would shout, "Soljer here!"

And my heart would start to race as I pulled them from the window to come to supper. Then, I would glimpse Matthew as he began his sentry's walk, up and down, the slow, measured gait, the musket on his shoulder, the way he turned on his heel and started back, and something would catch in my throat.

His form, outlined in the half-dark, etched

something on my mind, tugged at something in my memory that I could not name. My spirit felt a kinship with him. I became alive as I'd never been before, in his presence.

One night, the week before Christmas, Matthew gave me a small packet wrapped in burlap and tied with a bit of blue ribbon. The night was bright and cold. Stars lit the sky.

I'd brought a steaming mug of hot cider and some apple cake out for him. He warmed his hands on the mug, then set it aside to hand me the packet.

"Open it," he urged.

I did so. It was a book. *Pamela.*

"Oh, Matthew, I love it so. I do!" I clutched the book to my breast and looked up at him. "I've been wanting this very book. However did you know?"

"I went to Henry Knox's store. I told him I knew you. He suggested it."

Tears came to my eyes. When was the last time I'd had a present from anybody? I could not recollect.

"Why are you crying?" Matthew asked.

I shrugged.

He took my hand in his. "Rachel, I would like to see you more."

I was taken back. "You see me every night."

"I know. But I'm on duty and you have to sneak out. I'd like to see you in the day. I scarcely know what you look like by sunlight. Are you as beautiful as now?"

I laughed. I was trembling. "What a silly question, Matthew. Anyway, I'm not beautiful. I'm plain compared to the likes of Susie Sheaffe. *She's* the prettiest girl in Boston. Everyone says so."

"I don't care what everyone says. You are beautiful."

I blushed, grateful for the shadows. "Heavens, I don't know what to say to that."

"Say you'll walk out with me. On your day off. I'll try to get my day off changed. I'll arrange it."

"I might get in trouble with the Adamses."

"Do they tell you what to do on your day off?"

"No. But if they found out I was walking out with somebody, without their permission, let alone a British soldier, I don't know how it would sit with them. I'm accountable to them, Matthew. About my behavior, I mean."

He scowled. "Sometimes I don't understand you people at all."

"What people?" I asked.

"You Americans. You make such a fracas out of knowing your own minds and not being told what to do. And here I ask you just to walk out with me and you behave as if you have to ask permission from Parliament about it."

"Matthew Kilroy, I never said I had to *ask* anyone. And I *do* know my own mind. I've been on my own since I was twelve years old! I know what I want better than any girl my age!"

"Then apparently what you don't want is to walk out with me."

"I didn't say that."

"Then you *will* walk out with me?"

He was so earnest, so dear. And so close to me. I was leaning back against the house and he was in front of me, one hand holding mine, the other just over my shoulder, pressed against the house. His musket was propped up next to me. For a moment I thought he was going to kiss me, he was bending down so close.

Overhead, stars twinkled. In windows all up and down the street, candles glowed, but none gave a light so mellow or warm as Matthew's eyes.

"Yes," I said weakly, "I'll walk out with you. But I must go in now, it's late."

"So we're going to walk out together once a week," I told Jane the next day. She'd stopped by with a cinnamon cake for Christmas. We were sipping tea, alone in our kitchen.

"Be careful," she said, "or you'll be following

120

Susie Sheaffe and Molesworth down the aisle. They plan to marry in spring."

"It isn't like that, Jane. It's not romantic. It's a friendship."

"You've read enough of Henry Fielding by now to know better," she chided. "Where is this leading? Have you considered that question?"

"Must I?"

She sighed. "Yes, I'm afraid you must."

"I don't want to," I said. "Not right now. I just want to enjoy Matthew's friendship. Why can't I? I've never had a man for a friend before."

She sipped her tea and eyed me carefully. "Dear Rachel, there is no such thing as a man friend." She pronounced this with the same smug knowledge she displayed when telling me about secret meetings of the Sons of Liberty.

"There isn't?"

"No. A man can't be a friend to a woman."

"Why?"

"It just can't be."

"I thought I'd come close to it with Henry Knox."

"Has he ever told you your hair is beautiful?"

"No. He doesn't say things of that nature."

"What do you talk about?"

"Books."

"Ah, a safe subject. That's why you're friends.

121

If he started talking about your hair, if you started noticing the dimple in his face . . ."

"Henry Knox doesn't have a dimple in his face."

"You know what I'm saying, Rachel Marsh. Don't be dense."

"What are you saying?" I asked. "Say it plain."

She'd brought a copy of the Tory newspaper, the *Newsletter and Weekly Advertiser*. Instead of explaining, she opened the paper and showed me an ad in it, taken out by an anonymous British officer:

> *Wanted, to live with two single gentlemen, a young woman to act in the capacity of housekeeper, and who can occasionally put her hand to anything. Extravagant wages will be given and no character required. Any young woman who chooses to offer, may be further informed at the Royal Coffee House.*

We laughed over the advertisement. Then she grew solemn. "You see what I mean?" she asked.

"Jane! How can I compare my friendship with Matthew with that!"

She sipped her tea. "I hold you in high esteem, Rachel Marsh," she said. "I value your friendship, but I must tell you something."

I felt dread in my bones. "Tell then."

"There's word around that Kilroy is a scamp."

"What does *that* mean?"

"That even in the Twenty-ninth, which is full of scamps, like Molesworth, he's a bounder. They say he's robbed a Boston woman of almost all her outside clothing."

I went red in the face. "You'll be no more friend of mine, Jane, if you say such about him. I *know* Matthew. He's decent!"

She sighed. "I had to tell you. Of course, lots of what they say is rumor. But be careful, please? I don't want to see you give your heart to a bounder."

She was the third person to bid me be careful with Matthew. "No need for you to worry on *that* score, Jane. I'll never give my heart to a bounder."

"Many women have said such. Do you think they set out to do it? It just happens. With blue eyes like he has, what chance have you?"

"I'm going to better myself and become educated before I give my heart to anyone," I told her.

"Good," she said. But I had the feeling she did not believe me.

Late in December Mrs. Adams's baby was born. Doctor Lloyd stayed all night. It was bitter cold with winds whipping off the bay. Mr. Adams had Luke bringing wood in all night. Sukey and I stayed up, keeping coffee brewing in the kitchen. The tea was all gone.

We waited hours for that baby. But it just

wouldn't be born, it seemed. Then, finally, we heard its wail, thin as the morning sun coming through the windows. A girl. Sukey said the doctor couldn't get it to breathe right away, that he had to work on it for a while.

The winter days passed in what seemed a half-light, one colder than the next, darkness descending by four in the afternoon. All I remember was the cold and Baby Susanna's weak crying. And Mrs. Adams dragging herself around the house, trying to get her strength back. It was not a good winter. If it hadn't been for Matthew, who came to do his sentry duty each evening at dusk, I don't know what I would have done. No matter how cold, I'd sneak out to see him each night. Then run to bed where I'd bundle under my quilt and listen to the wind under the eaves and hear Mrs. Adams walking the floor with the baby and hear little Susanna's weak cry and shake with fear inside me. For what, I did not know. I could not name my fear. And that is the worst kind, I have come to know. Nameless, it takes on the names and faces of all who are dear to us.

I prayed for spring.

Chapter Eight

IT WAS A SILKEN DAY in May. Matthew and I were walking to Cold Lane near the millpond, on our way to see the new house the Adamses were soon to move into. Matthew was not happy about the move.

"I don't see why the landlord had to sell the Brattle Square house out from under them," he said.

"Someone offered to buy it," I told him.

"Why didn't the Adamses offer to purchase it?"

"They're not sure they want to buy a house in Boston right now."

"I thought you Americans were sure of everything."

"You needn't sound so bitter, Matthew."

"I'm not bitter. And you've no right to say such."

"You are and I do. And you say something mocking about Americans every time you're put out with me!"

I pulled my hand out of his. Hand-holding had become habit on our once-a-week walks. But lately Matthew had been pushing for more. His advances had started a few weeks ago. I was determined not to start down *that* path, and so had refused him.

Ever since, there had been trouble in the air between us. At first I'd put it down to spring. And the normal process of a young man's sap running. Besides which, since April the troops were drilling outside again, sassier than ever, glad to be free of the confinement of winter quarters. And they were all full of vinegar.

"I'm not put out with you," he murmured, reaching again for my hand, "but am angry because I'll be doing sentry duty in front of the house on Brattle Square and you'll no longer be there."

I accepted that, though I knew other matters were on his mind. And I knew what they were. My own feelings were in turmoil. Was it possible Jane had been right? That a man could never be friends with a woman without wanting more?

"Will you miss me?" he pushed.

"Of course, Matthew. But we'll still see each other once a week."

"Once a week!" He stopped and took both my

hands in his and turned me to look at him. "Here I am near crazy with what I feel for you and you keep pushing me away and then you tell me to be content with seeing you once a week."

"Well, what do you want, Matthew?"

"More than hand-holding once a week, I can tell you."

"I'm sorry. I can't give you any more. And don't hold my hands like that in public."

"There's no one about."

"It's still broad daylight. Don't you people think American girls have any scruples? Do you think we're all like Susie Sheaffe? Her name is bandied about on everyone's lips since she and Molesworth eloped a few weeks ago."

"Now *you're* hiding behind the fact that you're American and different."

"I'm not, Matthew. It's the way you see us. If we're different it's because your people have made us think so."

His blue eyes went sad. He released my hand and started walking ahead of me to the house. I hurried to catch up. There was a stubborn streak of pride in him that frightened me. Always, he seemed to give me the feeling that if matters did not go his way between us, we could no longer be friends.

We stood looking at the new house, which was

about fifty yards from the millpond. "It's nice," Matthew said, "but it's not made of brick. What of fire?"

Everyone in Boston had a terror of fire. On the night of January thirtieth, Matthew had been one of many British soldiers to help townsfolk fight the fire in the Queen Street jail. I had been one of the citizens to bring out hot coffee and food to the fire fighters.

Patriots, Tories, and soldiers had fought side by side. Matthew's uniform had been ripped and ruined. He'd acquitted himself gallantly and earned praise from his superiors. And now he had new clothes, which included white linen breeches for summer and a bright new red coat. He had a new swagger as well.

"Are you trying to frighten me with the thought of fire?" I asked. "The house is beautiful, and look at the view!"

The house had eight large rooms and was freshly painted, inside and out.

"I am looking at the view," Matthew said, "and it isn't the millpond." He pointed east, across Hanover Street to the bay. There, riding at anchor, sails furled, was His Majesty's brig *Rose*.

The ship was another bone of contention between us. We'd argued over that on our last day together. Now we began again.

"Your people didn't have to charge the American sailors with murder, Matthew."

"Those sailors killed a lieutenant from His Majesty's navy."

"I'd have killed him, too, if he boarded a ship I was on and tried to kidnap me. You may call it impressment, Matthew, but we call it kidnapping, and your people have been doing it for too long now. It's uncivilized."

"Those four sailors stabbed Lieutenant Panton with a harpoon! Is *that* civilized?"

"He was warned. They should have known you don't shilly-shally with whaling men."

"I can't believe you're saying such to me, Rachel. Any more than I can believe that your John Adams is defending those sailors."

I felt anger flood my veins. "He isn't *my* Mr. Adams. But if he is defending them it's because he's the best lawyer in Boston. Who else is there? You know James Otis got into a mad freak last night at the Royal Coffee House with some of your officers. Otis got his head cracked in a fight."

"Am I supposed to apologize for what happened to Otis?" he asked. "They say he was always crazy."

"He was a good man. All this trouble with the Crown made him crazy."

He smiled. "And look what it's doing to us,"

he said. "We're at each other's throats, saying *your people* and *my people*." He reached for my hand again.

I gave it, but I was troubled and made no bones about telling him. "This is Mr. Adams's first murder trial, Matthew. He's working night and day on it. I won't hear ill of him."

He stepped closer to me. "He should be confident. He won the case for Mr. Hancock, didn't he?"

"He is confident. Only he didn't win that case. The Crown dropped it."

The muscle in his jaw twitched. He'd filled out over the winter, thanks to my offerings of buns and smoked turkey, venison, ham, and bread. His face was set and firm. And sterner.

"Do you know what I think, Rachel Marsh?"

"No, but I suspect you're about to tell me."

"I think this isn't about the *Rose*. Or Mr. Adams defending those sailors. I think you are throwing all kinds of brickbats at me for the same reason the street urchins threw ice balls at our soldiers all winter."

"Oh? And what reason is that?"

"You're afraid of me."

"Afraid?" I laughed. "And why should I be? Because you've a fine new red coat?"

"No." His blue eyes reflected the sky and became bluer. There must be something about the new red coat, too, I decided. His shoulders seemed broader.

"You're afraid to let me kiss you." The words were said as softly as the May breeze. And they took my breath away.

"I'm not afraid of anything," I said.

"I don't blame you, mind. I understand you're afraid of how you'll act if I kiss you."

"Why, I never heard such arrogance, Matthew Kilroy! Your new clothes have likely gone to your head."

"Then why won't you let me kiss you?" His voice grew even softer, more insistent.

The word *seductive* came to mind. I'd heard it, but had never known what it meant until then. "Because I'm not Susie Sheaffe," I said.

"Heavens, I'm not asking you to elope with me."

"I let you hold my hand, and you're not satisfied. Now you're pushing for a kiss. What more will you want then? And if I grant it, we can't be friends anymore."

He laughed. "You're asking what I want and telling me I can't have it all in the same breath." Then he scowled. Even when he did that he was handsome. "Why couldn't we be friends anymore if you granted it?"

"We just can't, is all. It's the way of things."

131

"I suppose you read *that* in those books of yours."

"You're not gaining any ground with me, Matthew Kilroy, mocking my book reading."

That was when he kissed me. Without so much as a by-your-leave. I tried to push him off at first, but he was so strong. Except in the kissing, which was as gentle as the May breeze. And which was over before I knew what was happening, or that I wanted it to happen. Then he drew back, scowling.

"Have I gained any ground with you now, Rachel Marsh? What say you? Are we still friends?"

"I'm glad we're moving," I said. "I'm glad you won't be outside our house every night." And I turned and ran from him, back to Brattle Square. But I was not glad of it. And I was crying. I was so confused!

I ran around the back of the house so no one would see my tear-streaked face. Just outside the garden gate Chris Snider was waiting for me. He seemed to have grown taller this past winter, too. He was sprouted up like a weed.

"Hello, Rachel."

"Hello, Chris."

He handed me a copy of the new newspaper started up by Sam Adams and his friends, *The Journal of the Times*.

"Thank you, Chris." I scanned the newspaper. It was brimming with the story of the American sailors accused of murder. Sam Adams had started the paper outside Boston to force the removal of troops and warships. But it was living up to another purpose as well. Which was to inform people in other colonies of the terrible ways in which the soldiers were treating the townsfolk of Boston. Governor Bernard was incensed over the new paper. He called its reports "seditious lies."

"Glad to see Mr. Adams is defendin' the sailors," he said.

"Yes. So are we all, Chris."

"How's the baby?"

I was touched that he should ask. "Not well, Chris. She cries all the time. Dr. Warren comes every other day to suggest new gruels, but she won't eat." Matthew hadn't asked about the baby, I reminded myself.

Chris nodded solemnly. "The paper's sellin' as far away as Georgia," he said.

I nodded politely.

"The *Gazette* is startin' to print some items. Thanks to your Mr. Adams."

"You mean Mr. Adams from this house?"

He nodded. "Where you think he takes himself off to Saturday afternoons?"

"His political club," I said.

He grinned. "He's in the *Gazette* office, writin' articles. With Dr. Warren and others."

I could not believe it! "I didn't know," I said.

"Well, it's a secret, so don't bandy it about."

"And who would I bandy it to?"

He shrugged but did not answer. He was thinking of Matthew, of course.

"I wouldn't tell Private Kilroy," I said. "He's just a friend. I don't tell him things of that nature. I seem to be the last one to know things of that nature, anyway."

He smiled. "You didn't know your uncle Eb's shop windows were broken last night, did you?"

I drew in my breath. "For what?"

"For what else? For goin' against the non-importation agreement. He's been importin' fabric from England. We dragged some of his fabric through the streets. He won't be sellin' it the way it looks now. That agreement is the only weapon we got against the king right now."

The way he said that made me pay special mind. He stood there, shabby and fragile, looking like a good wind from the bay would knock him over, talking about a weapon against the king. And including himself in the "we."

"My uncle Eb must be in a frenzy, though I'm not sorry for him, the way he treated me. Be careful, Chris, please. He isn't one to take it sitting down."

"I'm careful," he said. "I ain't afraid of anythin'. You be careful, too, Miss Rachel."

I stood pondering on what he meant. He did

look thinner than when I'd last seen him. Was it because he'd grown so? Or because he hadn't enough to eat? Why had I never offered *him* any food when he came round? I would next time. He waved and something about the way he stood there, so cocky and ragged, tore at me. It was as if I were seeing him for the first time. Yes, I decided, that *was* hunger in his face. But not for food. For something else. What?

For liberty, I thought. He had the fever for it, like Jane, like Sam Adams and John Hancock and so many others. *Nonsense,* I told myself, going up the back steps. *That's romantic nonsense.* And I'd had more than enough of my share of that for one day.

Chapter Nine

"THE KING'S PEACE has been broken!"

The room was dark, though I had come in broad daylight. The inside shutters on the windows were closed and I was hard put to see the face of the man behind the desk. The man was Uncle Eb. I'd sworn that I'd never have to do with him again, yet earlier that morning when the note had come, I'd trembled for the news it brought. *I don't dast not go,* I told myself. And I'd come running.

Uncle Eb had been attacked the night before by the mob. It was the twenty-ninth of October, a bright blue day outside the warehouse, yet Uncle Eb sat in his office in back with one small candle giving light.

"Did you see my front windows?"

"Yes," I answered.

"They besmeared them with dirt. Outhouse dirt!"

"I saw your men cleaning them as I came in." The mood was hushed between us, as it is when someone dies.

He coughed and reached for his mug and took a drink. The candlelight flickered across his face and I saw the swollen eye, caught sight of the makeshift sling holding one arm firmly in front of him. "I can't scarce walk," he said. "They near broke my leg. I was with my friend Mein and his partner, John Fleeming."

"Mein is trouble," I told him.

"Trouble? Because he dared print the truth in his *Chronicle?*"

"He called John Hancock a milch cow in his paper. That is no truth." So, we were to debate then. Well, I was ready for it.

"I don't speak of that. I speak of the lists."

Everyone in Boston knew of the lists. In August Mein had started running Custom House records showing the names of merchants importing from England.

Many were Patriot merchants, breaking their own boycott.

Uncle Eb grinned. With the bruises on his face, it was a leer. "He proved that certain merchants in the Sons of Liberty are using the nonimportation agreement to destroy their competitors, didn't he? The self-righteous Sons of Perdition are importing! And attacking people like me!"

"Mein printed the lists to turn people against each other," I replied.

He grunted and began to eat from a plate of food on the desk. I could see it was painful for him to chew. "He has courage, though his life has been threatened. He's circulating those lists all over America."

"Then Mein is doing his best to break the king's peace," I reminded him.

He eyed me like a one-eyed vulture. "You defend that rabble?"

"I defend no one, Uncle Eb. I'm sorry you were attacked."

"It almost ended in tragedy. We were walking along King Street last evening. A crowd approached us, led by that mulatto, Attucks. They provoked argument. If Fleeming hadn't fired his pistol into the air and kept them at bay, like as not we wouldn't have made it to the king's troops, the Main Guard. Just as we were being slipped into the guardhouse, one of the rabble lashed out with a shovel. First Mein, then me. Near broke my shoulder and tore my eye out."

I said nothing. My mouth was dry.

"Only the bayonets of the sentries kept the mob from storming the guardhouse then and there. As it was, that benighted fool Sam Adams got a warrant for our arrest and they came for us in the guardhouse. We had to hide in the garret for an hour. I near fainted. I was bleeding. We had to put on soldiers' uniforms to escape."

"There isn't anything I can say, Uncle Eb. I've naught to do with any of it."

"Yesterday afternoon," he bellowed, leaning forward, "a group of Liberty Boys tarred and feathered one of their own because they thought he was informing. A sailor. He's near dead."

I sighed. There was nothing for it. I would have to hear him out, bear witness to his humiliation. He would have it no other way.

"The situation in Boston is beyond being salvaged since Governor Bernard went back to England." He spoke in a low and rumbling voice. "Hutchinson can't keep order. Mein asked him for protection. He as much as said he can't give it. He can't get the Justices of the Peace to honor their legal obligations. The soldiers are morally isolated. The civil courts give no help."

Morally isolated. I thought of Matthew. I must remember those words. "I'm sure you shouldn't be exerting yourself like this, Uncle Eb," I said.

"The army came here as peacekeepers! The citizens have made ill usage of the troops! Now they feel themselves in danger."

I felt anger. "Danger? Tell such to Private John Moyse of the Fourteenth who was convicted of breaking and entering."

"That was a contrivance. The judges sold him

into three years of indenture because he couldn't pay damages. When his superiors offered to buy him out he refused. He wanted to desert!"

I felt like John Adams himself standing there, arguing for the citizens. Up until that moment I'd managed to stay neutral, though I wavered occasionally, from one side to the other. But I was determined to argue in favor of the Devil himself if it meant standing up to Uncle Eb.

"Private John Riley of the Fourteenth traded punches with a man at the market in Faneuil Hall for no reason. When he was put in prison the grenadiers helped him break out. Is that keeping the king's peace?" I asked.

He just stared at me.

"Ensign John Ness stole wood from John Pierpoint. When Pierpoint went to get it back, Captain Molesworth told his soldiers that if any of the crowd struck them they were to use their bayonets."

"A soldier was punched in the face that day," he flung back. "And it was not a crowd, it was a mob."

We glared at each other in the flickering light. "Yes, and what of the day the people came to see the changing of the guard near the Town House? Molesworth called up the Yankee Doodle tune and pushed his way through the crowd shouting insults.

He is spiriting up his soldiers to murder the inhabitants."

"You've become saucy," he said. "A shrew."

"I've become educated, Uncle Eb."

"And this is what your book reading has done for you? You've become one of them?"

"I haven't. But I've heard too many good people say the army is a parcel of blackguard rascals."

"Let me tell you something, girl. The people here enjoy the blessing of as mild and good a government as any people upon the globe. Sooner or later they will see the absurdity of what they are doing."

I did not reply to that. Never had I spoken so passionately in defense of the rabble. I had not even known such feelings were in me. And never had I spoken so to Uncle Eb.

"Where are you getting your information?" he asked.

"I read the newspaper."

"The weekly dung barge, I suppose." That was what the Tories called the *Gazette*.

"And I have friends," I added.

"Jane Washburn?"

"Leave Jane out of this, Uncle Eb. Tell me the real reason for this meeting today."

"So you can see what they've done to me. To one of your family."

He seemed to have forgotten that the last time we met he'd disowned me. Now I was family. "I'm sorry you've been so ill-used," I said again. "If there's anything I can do for you . . ."

"There is."

I'd spoken too quickly, forgetting his penchant for intrigue. It was a trap then, this meeting. And I'd fallen into it again.

"Your friend Washburn . . ."

"Please, Uncle Eb, leave her out of this."

He waved his good hand in impatience. "I care not that you choose to be friends with her. She's trouble, but then as you say, so is my friend Mein. Come here, girl." He gestured that I should sit. His tone was kind.

I did so. He lowered his voice. "I hear that the Sons have threatened the life of Mackintosh."

Jane had cried telling me such. I'd had to comfort her, she who had never needed comforting.

"The Sons have come to realize that Mac knows more of their secret transactions than all the Tories in Boston. I hear they're afraid he'll turn informer."

"I've heard no such thing," I said. I was trembling.

"The Tories know that Mac can unravel for them all these bloody intrigues. Wouldn't you say it would profit the ministry, and Mac, if he were brought back to England?"

"What has this to do with me, Uncle Eb?"

He chuckled. "A little slip of a girl like you. Think of how you could help restore the king's peace. Wouldn't you want a part in that? Any small incident may trigger a catastrophe if we continue the way we're going."

My eyes were wide in fear. "Say it plain, Uncle Eb."

He said it plain. "I've been authorized by the ministry to get to Mac and suggest he go back to England. The best way to get to him is through Jane."

"And the best way to do that is through me," I said.

"Yes."

I got up, trembling so I could scarcely stand on my own two feet. What was there about this man? How could one be so conniving and evil? And what was there about me that I kept going back to him? Yes, he was family, and yes, that morning when the note had arrived I'd not hesitated to come. Why? To be welcomed back into the bosom of family again, even though there was a snake in that bosom? How could I be so weak?

"You should know better than to ask me, Uncle Eb. The answer is no."

He said nothing.

"How come you to think Jane would listen to me anyway?"

"I know she would." He chuckled. "Your uncle Eb knows a lot of things."

"Like what?"

"Mackintosh is married. And your Jane is hopelessly smitten with him. This would be her chance to go to England with him and get away."

I was dumbstruck. I hadn't known Mac was married. Poor Jane. How she must be suffering!

He was watching me. "Your uncle Eb knows other things that might interest you," he said.

"You might as well tell me then and get it over with. Since I don't think we're going to be seeing each other anymore." My voice was tight, lifeless.

"Your mother was in circumstances before she married your father," he said. He smiled with the telling of it. "Why else do you think she'd marry a Protestant-burning Frenchman like that?"

The candle was burning low on the desk. I clutched at the doorjamb. "You lie."

"I can produce the date of their marriage. And your birth."

I felt about to faint. Yet at the same time I was flooded with a sense of purpose to sustain me. "Good-bye, Uncle Eb. I hope your wounds heal."

His laughter followed me out. "Remember that when you walk out with that Private Kilroy. You'll come to the same end, you'll see."

I found my way out of the warehouse into the

bright blue October day. Fresh air restored me. But I took the blackness of that back room with me as I went on my way. The mob can tar and feather him next time, I vowed, and I will not come when he calls.

Chapter Ten

· 1770 ·

I WALKED, HEAD DOWN, against the bitter wind on Queen Street. I was on my way to fetch Mr. Adams from the *Gazette* office. It was Thursday, the eighth of February. He often helped in preparing Monday's paper, usually on Saturday. But this Saturday he would be in Braintree.

Baby Susanna had died the week before. Her little body lay wrapped in winding sheets in the parlor, awaiting the coffin made by Mr. Adams's brothers, Peter and Elihu. They had arrived with the coffin just before I left the house.

Mr. Adams would not have gone to the newspaper office that morning, but one of the Junius letters had just arrived from England. It was a bitter attack on the king and they needed his legal advice to print it. As well as his help.

As I mounted the stairs to the second floor, my heart was leaden. What would I say to him as we walked home? What words to ease his heart for the journey back to Braintree?

No words. There were none. I felt betrayed. All my book reading and I did not have words to help him or Abigail now when they so needed it. What good was book reading then? Had it just served to muddle my head, as Uncle Eb and Matthew often implied?

I stood a moment in the doorway of the office, taking in the scene. The room was full of old desks that were piled high with paper and inkstands and quill pens, books, plates with scraps of food left on them, and pewter mugs.

At one desk sat young Josiah Quincy, lawyer and brother to Hannah. He looked up and smiled. He was cross-eyed, but that did not detract from his appealing manner. At another desk was Dr. Warren, and off in a corner was the man who advertised himself betimes as a silversmith and other times as a dentist. Paul Revere did fix teeth.

Henry Knox had told me that Revere's latest venture, from his shop on Clark's Wharf, was doing sketches of Boston's riots. They were being published in the *Gazette*.

All nodded their polite hellos. They were all Sons of Liberty and had been to the house last evening along with John Hancock, Thomas Boylston, Martin Brimmer, Moses Gill, and others to pay their respects at the death of the baby.

"It's time, Mr. Adams," I said.

He nodded and got up. The others shook his hand and murmured words of comfort, then together he and I went out into the unrelenting cold.

We walked in benumbed silence. He spoke first.

"Mr. Revere's sketches are very good," he said, "but there are times I'm afraid he likes to stir up the pot with his etchings."

"He's a Son of Liberty. Isn't that what they do best, sir?"

"Yes, I'm afraid it is. And as a silversmith, he has no equal in America. I'd like to get Abigail one of his punch bowls. Perhaps for her next birthday."

"That would be nice, sir," I said.

"How is she, my Diana?"

He sometimes called her that, though I knew not why. "She's keeping, sir."

"I wish to God it was in my power to take this sorrow from her."

"I think she knows that, Mr. Adams."

"You've been a great comfort to her, Rachel."

"Not enough, sir. This business sits ill upon her."

He sighed. "Patience, forbearance are the lessons we grew up with. Yet how difficult to put them into practice. I don't know if we can live this winter out here in Boston, what with the troops and this sorrow. I was thinking of removing my family back to Braintree. What say you?"

He was asking my opinion! "I know Mrs. Adams likes it here, sir. Especially in the new house. She says it is most commodious."

"She does seem to like it, doesn't she? Perhaps I'm using my wife as an excuse to go back to Braintree, Rachel. I seem to be in a constant quandary here. Yet I've never done so well in my law practice."

"You got those sailors free of the murder charges last summer," I reminded him. "You've been a hero to the people since then."

He grunted. "I'm not sure I want to be such a hero. I'm losing my peace of mind. The Sons are demanding more and more of my time. And I'm allowing myself to be drawn into their politics. How much time can I give to the Cause? Will it swallow me up as it did Otis?"

He was talking more to himself than to me, so I kept a quiet tongue in my head.

"Truth to tell, Rachel, I've been in a fit of depression since that comet appeared in the sky last November. I'm not like most people who believe that comets bring bad things. Yet I sense some doom is about to befall us."

"It has, sir."

He stopped to peer down at me. "Of course it has. Yet I feel Susanna's death isn't all, that more will follow."

149

"It's the cold, sir. And February. My mother used to say that February will do mischief to the stoutest soul."

He smiled. "Your mother must have been a fine woman, Rachel."

We continued walking. He told me how someone had cut the heart out of Governor Bernard's portrait at Harvard College. "Resistance to authority always is present at Harvard, but now it's the spirit of the times all over. What's going on over there?"

I looked across the street. It was market day in town and a group of boys and country people were gathered around the town pump. On it was a board on which was painted a large hand. Beneath it was the word *Importer*.

The town's merchants had agreed not to import British goods until the first day of 1770. Those who had been caught importing had agreed to allow the Committee of Inspections to lock up their goods until merchants who hadn't been importing could do so. And have a fair chance to compete.

The hand on the sign pointed to Mr. Jackson's shop, The Sign of the Brazen Head. The boys were hurling snowballs at anyone who came out of the shop.

Another crowd of men, who seemed to be merchants, were watching in amusement.

"Stop that," Mr. Adams called. A cheer had just gone up as one of the shop's customers was hit with an ice ball.

No one heeded Mr. Adams. He started forward. "Molineaux," he murmured. "I should have known he'd be in the midst of it all."

"Isn't he a Son, Mr. Adams?"

"He's the new captain of the Liberty Boys. In charge of the Committee for Tarring and Feathering, no doubt. Disperse," he called, "disperse, I say, before someone is hurt and we have more trouble! Molineaux, get them in hand, can't you?"

Molineaux waved and grinned, then came toward us. "It's only an exhibition, Mr. Adams. To get Jackson's attention. The man is selling his goods before other merchants have a chance to import."

Mr. Adams was angry. "Wasn't he already visited by you people in January?"

Molineaux was a very large man of middle age. He was, himself, a hardware merchant. He had a dark and brooding look about him. "We're giving him a reminder, sir."

"Why are those boys out of school?"

"It's market day and a school holiday, sir."

"There are too many school holidays in Boston. Get them off the streets. Are you paying them to throw those ice balls?"

"Now, would I do such a thing, Mr. Adams?"

"Yes, you would. They don't call you the first leader in dirty matters for nothing. Get them off the streets, I say, before we have tragedy!"

Molineaux nodded his head, gave no further argument, and went back to becalm the boys. Within minutes he had them in hand and dispersed.

I looked up at Mr. Adams. "He minded you, sir."

"Wasn't that Chris Snider, who sometimes comes round to deliver my cousin's newspaper?" he asked.

He was right. It was Chris. I caught sight of him just before he rounded a corner, but I said nothing.

"Come along, Rachel."

And so we quickened our steps in the direction of home.

"Molineaux is trouble," he told me. "I can't abide the man. He looks as if he comes from the nether regions. By God, it's wrong to pay those boys for his sinister purposes. And one of these days we'll all suffer for it."

As we came up the hill to the house I saw the sled out front, hitched up to two fine farm horses. Mr. Adams stopped, seeing it, and paused in the cold. I saw his face go rigid.

"Rachel, Mrs. Adams will not be going on this trip to Braintree. She isn't well enough."

"Yes sir."

"I wish you to take care of her in my absence."

"I will, oh yes, I will, Mr. Adams."

He sighed and looked around him at the forbidding landscape. It was almost as if he were summoning up the courage to go inside the house and face the duty that lay ahead. "It's more than the death of Susanna. She's in circumstances again. I worry for her."

I brightened. "Oh, Mr. Adams, that could be just the thing to get her mind off her sorrow!"

"Do you think so?"

I blushed, minding how freely we were talking about such a delicate matter. "I'm sure, sir."

He nodded. "You have helped me much, Rachel. Thank you. I'll be overnight in Braintree. We won't be able to bury the baby. The ground is too frozen. My brother Peter has promised to cover the coffin with pine boughs and keep watch daily."

I shivered, nodding.

"You will not mention that to Mrs. Adams. Read to her, will you, Rachel? Something to make her happy. Don't let her dwell on melancholy reflections."

I promised that, too. He was just about to go into the house when, from around the corner of it, like a bright red bird in the snow, a British soldier appeared.

"Mr. Adams? It's Private Kilroy. I was sentry outside your house when you lived in Brattle Square, sir. I've come to offer my condolences. I remember the night the child was born."

John Adams straightened himself up and nodded. "Thank you, yes."

"Please convey my sentiments to Mrs. Adams, sir. She was most kind to me every time she came into the street."

"I will, yes, I will." Mr. Adams started up the steps.

"I just don't want you to feel, sir," Matthew added, "that we're all a parcel of blackguard rascals."

Mr. Adams stopped at the door. "Perhaps you can enlighten me about something, Private."

"Yes, sir."

"On the way home just now, we ran into a fracas on Queen Street. Why is it that whenever mobs of citizens gather for sinister purposes, you red-coated sentinels disappear into the mists?"

Matthew stood looking up at him with his mouth half open. Then he scowled and looked at his shoes. "We've been instructed to, sir."

"Instructed?"

"Yes, sir. By our superiors. We've been told to let most anything happen and not take action. We're ordered to do nothing that might deprive a man of his liberty."

Matthew raised his eyes and met those of John Adams as he said this. I'm sure Mr. Adams saw the defiance in those blue eyes. I did.

But all Mr. Adams said was, "Thank you, Private." And then he went into the house.

In spite of the cold and the death of Susanna, I had felt warm and happy inside. John Adams, one of the best lawyers in Boston, had spoken to me like I was . . . like I was Mercy Otis Warren! Like I wrote plays! Why, he'd even asked my opinion on things! And said I'd helped him!

My book reading has made this possible, I thought. *How could I have ever doubted it?*

Then I looked at Matthew, saw his misery, and everything was ruined.

"He thinks little of me," he said bitterly.

"Mr. Adams is not like that, Matthew."

"I saw the look on his face."

"And he saw the look on yours."

"And what does *that* mean?"

"You defied him."

"I only told him what our officers told us."

"It's stupid, them telling you such. And it mocks the very idea of what liberty is supposed to be. Mr. Adams knows that, because he's a lawyer. Even I know that. And surely you do."

We had walked around to the side of the house that overlooked the millpond. The afternoon sun shone brightly there. He set his musket, butt down, on the ground, leaning it against the house.

"Yes, I know it, Rachel. Why do you think I'm so unhappy? I'm in a strange land. I haven't been home in over two years. We came here to keep the peace and the people hate us."

I was getting the uncomfortable feeling that sooner or later this conversation would take a turn I did not want.

"The street urchins call us bloody-backs. Or lobsterbacks. When they aren't pelting us with dirt or ice balls. 'C'mon, boys,' they say, 'who'll buy lobsters tonight?' "

"They're street urchins, Matthew."

"Put up to it by the leaders of the mob. The other night a thief broke into Mr. John Gray's house. Do you know who the authorities blamed? One of our sentries, for standing there and allowing him to do it. He had *orders* not to challenge the thief. How do you think he feels? How do you think *I* feel, wearing my fine red coat, carrying this Brown Bess musket, and not being allowed to be a soldier?"

"I hadn't thought about it," I said.

"I'm not allowed to fire my musket. And I want to. I want to do the job I was trained to do! Be a soldier! I'm getting bloody tired of it all, I can tell you."

I heard a noise from inside the house. A door slammed. They would be putting little Susanna in her coffin now. I should be inside. I was needed. But I sensed I was needed out here, too. I felt torn.

"You've been away from home too long," I suggested gently.

He glared at me. "Do you know that in the year and a half I've been in Boston I've never been inside a house? Never sat by a hearth or taken a meal at a proper table? I walk sentry duty at night and see the candles glowing in the windows, see the people warm and safe inside, and I want to die for wanting to be inside a house again, Rachel." I saw a film of tears in his blue eyes.

"I feel the fault is part mine, Matthew," I said. "We haven't been able to see each other every night since last spring when we moved here."

He smiled ruefully. "Do you remember the day we came to see this house? And how we kissed?"

I blushed. "I mind it, Matthew."

He reached out to take my hand. "You've been hiding around corners from me ever since."

"I haven't! We've been seeing each other at least once a week on my day off."

"We haven't kissed since. I thought I'd give you time, and you'd come round. Then last fall something else happened."

"What?"

"I don't know. You became even more standoffish. I recollect the day it started. Right after you paid a visit to your uncle, when he was attacked. It was like you blamed me for his attack."

"I never did, Matthew. I never . . ."

"And you've been prissier than my aunt Mathilda ever since."

He was right. I looked away from him, toward the millpond. That had been the visit when Uncle Eb told me my mother had been in circumstances when she married my father.

I had shied away from Matthew ever since. I loved my mother, but I did not want what happened to her to happen to me. It was that simple.

"I've reasons you wouldn't understand, Matthew," I told him. "But you're still my friend. I like you very much."

"But not enough to kiss me again. Or tell me why you won't."

I reached out and put my hand on the red woolen coat sleeve. "Matthew, not today. I'm needed inside now."

He sighed. "It's always not today. I'm weary of it."

"I know. And you've behaved properly for so long. For which I hold you in high esteem. We'll speak of it soon, I promise, Matthew."

He slung his musket over his shoulder. "I'm going to take a job at the ropewalk works. I need the money. For food. They still don't feed us that well." He smiled. "I suppose I'll always be a beggar for your handouts."

"Matthew, don't work there! The soldiers are always fighting with the workers. Mr. Adams says it's a hotbed of trouble."

"Mr. Adams has a home, a profession, food on the table, and a family."

"Oh, Matthew, don't. You'll get into a fracas."

"Mayhap what I need is a fracas," he said bitterly. "I need to do something so people will respect me. Would it matter to you if I was in a fight, Rachel? No, don't answer that. Answer this. Don't you think I'm weary of being called a damned rascally scoundrel lobster, and I want to stand up for what I really am?"

"What are you, Matthew?"

"A soldier in His Majesty's army, the most powerful army in the world!"

And so saying, he took his leave. He walked across the expanse of whiteness, into the lane. I watched him go. I minded his broad shoulders, the way his cocked hat sat on his head, the swagger of him, with his musket across his shoulder, a lone red figure against the bleak landscape. A soldier far from home.

I shivered. Oh, Matthew! My heart went out to him. What had I done, hurting him, pushing him away, when all he'd wanted was to hold me and kiss me, to be comforted. And it wasn't as if I hadn't wanted it, too. Surely I could have allowed him such and still have kept him from compromising me. I'd kept him from kissing me for weeks on end, hadn't I?

I stood there, my heart wringing with anguish. *You love him, Rachel, why don't you tell him so,* I asked myself. *You know how you always look forward to your day off so you can see him. Call out to him. Bring him back.* But I did not, and the distance lengthened between us as he walked away. And I was needed inside.

I walked around to the front and up the steps. This was so unfair. I wasn't ready to give my heart to a man. I was too young. Surely, love didn't happen that way. Why, from everything I'd read, all those books I'd gotten at Henry Knox's shop, the heroines became smitten only when they were looking for love, when they were pining away.

I went inside. And then another thought came to me. I hadn't known I was so smitten with Matthew until he walked away. *Unfair, unfair,* I told myself. *Life is unfair.* And I went to help them with the dead baby.

Chapter Eleven

"IN ANSWER TO YOUR question, no, Rachel, you shouldn't have told him you're smitten with him. Has he told you?"

"Well, not in so many words, no. He tiptoes around the matter a lot."

"Of course he does. They all do." Jane's mouth was tight. Was she thinking of the tiptoeing Mackintosh had done? She busied herself briskly, laying the table in her small room upstairs in Sarah Welsteed's house.

I sat down on the window seat and watched her. She seemed much more serious these days. Some of the gaiety was gone. I'd never told her that I'd found out Mackintosh was married.

It would distress Jane to know I knew. She never spoke of it. Yet she still met with him regularly. Business, she called it.

"Your room is warm. The fire gives good light and heat," I said.

"It's not commodious, but it will do."

"I was so surprised at your invitation for tea. It isn't like you, Jane."

"Oh? And why?"

I giggled. "Well, for one thing, you prefer coffee."

"Do I?"

"Yes, you're always at the coffeehouses."

She scowled. "That's business. How do you know what I really like? Do any of us really know the other? We don't know ourselves."

"I think we know ourselves," I allowed. "I just don't think we're honest about what we know."

"Mayhap you're right." She poured tea. "Come sit. This invitation is by way of thanking you for refusing your uncle when he asked you to exert influence on me to convince Mackintosh to go to England."

I sat. "Mac isn't going then."

"Of course not. He's determined to fight to the end against the British. But I have another reason for inviting you today. The Whigs are promoting a no-tea-drinking subscription this week amongst Boston's fine ladies. This is made from labradore, a herb kindred to this area. Do you like it?"

I sipped. "It's very good. So is this cornbread. Did you bake it?"

"I do some baking on occasion for my mistress.

Would you take some tea home to Mrs. Adams and have her share it with her friends?"

"Yes."

"I think the fuss over this pernicious weed will never come to an end." She sighed. "England could repeal the Townsend Acts, but they'll never repeal the tax on tea. But then, I forgot!" She set her cup down. "Mrs. Adams is not well. Invalids are permitted to drink the real item."

"She isn't an invalid, Jane. She's just mourning the death of her baby. I worry about her. Sometimes I come home from errands in the afternoon and find her sitting there with a book in her lap. But she isn't reading. She's just staring. It's frightening."

She nodded. "We women do have a bad time of it, don't we? From the moment we meet our men until we raise their babies. If we're lucky enough to raise them."

"Mrs. Adams said if the men don't pay particular care and attention to the ladies, we are determined to ferment a rebellion of our own someday. But that, for now, we dare not exert our power in its full latitude."

She raised her cup. "A toast to Mrs. Adams."

"Are you having a bad time of it, Jane?"

She brightened quickly. "No. What makes you think that?"

"You seem sad."

"I'm busy helping the Liberty Boys. I've been selected to promote the no-tea-drinking business this week."

"Well, I'm having a bad time of it, and I don't mind saying. I haven't seen Matthew in near a fortnight, and I'm sore afflicted for the way I treated him."

She leaned forward. "He wants you to be sore afflicted."

"He does?"

"Yes, that way next time you meet, you'll do his bidding."

I shook my head no, vigorously. "I'll never do that."

She set her cup down gently. "I told you men could never be just friends, didn't I?"

"Yes, you did, Jane. And you were right, I'm sorry to say. Though I still have Henry Knox."

She bit her lower lip and scowled. "When did you last see Henry?"

"Right before the baby was buried. Why? Is something wrong?"

She got up and crossed the room and took a folded piece of paper out of a book. "I shouldn't divulge this, but the fat is already in the fire. The Loyalists know what side Henry's sympathies have favored." She handed the note to me.

It was from Henry Knox. To Jane? I looked at her. "Read it," she directed.

Dear Jane:

I write to advise you that I am under surveillance. And, though I would like to see you, concern for you obliges me to tender you my most sincere warning. Don't come until I can communicate to you that the way is clear.

I was openmouthed. "You know Henry? You're friends?"

"We work together. I am not permitted to say how."

"He's being watched? By the Loyalists?"

She nodded. "He's not allowed to leave Boston. I can say no more."

"I thought he was neutral?"

She smiled that secretive smile of hers and poured more tea. "As I said before, dear Rachel, who of us really knows the other? Or ourselves?"

My mind was playing leapfrog with its thoughts. I could not keep up with it. "Henry Knox, a sympathizer with the rebellious Americans?" I said. "I should have known."

"You sound pleased."

"I must pay him a visit."

"Do I determine, then, that you have made a decision to side with the rabble, too, Rachel?"

I stared at her. "I've made no such decision. Henry's a friend. He's helped me greatly with my book learning. And now he's in trouble."

"As you said before, Rachel, we know ourselves, but are not always honest about what we know."

She got up. I studied her tall slender frame as she put another log on the hearth. Jane had been right about Matthew. Was she right about this? Was my heart with the rabble? I pushed the thought aside. Arguing with Uncle Eb or Matthew in their defense was one thing. Being pulled into their Cause was another.

Jane came back and sat down. "Of course, Lucy's parents are against her courtship more than ever now. It's an embarrassment to her father, who is a high-toned Loyalist of great family pretensions. They've told her that if she marries Henry, she will be eating the moth-eaten loaf of poverty, while her sisters reap the benefits of the mother country."

"Is she still seeing Henry?"

"Of course."

"I must pay him a visit," I said again.

"Do. But don't let on I've told you of his trouble. Let him confide in you himself. But be careful you're not seen conspiring with him. He never knows who's in the shop, watching."

"Tell me about the Plains of Abraham," I said to Henry.

"What would you have me tell you?"

We were standing in an aisle between two

bookshelves, well away from some British officers who were browsing. Henry had greeted me cheerfully, and to get him alone I'd asked for a copy of *Robinson Crusoe*. He was searching the shelves for the book.

"My father was killed fighting there. But no one has ever told me about the battle. The name sounds like something from the Bible," I said.

"Like something mystical?"

"Yes." I smiled. I had always thought that but been fearful of saying it, lest anyone thought me weak in the head.

"It was July of 1759. The French still held Quebec; the English knew they had to take it. For seventy-five years the French had sent raiding parties that included Indians from that place, to raid us. Ah, here's the book you wanted."

He took it from the shelf, examined it, and handed it to me.

"Tell me," I looked up at him.

"Yes." He clasped his hands behind him and rocked on his heels. "Thousands of American lives had been lost in the wars. Then William Pitt, the great British statesman, sent us James Wolfe. And the largest number of ships they'd ever sent across the Atlantic. Twenty thousand men went in two hundred twenty-seven ships up the St. Lawrence. Many were Yankees. Fishermen and sailors."

"And?"

"And on shore young General Wolfe let nine thousand men on land, above the harbor. They met the French General Montcalm on the Plains of Abraham."

"My father was with Montcalm."

"Yes. Montcalm was killed. So was Wolfe. But the British won the battle and took Quebec. Everyone in America celebrated. Long live George II, who has freed us from the yoke of the French! No longer would we have the threat of the French. But George II died soon afterward and we got George III."

"He is our king now."

He closed his eyes. "Yes. Our royal sovereign."

"Henry, may I tell you something?"

"Yes."

"I don't feel like he's my king." I whispered the words. No one could hear us. "He means naught to me. I don't feel as if I need a king. And it isn't because his men killed my father. Is something wrong with me?"

He looked at me almost tenderly then. "There is nothing wrong with you, Rachel," he whispered. "You are a clever and thinking person."

"Then why do I feel this way?"

He put his hand on my shoulder and peered through the space above the books on the shelves.

Then he looked at me. His dark eyes seemed filmed with tears and his voice came in a hoarse whisper. "Because you are no longer a British American. You have become a plain American, Rachel. A true American."

I felt my own eyes go wide. "I have?"

"Yes, Rachel. Congratulations. You have finally become sensible of it. But don't go about telling just anyone how you feel. Let it be our secret, hey? Until we can talk more about it." He said no more, just patted my shoulder and walked away.

"Can I help you, gentlemen?" I heard him ask the British officers.

I clutched my copy of *Robinson Crusoe* close to my breast. My heart was hammering. I could still feel Henry Knox's hand on my shoulder. *You have become a plain American, Rachel. A true American.*

I felt a rush of comforting warmth go through me at the words. It was as if there was a bond between us. I felt like a child sharing some delicious secret, and at the same time like a grown woman just being admitted into an honored circle of people. I closed my eyes, holding the moment close to me. Why had I never understood this before? This was what all the rioting and fracas was about on Boston's streets.

A new breed of people was being born. And

the tumult and trouble going on out there were the labor pains.

Congratulations, Rachel, you have finally become sensible of it.

Was that how it happened, then, becoming a true American? Was it something you had to become sensible of? And understand? If so then, yes, I had become one. I smiled at Henry Knox as I left the shop. He was still waiting on the two British officers.

It was not until I was outside in the February cold that another thought came to me. Becoming a true American was something anybody could do. You needed no family pretensions, no monied background. But more than that, *I had been accepted.* Without question. Just because I wanted to be.

I walked home through the snowy streets. For the first time in my life I felt close to some truth. But I did not know what that truth was.

Life did not get any easier once I felt closer to my truth. I don't know what I expected, but deciding one was a true American in Boston in February of 1770 did not suddenly give one the power of second sight. It only made matters more complicated.

For one thing, I could not go home and announce to anyone what I had become. Not even to

Mr. or Mrs. Adams. When I did go home from Henry Knox's that day I found Mrs. Adams in the same chair in the parlor again, this time with some crewelwork in her hands. But she was not making any stitches. She was just staring.

The children were making free with themselves in the house. Sukey was busy cooking. So, though it was my day off, I took matters in hand. I sat the children down with the new copy of *Robinson Crusoe,* read to them a bit, and then put them down for their naps. Then I attended to my mistress.

"Ma'am? Would you like some tea? I've fixed some on a tray with some little cakes Sukey made. It's the tea Jane sent."

"Yes, Rachel, how sweet of you."

"You shouldn't sit in the dark, ma'am."

"Is it dark then? So soon?"

"Yes. You know the dusk comes earlier in February. I'm lighting the candles."

"I have melancholy reflections, Rachel."

"You mustn't. You have so much to be thankful for."

"There are times I feel as if something terrible is about to befall us all. As if hope, the anchor of my soul, is lost."

"You will find it again. My mama felt that way when my father was killed. She told me so when I was old enough to understand. She felt like she

171

was wandering in a desert. But she recovered her senses."

"How did she do that, Rachel?"

"I don't know, ma'am. But she did it. And if she did, you can do it, too."

"You are such a good girl, Rachel. How long have you been with us now?"

"Almost four years, ma'am."

"I think it is time for us to talk about the linen part of your dowry."

"Oh, ma'am!" My hand flew to my heart.

"Yes. I must rouse myself from this self-imposed lethargy. Most girls begin their dowry at fourteen. Of course, if we were back in Braintree, you could hand weave on our old loom. I did all my table linens and towels, bed sheets and pillow-cases. Have you ever used a loom?"

"My mama did her own weaving and taught me some. But then she died."

"I left my loom in Braintree. And you're too busy caring for the children. We'll buy some fabric. Not imported, no. But there is plenty of home-woven material here in Boston. You can then hem and embroider your sheets and pillowcases and table linen. And on some of our trips out, we might start to bargain for some kitchen items. A skillet on legs, I think. Some good pots. Some pewter mugs."

I was flooded with happiness. "Thank you, Mrs. Adams," I said.

"Thank *you*, Rachel. Just speaking of it has given life to me again. Perhaps we can go out tomorrow and search for some fabric."

By the time Mr. Adams got home, the color was back in her face and she was in much better spirits and ready to listen to all his news of the outside world.

"There was another fight at Gray's Ropewalk Works today," he told her. "The British should not allow their soldiers to work there."

I felt a catch in my throat. Had Matthew been in the fight?

"Also, Abigail," he went on, "I saw another painted hand on a wooden post. It was set up in front of Mr. Theophilus Lillie's shop. All these signs and harassment of merchants. Sooner or later there is going to be real trouble. It can't be avoided the way things are going."

Chapter Twelve

TRUE TO HER WORD, the next day when the children were napping, Mrs. Adams announced that we were going out to shop for fabric for my dowry. She was very excited as she dressed. Her cheeks had a pinkness for the first time in weeks.

"I've always loved shopping," she confided. "Especially in Boston."

And so we set out with our wicker baskets on our arms.

"In New England," she explained to me, "shopping is a sport, with a purpose and a challenge."

"Ma'am?"

"It is a matter of honor, no matter how well off the shopper, to get the most for one's money."

She told me then how Boston had been when she'd come here as a child. "I remember house paints and patterned wallpaper from England, woolens and satins and brocades. All before the nonimportation agreement, of course." And she sighed.

But she knew where the shops were to buy the good fabric. Shops where you heard the thumping of the hand looms before you walked in the door. Shops where the fabric was held up to the light and exclaimed over. Then the dickering in price. And I was surprised to find that Mrs. Adams could dicker as well as any indentured servant doing business on Long Wharf.

Within two hours we had visited three shops and come away with yards of good linen and the softest of cotton homespun. And silken thread to embroider with. And even some handmade lace.

She showed me then how to make pillowcases and how to trim them with lace. "You will wait to embroider your initials, of course," she advised, "until you know the name of the man you will marry."

Before I went to my room that night to pore over my beautiful booty, she sat and wrote a letter to her husband's brother Elihu back in Braintree, instructing him to make me a dowry chest. And she included the exact measurements.

I went to bed happier than I remembered being in a long time.

At two and a half, little Johnnie was a very bright and handsome little boy. He had many winning ways that had affixed him a special place in my heart. Nabby, at four and a half, was already a serious little woman, standoffish and not nearly as affectionate.

They each had their own bedroom, though lately I'd been sleeping on the narrow cot in Johnnie's room. He'd taken to having nightmares. Mrs. Adams said it was the presence of the soldiers, the constant fifing and drumming, the tramplings of the Light Horse regiments.

The day after our shopping expedition, it snowed. It was the twenty-second of February. Johnnie had slept fitfully and I'd been up with him. He was still sleeping at nine-thirty when I went down to breakfast, having overslept myself. I must have looked terrible, for Mrs. Adams advised me to take my bean porridge, ham, biscuits, and coffee back upstairs and rest myself. I ensconced myself on the little cot in Johnnie's room and ate. The house was quiet. Mr. Adams had gone out. Sleet fell against the windows.

I must have fallen asleep, because the next thing I knew, Johnnie was standing over me. "Wachel, get up," he said.

I roused myself. "What is it? Have you had a nightmare?"

"Guns, Wachel. I hear guns."

"No guns, baby." I took him on my lap and

hugged him close. "No guns. You must have been dreaming."

"Guns. I'se fwightened. And bells are winging."

I heard the bells then. They seemed to be coming from the New Brick Church on Hanover Street. "Why don't you get dressed?" I suggested. "And then we'll go down and find your mama?"

My fingers were trembling as I helped him dress. *Do little boys have second sight,* I pondered, *when it comes to guns and trouble?* We went downstairs to find Mrs. Adams in the parlor. But she would not let us go out. I peered out the front windows. There was an eerie yellow light outside, as sometimes fills the sky when it is snowing.

It was eleven-thirty in the morning. We stood in the parlor. Johnnie clung to his mother's skirts. Mrs. Adams sat and read to the children, looking up as footsteps sounded outside. I knew she was worried for her husband.

Sukey and I paced. All of Boston's church bells were now ringing. In a little while Luke came in the back door. Sukey and I ran to ask him what had happened.

"Riot," he said.

"Where?" we asked in unison.

"North End. Theophilus Lillie's shop. Bunch of boys were keeping people from goin' inside. An' peltin' the place with ice. Then Ebenezer Richard come over. He lives next door. The boys threw sticks and dirt and stones at him. He went into Lillie's. More sticks and stones and eggs flew through the air. Then another man came to help them. Some windows got broken."

He paused for breath. His thin face was red, despite the cold. And scratched. And his coat was torn. As houseboy to the Adamses, Luke never went about like that. He was clean and neat, always. Had he been involved in the riot?

Just as the thought came to me, Sukey went to him. "Take off your coat," she said. She took it from him, then gave him a bit of flannel to wipe his face. And some water. We waited while he drank.

Why, I thought, *Luke is one of those boys. Like Chris Snider. And Sukey knows it.* The thought made me dizzy, yet it made sense. Luke was only fourteen and often ran the streets.

He went on. "Richardson went an' got some guns. The crowd wuz sayin' to hang Richardson. Then Richardson pokes his musket through a window. Mob broke through the front door. Richardson fired."

"And who was shot?" The clear voice came from behind us. Sukey and I turned to find Mrs. Adams standing there, alone.

Luke set his cup down on the table. "Chris Snider," he said.

My feet were cold, so cold that they seemed not to be a part of me anymore. In my private notions, as I walked, all I could think of was the pain in my poor toes. Then I felt guilty thinking of my own discomfort when up ahead, in a coffin carried by six young people, lay Chris Snider. Dead.

I was not unacquainted with death. I'd lost both my mother and father when a young child. So, when baby Susanna had died in February, I thought I would recognize all the miseries one felt. But I'd found, back then, that there are, attached to the death of every different person in our lives, different feelings. With baby Susanna I had cried because she had not had a chance to live. And I had cried for her parents.

With Chris Snider I cried for having lost something. And I did not know what. I don't think any of us knew what we had lost as we marched the snow-filled streets of Boston on that solemn Monday, the twenty-sixth of February.

Two thousand souls assembled at the Liberty Tree on Deacon Elliot's corner at five in the afternoon to take part in Chris Snider's funeral procession.

I had never seen such a funeral in all my born

days. And sensed I probably would never see such again.

Oh, I had known that the mourners would be more than Chris's family and a few friends, for I'd heard Mr. Adams speaking of the funeral beforehand. "My cousin Sam is determined to make a martyr of the boy for the cause of Liberty," he'd told Abigail.

I had not understood what that meant until I marched in the procession. Someone said there were five hundred schoolboys walking ahead of the coffin. And that the coffin itself bore an inscription from the Bible about the murdered innocents.

There were at least thirty chariots and chaises, and the procession took up half a mile as it wound through Boston's streets. Up ahead marched John Adams himself.

All of Boston's church bells tolled mournfully, echoing off the snow.

We'd been marching for what seemed miles. Up ahead, for some reason, the procession stopped. I heard the sound of muffled drums. "I'm cold," I told Jane.

"So am I. But we're doing it for Chris."

"I could never think that so many people knew him."

"They didn't. This is to raise the passions of the people and strengthen the Cause."

"It doesn't seem right to me somehow. Does it to you?"

"And why is that?"

"To use the death of Chris this way. What would he think? He was ragged and poor. Where were all these people when he was running the streets, doing his chores for a pittance, and always looking so hungry and cold?"

"He is of more value to them shot dead by that Tory, Richardson, than he was working for the Sons for that pittance," she said. "He is more help to the Cause now."

"Jane!" I was horrified.

"It's the truth, and I don't think Chris would mind it. I think he would be proud."

I pondered on that. I minded what Chris had said to me once, a while back, about having a weapon against the king. But would he be *proud* of being dead? *He* was the weapon the Sons of Liberty were using now. Would he be proud of that?

The procession started again and I drew my cloak around me. There had been a terrible storm two days ago, with thunder and lightning, that had blanketed us under several inches of snow. But not even that had stopped plans for this fancy funeral.

"I'm confused," I told Jane. "I was not a dear friend to Chris, but I know I'll miss him."

"You're feeling what we all feel," she said, "that

we can never go back now. The Crown has shot one of our own. And we can only press forward. Any hope of reconciliation is what is lost."

I reminded myself that I was now a plain American. And I should be filled with a sense of purpose like all those around me. But I did not feel that way. Chris's death was stupid to me. A waste. *Perhaps I am not a true American at all,* I thought.

As we continued on our way I noticed the absence of the red-coated soldiers. Not a one of them was to be seen anywhere in the streets. I thought about Matthew. I had not seen him in weeks. I knew he had a job at the ropeworks. *I must speak with him,* I told myself. I felt a dread in my bones. Dear God, the last time we spoke we fought. I must make things right.

The desire to do so, fused by Chris Snider's death, suddenly became like a fever in my bones.

There was a hard edge about Jane that I wished I had. I knew I could never be like that, however. And at no time was I more sensible of it than late in the afternoon almost a week later when I spoke with the guard at the gate at Gray's Ropewalk Works.

"Private Kilroy? Let's see," and he scanned a list in his hands. "Yes, he's here. Though myself, I'm thinkin' he was a fool to come back after that fracas yesterday."

The fracas was why I had come. Yesterday, on my day off, I'd been with Jane in the apothecary and we'd heard about it. Some soldiers working at Gray's had tangled with the ropemen. Outmanned, the soldiers had fled, only to return in fifteen minutes with forty more, armed with clubs.

The civilians had driven the soldiers out. The street urchin, who gave us the news, took a shilling and a sweet from Jane and ran off. But not before telling us that "Private Kilroy fought well."

And so, after fetching fresh produce for Mrs. Adams next day, I walked to the ropeworks to find Matthew. It was the only place I knew to look. I stood shivering in the cold while the guard went inside. It was a massive building that seemed to go on forever. He'll never find Matthew, I moaned to myself. I was determined to wait ten minutes, no more, else how would I explain my tardiness to Mrs. Adams? I was about to leave when the guard came back out, a bedraggled Matthew with him.

He stopped when he saw me. He scowled. The guard went back into his little shed. "What are you doing here?" Matthew asked.

"Well, heavens, I'm glad you're happy to see me."

He gave that little crooked smile of his, the one that showed his dimple. And my heart lurched. He looked terrible. His fine red coat was torn and muddied. His woolen breeches besmattered with dirt. There was a bruise on one cheekbone, which was turning purple.

"Matthew!" I set my basket with the produce down. Tears came to my eyes. I ran to him. "I've been so worried that you haven't been around."

"It's been weeks. Why the sudden concern?"

"We heard about the fight."

"Well, if I'd known it would take such to bring you to me like this, I'd have gotten in a fight sooner." His voice had an edge to it and was not at all kind. "Don't worry, we gave as good as we got."

"Why are you being so mean to me, Matthew? I'm worried for you. You're liable to be killed. Like Chris Snider. I've lost one friend. Do you think I want to lose another?"

"Look here, Rachel, you drove me to this. So don't come around sniveling now."

I felt my eyes go wide. "I drove you to what?"

"Working here. And what comes with it."

"That's so unfair, Matthew. To blame me."

"Is it? I sought solace from you. Only you were too high-and-mighty to give it."

I thought quickly. "You said you wanted to work here because you were looking for a fracas. To stand up for what you are. Because the street urchins were tormenting you so."

"And because you were taunting me, Rachel."

184

"I?"

"Yes. I wanted a fracas to get rid of my pent-up passions."

"It's cruel of you to blame me." My chin was trembling. "But Jane said you'd do this."

"Jane? That beanpole friend of yours who trails around with Mackintosh? He's married, you know. You've been confiding in her about us?"

"She's my friend. Don't speak ill of her, Matthew."

His blue eyes took on the gray of the surrounding landscape. "What did she say I'd do?"

"I told her I was sore afflicted for the way I treated you. She said you wanted me to be sore afflicted so that next time we met I would do your bidding."

He laughed. "Am I asking anything of you now, Rachel? Did I ask you to come here?"

"No."

"And I'll not ask in the future. I have my pride, you know."

There was a catch in his voice. I felt terrible. I stepped closer to him. "But I would ask something of *you*," I murmured. I was so close I could see the stubble of beard on his face. His eyes grew soft. And for a moment we looked at each other and the old friendship was there.

"What?" he asked.

"Leave this place, Matthew. Before you get hurt."

"You care if I get hurt?"

"Yes."

He took my hand. "How much do you care?"

There was no mistaking his meaning. Or the huskiness in his voice. "Matthew, don't make it like that."

"Like what?"

"You know. Can't I just care about what happens to you without backing up my concern with promises of my favors?"

His jaw went hard. "There is no separating one kind of caring from the other, Rachel."

"Of course there is, Matthew!"

"Not the way I look at it."

"Oh, Matthew!" I was weary of the whole business already. I picked up my basket. "Why must you always lump friendship in with your basest needs!"

"My basest needs!" He hooted. "Is that how you think of my feelings for you?"

"No, but apparently it's how *you* think of them. Oh, there's no profit in this, Matthew. We go round and round, and always it comes back to the same thing. Why won't you understand?"

"Understand what?"

I hesitated, groping for the right words. "That

people can care for one another as I care for you, Matthew. Without putting any corrupt intentions on the caring."

He shrugged.

"That I want us to be friends. That I want no harm to come to you. That I want us to help one another and not let these silly arguments tear us apart."

"That's exactly what the Crown is saying to the colonies, Rachel."

My mouth fell open. I stared at him.

He returned my look with one of mock defiance. "It can never be. Don't you see that it can't?"

"I'm not talking about the Crown and the colonies. I'm speaking of you and me. The trouble with you is that you don't know what real friendship is! Didn't you ever have a friend in your childhood?"

"Yes, I had one." His voice came tight and strangled. "He was not only my best friend. He was my brother. Do you want to know what he did to me?"

He had never mentioned his family to me. I knew he had a mother back in Derbyshire County, that the family was poor, that his father had died from gout in the stomach. I had never pushed him for information. Having a background of which I was secretive, I understood his desire for privacy.

"What?" I asked.

"The care and feeding of the young ones fell to us after my father died. Francis was the eldest. We worked hard and managed to make a sufficient living from selling the produce from our gardens. But Francis took to gambling. He owed debts. One night he took me to a tavern and got me in my cups. A gentleman was there who was paid by the Crown for each soldier he enlisted in his regiment. I was stone drunk. They forced a shilling into my fist, and I signed on. I found out later that the recruiter was the one Francis owed the gambling debt to."

I ran my tongue along my lips, waiting. This painful admission from him was almost as surprising as the story itself.

"They took me that night. I never saw my mum or my home again." His voice was hoarse. I saw tears in his eyes.

I wanted to run to him, to throw my arms around him and let him cry his anguish out on my shoulder. Oh, I know what Jane would have said. It was but another ploy of his to gain my sympathy. But I prided myself on being able to tell when someone was lying. I always knew it with Uncle Eb. And Matthew was not lying, I was certain of it.

Yet, I said nothing.

He smiled at me weakly. "I wanted no part of this man's army, Rachel. And that's what my best friend, and my brother, did to me. To pay his gambling debt. And since I've been one of the king's own, every bit of my pay goes back home. To help with the support of my family. Why do you think I am always hungry?"

"I'm sorry, Matthew," I said.

"Are you?"

"Yes, but you're wrong. People can be friends. As I want to be to you."

"I put no store in it," he said.

"And so what will you do now? Stay here and fight with the workers again?"

"If need be, yes. At least it's a way to give back some of what we get when we're on duty."

"No good will come of it, Matthew."

"Mayhap you're right, Rachel." He said it sadly and with a finality that frightened me. He was out to prove something, I decided as we parted. I watched him go back inside the gates, then I started for home.

What do I do now, I pondered. He's going to be killed if he keeps working in there. Or kill someone. He's determined it's the way to settle the misery inside him.

Oh, I should have made it my business to find out sooner what he was all about, I minded. *Somehow, I should have made him tell me.* But it was too late now, the telling. I felt as if I had not done right by him at all.

Chapter Thirteen

"JANE, WHAT'S amiss?" I asked.

We were in the kitchen of the Welsteed mansion. Ten minutes into my visit I realized that something was wrong. Jane was distracted and disturbed. And she looked as if she hadn't slept all night.

It was Monday morning, the fifth of March. Mrs. Adams had awakened nauseated. I had come for more of the labradore tea.

"I spent last evening with some ropewalk workers." She was sitting at the old oak table, ladling the tea into a small sack. She raised her eyes to me. "There's going to be trouble tonight, Rachel."

"Trouble?" The way she said it sounded a knell in my bones.

"Yes. I wish I hadn't gone to the coffeehouse last night. I wish I wasn't privy to this information, but I am. They're planning a battle. Between the citizens and the troops."

"Who?"

"Enough to say that I know, Rachel. You know I can't say who."

I nodded. My mind was working fast. It was the first time I'd ever known Jane to be so benumbed about anything.

"Tonight the Sons are planning on having a boy climb up to the belfry of the Brick Church and ring the bell for fire. To assemble the people."

I just sat there in the quiet kitchen, listening to the crackling of the fire in the hearth, hearing the sounds of life in distant rooms in the rest of the house. Everything seemed so peaceful. Outside it was snowing. People were going about their business as if getting about on the ice-covered streets was all they had on their minds.

"So, it's come then," I said.

"Yes, I'm afraid so," Jane said quietly. "The talk is that tonight the townsfolk will fight it out with the soldiers."

I watched her measure out the tea. "Someone could be killed," I said. I thought of Matthew.

"Yes," she agreed.

"What are you going to do about it?"

"I?" She regarded me with her blue eyes. "What can I do about it?"

"I don't know, Jane. But you should do something. Or someone could be killed. Someone innocent, like Chris Snider."

She gave me no argument, which surprised me

in itself. She closed the cover on the canister of tea and tied the small sack and pushed it across the table to me.

"The mob is daft," she said. "All of them. Oh, mind you, they have their reasons. And they're all good reasons. No one is for liberty as much as I. You know that, Rachel. But sometimes they lose possession of their senses."

She said it with a certain sadness. *Was the sadness for Mac,* I wondered?

"But you have not lost possession of your senses. You are like Henry Knox. You are for moderation."

She smiled. "My, that's a big word. You *are* becoming educated, aren't you?"

I blushed. "You must warn someone, Jane," I said.

"Who?"

I pondered for a moment. Then it came to me. "Your mistress. She is sister to Lieutenant Governor Hutchinson."

She got up and went to put a piece of wood on the fire. "I don't know if I can do that," she said.

I stood up and took my cloak from a chair. "If you can't, Jane, I shall do it. I shall tell Mrs. Adams."

She turned. Her face was flushed from the fire. Then she came forward, smiling at me. "My, my,

Rachel, I never thought I'd see the day when you would be so sure of yourself. When we first met, you were a shy little moth."

"Well, I've learned a lot, Jane. And I'm learning even more. Mrs. Adams has started me on my linen dowry. I sew on pillow slips and table linens, every night when I get the chance."

Her eyes widened. "A dowry!"

"Yes. I never thought I'd be so happy doing it. Of course, Mrs. Adams says we women are all domestic beings."

"I envy you." I took her words to be true. For the look in her eyes did not deny it.

"Yes. And Mr. Adams's brother Elihu is making me a dowry chest. It will be sent down soon, from Braintree. Oh Jane, I have you to thank if I'm not a little moth anymore. And Mrs. Adams. And Henry Knox."

"You have only yourself," she said. "You made up your mind to better yourself. You've become the mainstay of Mrs. Adams, and you've managed to fend off the advances of Matthew and still remain a friend. You've done well, Rachel Marsh."

"I don't know if I've done that, Jane. Matthew doesn't seem to know what a friend is."

"I ponder if *I* did before today."

"What?"

"Never mind. Would I be a better friend to

Mac if I told my mistress what's going on? Or if I kept my mouth shut?"

"If you told her," I said. "Promise me you will, before I leave here."

She promised. And I left with a clear mind. Her mistress, Sarah Welsteed, could sometimes be flighty and frivolous. But she adored her brother, the lieutenant governor. So I felt sure the information would get to him.

It did not. But the fault was not Jane's. She told me afterward that she had gone directly to her mistress and advised her of the impending fight. But somehow her mistress never passed the information along to Hutchinson. Nobody knew why.

The children could not go out that day because of the snow, so I did my best to keep them occupied. Supper was early because Mr. Adams had a meeting at Henderson Inches's house. Around suppertime the snow stopped and the sky grew red with the setting sun. A quarter moon appeared on the horizon. The wind picked up. Gangs of boys appeared on the streets.

I had just gotten the children settled in bed and was in my room working on the seam of a bed sheet, dreaming and wondering who the man was that I would someday be sharing these lovely linens with. I was caught up in my pleasant fancies when the bells started ringing.

Bells! They were coming from the direction of the North End. The Brick Church! And they were fire bells. Just as Jane had said would happen!

I jumped out of bed and threw on a wrapper. Mrs. Adams was in the hall.

"Fire," she said. "Oh, dear, I wonder where." And she started up the stairs to the dormer rooms on top of the house where she could see what was going on. I followed.

Sukey came into the room and the three of us stood looking out, toward town. But we could see no flames, no smoke. I was trembling.

"Where is Luke?" Mrs. Adams asked.

"Doan know, ma'am. He went out earlier," Sukey answered.

Mrs. Adams drew her wrapper around her. "Well, there's no fire. We'll just have to wait until Mr. Adams comes home. I'm sure it's just another fracas in town. I'll check on the children. Go back to bed, both of you. The house is cold."

The house settled down to quiet again. I went back to my room and got into bed, but I could not abide not knowing what was happening. My heart was racing. I got out of bed and got dressed. I would go out, I determined. I would take a lantern and walk to town. I opened the door of my room and listened. No one was about.

Just then there was a sound at my window. I ran to look out. My room was in back on the second floor and, by the light of the moon reflected on the snow and ice, I could see a figure standing in the midst of the frozen garden below.

"Jane?" I asked. I struggled with the window latch. It was frozen. I skinned my fingers trying to get it open and finally accomplished my goal. Cold air rushed in. "Jane?" I called out. "Is it you?"

"Can you get out without being noticed?"

"What's happened?" I stuck my head out the window so my voice wouldn't be heard.

"Trouble."

"Where?"

"On King Street. At the Custom House. Come quick!"

I did not hesitate. I locked the window and, wearing my moccasins so as not to make noise, with my sturdy shoes in one hand and a lantern in the other, I made my way downstairs and out the back door. Thank heavens Sukey was tired. Thank heavens she was known to sleep as soon as her head hit the pillow. Thank heavens she was a heavy sleeper.

Outside the night was clear and bright enough so there was no need for a lantern. I set it down on the back steps, put my shoes on hurriedly, and followed Jane.

As we ran down Cold Lane, neither of us spoke. There was only the sound of our labored breathing in the cold. I knew it was right to go. I could not have stopped myself if I wanted to, and I did not want to.

Something inside urged me on. It was as if I had been moving through eternity toward this night since the day I had come to Boston. I cared not for the consequences of leaving without my mistress's permission. Something was happening this night, something at once terrible and fascinating and predestined. I had to be there.

But I did not know if it was because it most likely concerned Matthew or because I had finally harkened to the plight of the rabble and become a plain American.

I shall never forget that night as long as I live. Its sounds and sights shall stay with me forever.

"Town born, town born, turn out, turn out!" came the voices as people rushed out of the darkness to rap on doors. It was a sound of alarm. There was an urgency about the cries. It was a plea to harken to the future and yet it came out of a past filled with bad treatment and old-held grievances.

Jane and I rushed along. The snow crunched under our feet. The light from the pine knot torches made the icicles dripping from the house eaves look like silver. The crowd seemed to grow around us, pushing us toward King Street.

Then everyone came to a halt in the middle of Dock Square.

There, on some sort of crate, to elevate himself, stood a tall man. He wore a white wig and a bright red cloak. He raised a hand and the crowd quickly drew about him.

Jane and I stood to the back of the people. I could not hear the man's words. But it was clear he was urging the crowd on. He pointed, he raised both arms as if in a blessing. The people in Dock Square threw their hats in the air and gave a 'oud cheer. They whistled and stomped. Those of them who were armed with clubs banged them on storefronts as they surged away.

"Who is that man?" I stood staring at him.

Jane pulled my arm. "I don't know. Come on."

I stumbled after her, still turning to look at the tall man in the bright red cloak. By torchlight I thought I recognized his face, but I could not be sure.

Nobody was recognizable that night. And yet, as I caught glimpses of the people around us, I thought I knew everybody. Or was it only that I felt a kinship with the hungry, angry, and determined looks on their faces?

That was it, I decided, between quick breaths as I ran. These people look the way I have *felt* so often. And there were so many of them rushing forward. For what? It was as if they had an appointment and were late for it. They were street fighters, young boys, even women. Their cries rang over our heads and cut the night with a frightening clarity.

"The regulars are slashing at people with their swords!"

"They have cut down the Liberty Tree!"

"They've near killed a boy!"

I felt the excitement mount in me. And the fear.

"They've near killed a boy!" The cry was torn out of the man's throat as he went past us. Jane grabbed at his sleeve. "Who?"

His face was dirty, his mouth a mean slash, his eyes round with terror. "That young apprentice of Piermont's, the wig-maker. They've near killed him! He went to collect some money from Captain Goldfinch of the Fourteenth, and Goldfinch knocked him about." The man pulled away and ran.

People came out of houses with fire buckets in hand. The bell of Old Meeting began to ring with the signal for fire. I sensed doors and windows being flung open all around us.

"Say you, what's happened?"

"The regulars have near killed a boy!"

"Light the tar barrels on Beacon Hill! Send word!"

"It's come, it's finally come, what we said would happen!"

"Bloody-backs! Damned lousy rascal soldiers!"

"Teach 'em a lesson!

"There's no fire, it's the soldiers! Damn it, I'm glad of it. Damn their bloods!"

"There's Attucks. He'll do what has to be done. Follow him!"

"Get my coat, Shadrack. I'm going out. Where's that damned apprentice? Never here when I need him."

"Have you seen my Samuel?"

I recognized Mrs. Maverick. She was a widow who ran a notions shop. She was hastily tying the strings of her cloak hood. Her face was pale, her eyes frantic. "My Samuel's out here, I'm sure of it. If there's trouble, he's bound to be in it. Oh, I must find him!" And she dashed off into the crowd.

"I know her Sam," Jane said as we rushed along. "His half-sister, Elizabeth, is married to my Mac. And his mother is right. If there's trouble, Sam will be in the middle of it."

It was the first she'd made mention of Mac being married, I thought as we rushed onward. We were fast approaching the Custom House. A red-coated sentinel was on the steps. People were throwing chunks of wood and ice at him. He stood his ground, musket in front of him. But he was dancing to avoid the sharp objects.

"I need help out here!" he yelled. Then he started shoving the ramrod of his musket down the barrel, preparing to fire.

A door slammed across the street. "Cease that. Disperse from the King's Common! Clear the way!"

Everyone turned. Murray's Barracks was across the street. A young officer trotted across the snow, several men behind him. I recognized Captain Preston. Matthew had once pointed him out to me.

And then I saw Matthew in the column of soldiers. "Oh, Jane!" We stopped and I clutched her cloak.

"Yes," she said, seeing Matthew. "Yes." That was all.

The soldiers walked toward the crowd. Their bayonets were affixed to their muskets, and they made as if to jab at the people. I saw Nathaniel Hurd, the engraver, get his hat knocked off by a bayonet. He himself was roughly pushed aside.

"Why are you pushing me?" he demanded loudly.

"Damn your blood," Matthew ordered. "Out of the way!"

Oh no, I thought, *no, Matthew.*

"I will not," said Hurd. "I am doing no harm to any man and I will not stand aside for anyone."

Everyone's attention was now turned on this exchange. I held my breath. Matthew stood his ground and he and Hurd glared at each other like angry dogs. Then Preston gave an order and the column of soldiers passed around Hurd.

I sighed in gratitude.

"I don't see Mac," Jane said. "Or any of the Liberty Boys. Who organized this?"

"What does it matter?" I said. "Someone should do something!"

I was starting to expect the worst. The crowd was getting angrier as Preston and his men took their places on the Custom House steps.

"Disperse!" Preston ordered.

No one moved. "Lobsters! Bloody-backs!" That was all. Jeers, mumbles, hisses.

"Load and prime," Preston's order rang out in the cold. His men busied themselves, preparing their muskets.

A hush came over the crowd. You could hear the rattling of the ramrods being shoved down the musket barrels. And in that moment I felt faint with fear. I looked around for someone to step forward and stop everyone. But at the same time I knew it was too late to mend the moment. It seemed like something pulled out of time, something roughly torn out of the fabric of our everyday lives, which would make us stand apart from the rest of mankind, forever.

"You dare to fire on the people?" a voice from

the crowd bellowed. "Let's see you fire, Preston. You don't dare!"

From the crowd came a piece of ice, flung into the face of one of the soldiers. It hit him on the forehead. He slipped and fell. His musket went flying and landed with a clatter. The crowd roared and seemed to take on a new life. They booed and hissed. They jumped and shoved one another. And others kept running out of dark corners of the night to join the fracas.

In one surge, the crowd seemed to come backward, to make room for the newcomers. Back, like a wave, they came. Jane and I were standing on the edge. Someone pushed against me, roughly, and I was knocked over.

I went down, hard, on the ice-covered ground. My whole being was dazed. Still people were pushing and shoving. I could not get up. All I could see was shoes and stockings, the dirty edges of women's petticoats. Someone stepped on my cloak and then I couldn't move.

"Jane!" I yelled.

I could not see her. I struggled. And then something cold and hard grabbed at my innards.

Fear. *I'm going to be killed,* I told myself. *I'm going to be trampled to death. In a moment the soldiers are going to start shooting and the crowd will surge back and trample me into the ground!*

Oh, what was I doing here? Why had I come? All those riots I heard about while I was safe in the comfort of the Adamses's house and now I was in the middle of one.

Why had I come? I did not belong here, I was not part of the rabble. People had been killed in riots just like this. My mind rambled on while I struggled trying to get my cloak out from under the boots of the man who was standing on it.

People had been killed and no one ever knew how it started! Is this how Chris Snider felt, just before he was shot? Did he know this fear? And if I die here and now, will they have a funeral for me like they had for Chris? Will they call me a martyr?

I don't want to be a martyr!

What will the Adamses say of me? Will Uncle Eb be sorry for those things he said? Will anyone miss me?

"For God's sake!" I heard a familiar voice ring out from above the crowd. "Preston, keep your men in line. For God's sake, take your men back. If you fire, your life must answer for it!"

Henry Knox. Thank God! The voice of reason! It gave me strength. *I must see Henry,* I thought. *He's here, and I won't die this way, like a dog in the street, trampled underfoot. Not while Henry is so near.*

So I pulled at my cloak. I punched the man's ankles. I pinched his leg. He yelled and my cloak came free and I scrambled to my feet. Jane was gone. Nowhere in sight. I was alone.

"Contain your men!" I heard Henry's voice bellowing out of that great frame of his. "Do you mean to fire upon the inhabitants?"

"By no means," came Preston's reply. "Back, people, back. Go home. Disperse or I will not be able to restrain my men. You fools, don't ask for trouble!" Preston was begging them.

But the crowd was no longer a group of individuals. It was a vibrant terrible *thing,* a headless mass with thousands of arms and legs and a voice that was like the sound of rushing floodwaters. And above the sound was Henry Knox's voice, pleading for reason.

"Jane!" I yelled. I bumped into a young man with a catstick, the kind of bat they used in stickball. He turned on me. His face was thin and drawn and when he grinned it looked like a death's head. "We'll get them bloody-backs tonight," he said.

I ran from him, from his leer, from the smell of him. It was raw and dank. Like rotting matter around the wharves. I danced around the edge of the crowd, looking for Jane.

Before I knew it, I found myself on the side of the Custom House steps, in the shadows. And I could see everything plain.

I saw a man step forward out of the crowd.

He was well dressed and well spoken, and for a moment I thought he would be able to do what no one else could.

"Are your men loaded?" he asked Preston politely.

"Yes," Preston said with equal politeness.

"Are they going to fire?" the man pushed.

"They cannot fire without my orders," Preston said calmly.

And I thought, *We are all mad. They are speaking as if they are in someone's parlor.* Some in the front of the crowd heard the exchange and hissed. And the rest of the mob started hissing and cheering again.

And then I saw, head and shoulders above those in front of the crowd, the mulatto, Crispus Attucks. In a flash he hurled a large club.

It hit one of the soldiers, who then fell down. Attucks came forward and the two of them scrambled for the soldier's musket. The soldier retrieved it.

Those in front of the mob surged forward then, pushing against the soldiers. Again I heard Henry Knox's voice from somewhere close, pleading for sanity. But it was too late. The mob and the soldiers were pressing on each other, so close you couldn't tell one from the other. Shouts and curses filled the air.

Then I heard the order ring through the night.

"Fire!"

The world exploded in my ears. The sound echoed in my soul. I shut my eyes tight as muskets went off. I smelled the black powder, like the stench of rotten eggs in the air. I put my hands over my ears and closed my eyes tight.

When I opened them I saw Attucks on the ground, bleeding. And Matthew was pointing his musket at Sam Gray of the ropewalk works. Matthew's face seemed etched in stone. His fingers were on the trigger.

"No!" I screamed.

Again the world exploded and I saw smoke coming out of Matthew's musket, saw Gray go down.

A man in the crowd threw up his hands. "Fire away, you damned lobsterbacks!" he yelled.

In the next moment he crumpled to the ground. Everyone was screaming and the crowd started retreating.

The soldiers were firing into it.

And the mob broke into pieces then and became just people, frightened, scrambling people who ran, knocking one another over, leaving pieces of clothing on the streets.

On the ground in front of me were those who'd been shot. Some cried out, still alive. Then I saw

Matthew step forward and thrust his bayonet into Sam Gray's body.

"Matthew!" I screamed. And I kept right on screaming it, over and over.

"Rachel! What are you doing here?" Someone grabbed my arm and pulled me away. I turned and looked into the face of Henry Knox. It was like finding an island when adrift in the sea.

"Come away, Rachel," he said kindly. "You don't want to see this."

I allowed him to lead me away. I was blubbering and hiccupping. "Matthew," I kept saying. I was trembling, not from the cold outside but from the cold inside me. A coldness from which one can never get warm again.

Out of the night came the sound of drums, beating their tattoo, to arms, to arms. Soldiers and officers came rushing forward, out of barracks and houses. Some were half-dressed, but all had muskets with fixed bayonets. Their officers barked orders and they fell into their places. Their faces looked terrible, stony and white.

Henry Knox was leading me past the Royal Exchange, down King Lane.

"Come now," he was saying, "we must get you home."

"Matthew is my friend," I told him.

"Yes, I know."

"What will happen now? How can we be friends anymore?"

"Dear child," Henry said, "how can any of us be friends anymore with them? Dear God, what has been unleashed tonight? I pray He saves us all."

I turned to look back. The last thing I saw was Captain Preston standing in front of his men. He was pushing their muskets back, ordering them to fire no more.

I never did see what happened to Jane.

Chapter Fourteen

HENRY KNOX WALKED me all the way home. Approaching the house, I saw one lone candle in Mrs. Adams's room upstairs.

"I'll keep," I told Henry. "Thank you. Mrs. Adams doesn't know I went out."

"Will you be in trouble?"

"Not if I can sneak in the back door and upstairs. I just want to hide. And not tell anyone I was there. Would that be wrong?"

He stamped his feet in the snow. "I think we all wish we could hide tonight," he said.

"You won't tell anyone I was there?"

"I think the good people of Boston have a lot more to worry about than where you were tonight, Rachel. No, I'll keep your secret. I know you're keeping mine."

I looked up into his ruddy face, beneath the cocked hat. It had become very dear to me, that face. So, he was working for the Patriots then. And he sensed I knew. We smiled at each other. "Thank you, Henry," I said. No other words were necessary between us.

I managed to sneak in the back door. The kitchen was dark and I made my way carefully. Once I bumped into a small table and a dish rattled. Sukey came out of her room off to the side.

"Where you been?"

Moonlight, made brighter by the snow, slanted in through the window. "Out. Getting some air. I couldn't sleep."

"You lie. You been to town to see what happened."

In the darkness I could scarcely make out her face. "Don't tell, please," I said.

"What happened?"

"Promise you won't tell?"

"Ain't you learned yet? You be a nigra, you doan open your mouth lessen you gots to. An' sometimes not even then."

"People were killed."

"Who?"

"People. By the British. That mulatto, Crispus Attucks, was one."

Silence. I knew Sukey admired him. "Dead?" Her voice cracked when she finally spoke. "He be dead?"

211

"Yes. He was shot in the chest. I saw him fall."

"Who else?" Her voice was flat.

"Sam Gray from the ropeworks. Oh, Sukey, Matthew shot him."

We were whispering in the near dark. I was trembling. I put my hands over my face and sobbed.

She came to me and touched my arm. The floor creaked under her feet. We stood, wrapped in the misery of the moment. "I'se sorry," she said.

Something in the way she said it becalmed me. So did her touch. I nodded and struggled to stop my crying. Sukey would not respect that. And somehow I knew suddenly that I wanted the respect of this fragile and strong-willed creature.

"I'm sorry, too, for you, Sukey. I know you held Attucks in great esteem."

She nodded. "He wuz a slave," she said. "But he done somethin'. He stood fer somethin'. People, they looked up to him. They respected him."

"Yes," I said.

She hugged me, then. "Gonna be a long hard way now. Somethin' like this started, there be no turnin' back."

"Yes," I said again.

Just then we heard footsteps outside. She put her finger to her lips. "Mr. Adams! He comin' home from his meetin'. You go upstairs now, an' hush."

I went upstairs and hushed. I did more than

that. I hid under my quilt. I went into hiding, where I trembled and shook and did not fall asleep until the first gray light of dawn was peeping through the window.

Next morning the house was pandemonium. I woke to find Johnnie tugging at my arm. "Wanna get dwessed, Wachel. We got company an' wanna go down and see. Nabby gone down. Wanna go, too."

I opened my eyes to the sight of Johnnie's sweet face. For a moment all was well. Then the memory of last night came crashing down on my head, accounting for the peculiar way it hurt. I sat up. Downstairs I heard the tall clock chime. Seven bells. I'd overslept!

I told Johnnie to sit in front of the hearth, while I warmed his clothing. "I heard guns last night," Johnnie told me as I buckled his shoes.

"No guns," I said.

"Yes, Wachel. I heard guns. I was fwightened."

"You must have been dreaming."

I sent him downstairs, saying I'd be right along. Then I dressed. Every move made my head hurt more. My fingers seemed numb as I tied the laces of my short gown. I went downstairs.

The dining room was full of people. Men. They milled around the sideboard, waiting for Sukey to serve them food. Sukey was rushing back and forth trying to do six things at once and I went to help her. No one chided me for being late.

"You jus' keep servin'," she whispered, "while I fetches more coffee and biscuits."

As I heaped the plates with food and gave them over to waiting hands, I'd look up at the faces. I recognized Benjamin Edes from the *Gazette*. And Mr. Crafts, the painter. And Mr. Swift of the North End gang. Two others I did not recognize. Luke was bringing some straight-backed chairs in from the parlor and the men sat, gathering in a little group a bit away from the table, near the hearth.

Mrs. Adams smiled at me and gestured I should take my place at the table with the children. I took some coffee and one of Sukey's light fluffy biscuits and sat.

For a moment everyone seemed to be talking at once. I could scarcely sort it out.

"People are carrying muskets in the street. Gonna be more trouble, Mr. Adams." This from Benjamin Edes.

"We must put a stop to it," John Adams agreed.

"They aren't town-born, those with the muskets," put in Mr. Crafts. "They're in from Roxbury and Dorchester. Molineaux sent for them."

Everyone agreed they must be sent back. "Where's my cousin Sam?" Mr. Adams asked.

There was conjecture about that. Turned out nobody knew where Sam was. A man whose name I did not know said he was probably at Faneuil Hall.

"The people are gathering there even as we sit and speak," he said. "There's rumor your cousin will now press to get the troops removed from Boston."

John Adams listened. His face never changed expression. "My cousin must be found and a citizens' watch set up for tonight to avoid more trouble."

There was more buzzing talk amongst the guests about that. Someone offered to do the errand.

"How many were killed?" John Adams asked.

"Four," Swift said. "Crispus Attucks, the mulatto. They've taken his body to the Royal Exchange Tavern. Dr. Church is doing an autopsy."

"Patrick Carr," said Mr. Crafts. "He's an Irish lad of seventeen. He's just now dying. Dr. Warren is with him."

"A man named Caldwell, a sailor, who'd been just standing in the middle of King Street," said Mr. Edes. "And Sam Gray from the ropeworks. He's the one who fought with the soldier at the works on Friday."

I shuddered at the name Gray. And the mention of the soldier. It was Matthew. My friend. But now, after this, he was "the soldier who fought with Gray at the ropeworks on Friday." He was tagged and known by all.

And would he soon be known by all as "the soldier who stabbed the dead body of Gray with his bayonet"? Was that my friend, Matthew, too? Oh, my head hurt as the enormity of what had happened exploded over and over again inside it.

"Others are wounded," Swift said.

John Adams nodded. For a brief moment everyone fell silent. Coffee cups were refilled by Sukey, using the new silver pot Mr. Adams had given his wife for her last birthday. It had been made by Paul Revere.

I found myself staring at the pot, then at Mrs. Adams. She was looking at it, too. Were we both thinking the same thing? How could anyone who made such beautiful things run with the Sons, who practiced such violence? And were there, then, two sides to everybody? As I knew there to be with Matthew?

There came a rapping on the door. Sukey went to answer it.

Everyone looked up as a man came into the room. His clothes were dirty and tattered. Everyone stared at him.

"Well, if it isn't the Irish Infant," Swift said. "What are you doing here, Forrest? Thought you'd be taking your dram at the British Coffee House this morning with your friends, the British officers."

The man called Forrest held his hat in his hand. He had eyes only for John Adams. "Mr. Adams, sir, sure'n if I could speak with you."

John Adams nodded. "You may, Mr. Forrest."

"Alone, sir. Please!" The man was begging. John looked at the other men in the room and nodded and gestured with his head. One by one, they got up and set down their coffee cups and bowed to Mrs. Adams and took their leave. Sukey saw them out.

Mr. Forrest looked at the floor as they passed him. He still held his hat in his hands.

"Come sit, Mr. Forrest," Mrs. Adams said. "We can't give you a dram, but Sukey makes good coffee. You look as if you need some. And some slices of ham and fresh preserves and bread."

"Grateful, ma'am." He pulled up a chair a distance from the table. I served him a cup of hot coffee and put food down in front of him. The food he did not touch.

"Mr. Adams, we need your help," he said.

Both John and Abigail waited.

"I've just come from Captain Preston. He's in prison. A terrible state he's in, too, all bruised and beaten."

"There are others, as I understand it, Mr. Forrest, who are even in a worse state this morning," Mr. Adams said testily.

"To be sure, sir. 'Tis a tragedy of the utmost proportions. But Preston is not to blame, sir. All night they questioned him. Tried to get him to admit he gave the order to fire."

"State your purpose, Mr. Forrest," Mr. Adams said.

"He never did that, sir. Never gave that sinister order. Nobody knows who did, but they can't put the blame on him. He's a good man, sir. A sober, honest man and a good officer. Even the radicals have said such about him."

"So I've heard," Mr. Adams said.

"Already this mornin', Mr. Adams, I've been to call on three of the Crown's lawyers. They refuse to defend Preston. Then I went to Mr. Auchmuty, the admiralty judge. He said he would act on Preston's behalf. But with one condition."

Here the man paused and took a deep breath. It was almost a sob.

"I'm listening, Mr. Forrest," John Adams said.

The man raised his eyes. "That condition bein', sir, that you serve as counsel with him."

I thought I heard Mrs. Adams gasp. Then the room was perfectly quiet.

Nobody knows why they call Mr. Forrest the Irish Infant. The name just evolved in Boston, a place of many colorful characters who had many distinctive names. But in that moment, seeing the way he was looking at Mr. Adams, I minded it was with the eyes of a child, appealing for help from a father.

"Go on," John Adams said.

"Yes, well, sir, after that I took myself to see Josiah Quincy, Jr. He said the same thing. He would take the case for Preston and the other eight who are also in jail for murder, sir, if you will act with him."

Murder! All nine! A shudder went through me.

We all stared at Mr. Forrest. Even little Johnnie and Nabby had their mouths open and were bedazzled by the man's performance. For tears were coming down his face. Murder.

John Adams got to his feet, heavily. He set down his linen napkin. "Mr. Forrest, if I took this case, do you realize what would happen to me?"

"No, sir."

"It would compel me to differ in opinion from all my friends. To set at defiance all their advice. As well as their remonstrances, their ridicule, their censure, and their sarcasm. Without acquiring one symptom of pity from my enemies."

We all stared now at Mr. Adams. Johnnie and Nabby were positively enraptured. They were too young to understand what was going on, of course.

But they sensed, as children do, that the moment had great drama. And of course, they never tired of hearing their father talk his lawyer's talk.

As for myself and Mr. Forrest, we waited to have that lawyer's talk interpreted for us.

"What I mean, Mr. Forrest," John Adams went on, "is that if I take this case I will not have a friend or a client left. I will be forced to go back to Braintree and tend to my cows."

"Yes, sir," Forrest said. He bowed his head, beaten.

"Having said such, Mr. Forrest, we will now retire to my office for further discussion. Take your coffee. Take your food if you wish. You look as if you need nourishment."

The streets were full of people, all seeming to be rushing somewhere. As I approached town that afternoon, basket on my arm, I saw they were coming out of Faneuil Hall in droves and rushing off in the direction of the Old South Meeting House, about a quarter of a mile away.

I was going to market for Mrs. Adams. Light snow was falling. *Oh no,* I thought, watching the crowd rush off ahead of me, *not another riot.*

"Rachel! Rachel Marsh!"

There was no mistaking the voice. It was Jane's. Up ahead she was running toward me. "Rachel, I was worried when we got separated the other night. Then I saw Luke this morning and he said you were busy. That the house was full of people. So I knew you were all right."

"Luke?" I searched her face. "Did you tell him I was there the other night?"

"Of course not. You'll never guess what's happened. So many people met at Faneuil Hall they couldn't fit them, so they've removed to Old South Meeting. Sam Adams sent a message to Lieutenant Governor Hutchinson that if he doesn't remove the troops immediately the province will raise fifteen thousand men and the town won't answer for the consequences. What's the matter, Rachel?"

I looked at her. "Jane, don't you ever weary of it all? After what happened last night?"

"There's no wearying of it, Rachel. Once you start something like this you don't turn back."

"But those people who were killed!"

"If we gave up now, it would be for nothing. Don't you see?"

"I have to go to market for food."

"I'll go with you."

"Suit yourself."

"Rachel Marsh, what *is* ailing you?"

"We need food. I'm to pick out a saddle of mutton for supper. And some pimentos and limes. A ship is just in from the West Indies."

"It's Matthew, isn't it?"

I stopped in my tracks. "They're going to try the soldiers for murder," I said.

"Well, of course. They *committed* murder."

I nodded vaguely and we commenced walking. "All morning, while tending the children, it was all I could think about, Jane. Mr. Forrest is at the house now. Begging Mr. Adams to defend them."

Now she stopped. *"John Adams? Defend the British soldiers?"*

"He hasn't decided yet."

"It would ruin him."

"He knows that, Jane." We walked in silence for a while, each with our own thoughts. My head had cleared, finally, thanks to a good noon meal and Mrs. Adams's kindness. She had given me one of her headache powders. But now my heart was muddled.

John Adams had been hours in his office with Forrest. When I'd brought them both a noon meal, Josiah Quincy, Jr., had burst in to see Mr. Adams. Josiah was a cousin of Abigail's, twenty-six, with the most beautiful eyes and voice. His older brother was Solicitor General for the Crown. His father was a staunch Patriot.

"John," Josiah had said, breathlessly. "I've news. Patrick Carr is not yet dead. They've questioned him. He said that the soldiers were greatly abused by the citizens and fired in self-defense."

Mr. Adams had looked up from his desk at the young man. "Carr is Catholic," he said. "Isn't he?"

"Yes."

"Then you should know, better than I, Josiah, how prejudiced people are. No one will put store in what he says."

The young man was not to be discouraged. "I've told Captain Preston that I will take his case, though I am a staunch Patriot," he said. "Perhaps people will take example from that."

"Ah, the enthusiasm of youth," Mr. Adams said dryly.

My heart was beating rapidly, watching Josiah Quincy. Mrs. Adams had told me about him. The Supreme Court refused to grant him the barrister's long robe to wear in court. Because he'd written so many passionate articles against the Crown. So he argued cases in his everyday clothing.

I liked the young man on sight. And I was praying that Mr. Adams would take the case, too. Else, I knew, Matthew and the others would go to the gallows.

"But I need you," Josiah had said. "Have you decided?"

"Not yet, Josiah. I need time. I'm not as young as you. I haven't the years to make up for what it will do to me."

Josiah had left then. But I knew Mr. Adams to be wrong. Mrs. Adams had also told me that another of Josiah's brothers had died of consumption. And that Josiah had it, too. And knew he didn't have that much longer to live.

". . . to see Matthew in jail," Jane was saying.

I pulled myself back to where I was. The cold street, on my way to market. "What?"

"I said it's only a short distance from here if you want to go and see Matthew in prison."

I stared at her. The idea had never occurred to me. "Would they let us in?"

"Why not? You want to see him, don't you?"

"I don't know. I feel guilty because he's in jail. I feel the fault is mine. He told me he wanted a fracas to rid himself of his pent-up passions."

"I told you he was going to say such to you, didn't I?"

"Yes, Jane. But he still did what he did. I think it was to get my attention."

"He did what he did because he's one of the king's own, Rachel. They're trained to kill."

I shuddered. Matthew of the blue eyes and dimple in the face? Trained to kill? I knew him only as a lonesome, cold, and hungry soldier, far away from home, sold into bondage by his brother. Sometimes petulant and angry, yes. But Matthew was not a killer. I was sure of it.

224

And then I recollected how he'd stabbed Gray's dead body.

"Here we are," Jane was saying. "Want to go inside?"

I looked at Jane. Oh, I was so confused! Was he my sweet Matthew? Or a killer?

We were on Queen Street. At the jail. I drew in my breath. "Yes," I said.

The waiting place was dingy and damp, and when the guard finally returned from the inner reaches of the compound to gesture that I should follow, he took my basket from me. I left Jane sitting there on the bench.

Matthew was in a cell by himself. He looked tired and pale and the narrow bed was rumpled. The linen looked none too clean.

"Rachel."

"I've come to see you." It was a silly thing to say. I could think of nothing bright. This was not the place to be saucy or cheerful. He only nodded.

"How are you, Matthew?"

There was a dark bruise over his left eye. His linen was dirty, his coat even shabbier than when we'd last met. It was a stupid question, but I could think of nothing else.

"I'm a sorry thing this day," he said.

"Do they feed you?"

"Gruel and a bit of salt meat."

"I'm so sorry, Matthew. So sorry to see you this way."

His smile was lopsided. "So am I."

The smile warmed me, reminded me of happier days. Then I sobered. "They're going to try you and the others for murder," I said. "Oh, Matthew, what's going to happen to you?"

"I did no murder, Rachel. I did my job. We all did. That crowd was looking for blood. You had people in it not even from the town. That mulatto, Attucks, was from somewhere else, stirring things up. So was Carr, the Irishman. They were brought in to stir things up. They set upon us, and we defended ourselves."

"If only you hadn't shot Gray," I whispered. I leaned my head against the bars of his cubicle. They were cold on my throbbing head. The whole place was cold and damp.

"I was doing my duty," he said. "We were insulted and abused. The crowd knew what they were about, Rachel. They knew the danger. I have no fears."

His duty. I looked at him. Yes, that is what he would say. The soldier in him was speaking. So sure of himself. So proud.

But you stabbed Gray after he was dead, I wanted to say. Was that your duty, too? Only I

226

didn't say it. Because I did not know what orders soldiers were given and what they were trained to do. And I had learned one thing about Matthew: he was a soldier before anything else, much as he never wanted to be one.

"They could hang you," I said.

"Most likely they'll try. The townsfolk think the life of a soldier has very little value. They'd think naught of it."

"I couldn't abide it, Matthew."

"I went to the ropeworks looking for work. Gray asked me if I wanted a job. I said yes. Do you know what he said to me? He said, 'Then clean my outhouse.' That's what he said."

I heard a noise, dripping water someplace. Outside the window an icicle was melting. Sun shone off it. In that moment, seeing the sunlight on that icicle, wearing it away, drip by drip, I minded how the townsfolk had worn away at the patience of the soldiers. And their dignity, insulting them, throwing things at them, demeaning them in every way possible. You couldn't live in Boston that last year and a half and not be sensible of it. And so it was given to me in that moment to know what I would do.

"I'm going to help you, Matthew," I said.

He shrugged. "You're a mere girl, Rachel. You'd best go from this place and not be seen with me again."

"I may be a mere girl, but I work for Mr. John Adams. Mr. Forrest is at his house this minute, begging him to take on the defense of Preston and the other soldiers."

His blue eyes went wide. "Why would he do such?"

"I don't know as he will. But I'm going to ask him to."

"And he'd do it if you asked?"

"I don't know that, either. But that doesn't stop the asking."

"Why?"

"Because we're friends. I tried to tell you that before. But you wouldn't hear of it."

"You could get in trouble. You've told me the Adamses don't know how many times we've walked out together. And now this," he gestured to his surroundings. "You could lose your place, Rachel. It's all you have. You mustn't."

"Exactly why I must," I said.

"I don't understand."

"Of course you don't. But you will. It's easy to say one is a friend when the sun is out and the larder is full."

"What have the sun and a full larder to do with it?"

"My mother used to say that when the sun is out and the larder is full, one has nothing to lose,

Matthew. But a true friend proves herself when the larder is empty and the night is dark."

He reached through the bars for my hand. "Are all American girls as daft as you, Rachel?"

"I would hope so," I said.

"I never could understand you." He sighed.

"And you never will, Matthew." I said it sadly, then I left.

Once I knew what I had to do, everything fell into place. That night I sought out Mr. Adams.

He was in his office, dressing to go out. In his hands was a musket, to which he was affixing a bayonet. "Mr. Adams!" I gasped.

He turned and smiled on seeing me. "I've always had a hankering for the military life, Rachel," he said. "How do I look?"

A cartridge box was slung over his shoulder. He was wearing a sword, also. A scarf was tied around his head and over his ears under the cocked hat.

He looked silly.

"Where are you going?"

"I'm taking part in the civilian night watch. All responsible citizens are taking turns at guard duty. Tonight I take my station behind the Town House. Where is my lantern?"

He picked up a small lantern made of tin. "My

captain is Mr. Paddock, the coachmaker. I'm actually looking forward to this, Rachel. At least I'll be able to tell the children I did my part when the time came."

Tears came to my eyes, watching him. He would go for a soldier if they needed him. Learned as he was, he would take orders from a coachmaker.

"I would ask something of you, sir. But if you are too busy . . ."

"No, no, Rachel, I can tarry a bit. What is it?"

"Well, I know Mr. Forrest was here earlier today, asking if you would defend the soldiers."

"Begging, you mean."

"Yes sir, well, I would beg you, also."

He raised his eyebrows. For a moment he contemplated me. Then he knew. "It's that young Kilroy, is it?"

"Yes, sir."

"He hasn't been around that much since we moved here, has he?"

"No, sir, but I have been seeing him."

He nodded slowly. "He's in a great deal of trouble, Rachel. They would hang him."

"I know that, sir."

"The mere mention of it distresses you. Have you then become that enamored of him?"

"I've done nothing wrong, sir. I've always behaved most proper. But I was there last night and

I saw the civilians provoking the soldiers, and Matthew was only doing his job. He shouldn't go to the gallows for it."

"You were *there* last night?"

I clapped my hand over my mouth. "Yes, sir."

He set his musket aside and removed his hat. He loosened the scarf around his neck. "How came you to be there, Rachel?"

"I slipped out of the house, sir. I knew there was going to be trouble. I heard talk. So I went."

"Does Mrs. Adams know this?"

"No, sir, I haven't told her."

"It seems you've a whole life we don't know of then."

"I have friends, sir. On both sides. Matthew is one of them. Which is why I've come to beg you to take the case. It isn't fair he be sent to hang, sir. I know you'll be angry at me now. Perhaps you'll even dismiss me. I've thought on it all. And I've decided that Matthew needs your help more than I need this position, though it's all I have."

He put on his scarf again, then the hat. "I appreciate your honesty, Rachel, though my wife and I would have appreciated it a bit earlier on in the game."

"Yes, sir," I said meekly.

"I must go now and take my place."

"Will you do it, Mr. Adams? Will you defend

them, please? It would mean much to me, though I haven't the right to ask."

He paused at the doorway. "It is all over town already, Rachel. I'm surprised you haven't heard. I accepted Mr. Forrest's guinea as a retainer this afternoon, to defend Captain Preston and the soldiers."

"Oh, sir!"

"I did it not for Preston. Or any of the soldiers. But because good legal counsel should be the very last thing a person should be in want of in a free country."

I said nothing. He picked up his musket. "I must go now, Rachel."

"Yes, sir."

He was angry with me, I could feel it. A coldness had come between us. He was angry that I had deceived him about Matthew. I hadn't meant to deceive. It was just that there had been nothing to tell. I had not known the day would come when I would have to beg for Matthew's life. Or that I would willingly sacrifice my place, that meant so much to me, to do it.

Chapter Fifteen

ALL OF BOSTON was in turmoil. No matter where you went in the days following the killings, people were gathered in knots on the corners, arguing heatedly about who yelled "Fire!" and who threw what and how the bloody lobsterback soldiers had been waiting for the first opportunity to shoot at the citizens.

In churches, even in the middle of the week, the reverends were using the tragedy to deliver booming sermons about hellfire and damnation. Schools were closed. Shops were shuttered. Shopkeepers made you ring the bell and admitted only those they wanted to admit.

People walked the streets like crows, huddled in their cloaks, sidestepping friend and foe alike, hurrying on their errands. Children were not allowed out at night anymore.

And suddenly shopkeepers and vendors started

ignoring Mrs. Adams. And anyone who worked for her.

The first indication we had of such treatment was in the saddle of mutton I brought home the day I visited Matthew in jail.

For supper that night we had leftover stew. "Where is the mutton, Sukey?" Mrs. Adams asked as Sukey set the tureen down on the table.

"Had a bad smell," Sukey said.

Mrs. Adams raised her eyebrows and looked at me. "Rachel? Did you buy a piece of spoiled meat?"

Before I could reply, Sukey spoke up in my defense. "Wasn't 'til it started cookin', I noticed the smell, ma'am," she said.

We ate the leftover stew.

"Somethin' else you should know, ma'am," Sukey went on. "Mr. Samson, the butter-milk-and-eggs vendor, didn't stop by this mornin'."

Across the table I saw Mr. Adams exchange a look with his wife. "I fear, my dear, that this is a result of my agreeing to defend the British soldiers. The common man of Boston has turned against us."

Mrs. Adams smiled. "Tomorrow I shall go out myself, with Rachel," she said. "If you can defend the soldiers, I can face the common man."

"Do you think you should?" he asked.

"We must eat, John."

"Yes, and we'll soon have another mouth to feed. I've asked my new young law clerk, Johnathan

Austin, to give me even more hours a day now that we're rounding up and interrogating hundreds of eyewitnesses to the shooting. No doubt Austin and I will be working late many a night and will require food in my office."

Next morning, early, we set out to buy food. I had never seen Mrs. Adams so determined. Neither had I ever seen her so unjustly treated.

At Long Wharf, where, in the past, people would always move aside as she approached a stall, no one even acknowledged her. The tradesmen made her wait her turn. She did so, cheerfully. Once or twice people pushed ahead of us. A large woman actually stepped on her foot.

"There's no cause for such rudeness," I told the woman.

"Hush, Rachel," Mrs. Adams chided. "She didn't mean it."

"Yes, she did. Now show me the lobster you want and I'll get it for you."

She pointed it out. "Twopence," the man behind the stall said.

"The sign says halfpenny apiece," I told him.

"That's yesterday's sign. Didn't have time to change it."

"You must honor your sign," I insisted. "All the tradesmen do."

Mrs. Adams put a restraining hand on my arm.

But I held my ground and the man gave in. We got two lobsters for halfpenny apiece. The man wrapped them and I put them in my basket.

And so it went. I argued all morning. Sometimes I lost. We paid three shillings for a good turkey instead of two. It made me angry. I'd learned to dicker from both Jane and Mrs. Adams. But Mrs. Adams had no heart for it and we paid the three shillings.

"My family is coming to visit and we must have the best food," she said. "Elihu writes that he's bringing your dower chest. Come, let's visit Mr. Revere's shop. I want to see what new pots he's gotten in."

Paul Revere sometimes sold pots. As well as clock faces, sword hilts, babies' rattles, silver chains, and baptismal fonts. A little bell rang as we entered the shop.

"Mrs. Adams, how nice to see you."

"You're the only tradesman in Boston to think so, sir," she said.

He took her bundles and offered us chairs. He even brought forth hot cider in pewter mugs. "I'm a staunch member of the Sons, Mrs. Adams. Which is how I come to know that your husband's cousin Sam is happy your husband is taking the case. John Adams will be sure to keep the name of the good citizens of Boston intact."

"Thank you, Mr. Revere. Now may I see the drawings for the design of the silver baby's rattle?"

He brought forth his sketch. "It's lovely," she said. "I hear you have done an engraving of the massacre."

He was delighted to show it off. "I've sold hundreds of copies already," he said. "And it's going to be in the *Gazette*."

I spoke, then, out of turn. "But it wasn't like that," I said.

They both stared at me. I felt the color rushing to my face. "The crowd was holding sticks and clubs." I looked into Mr. Revere's brown eyes. "And the British soldiers weren't all lined up straight like that. The crowd was provoking them, Mr. Revere."

"You were there?"

"Yes, sir," I said.

He and Mrs. Adams exchanged glances. She became flustered. "Let us see what you have in the way of pots today," she said.

He brought out the pots. She selected three for my dowry. He said he would have them delivered. Outside, Mrs. Adams commenced to walk briskly. But she did not speak.

"I'm sorry, ma'am," I said. "I suppose I should have held my tongue."

"It isn't that, Rachel. How came you to be there?"

She stopped walking and I met her eyes. "I sneaked out that night. I heard the bells. Jane had told me there was talk of trouble. I was worried about Matthew."

She sighed. "You shouldn't have gone, Rachel."

"Yes, ma'am."

"I can't have you running the streets at night. Like part of the rabble."

She had never scolded me before. Tears came to my eyes. "I didn't think," I said.

"We know you to be a plain and decent girl, Rachel. It's important you be such, for the children. Did anyone see you there?"

"Only Mr. Knox."

She sighed and tightened her lips. "Henry will hold his tongue. But you mustn't tell anyone else you were there, Rachel."

"But I was," I said dismally. "And I saw what happened. And it wasn't like Mr. Revere's engraving. And if he's sold hundreds, and it's going to be printed in the *Gazette,* then people will think that's how it was."

She continued on, walking. "That's not for you to concern yourself with, Rachel. If Mr. Revere's engraving takes liberties, that is political license. People will take that into consideration. It is Mr. Adams's job, as lawyer for the defense, to bring out the truth."

238

"But I was *there*. And I can help him!"

Again she stopped walking. "What are you suggesting, Rachel?"

What, indeed? I had not known myself, until that moment. "I could testify," I said. "Couldn't I? Couldn't I tell the people what I saw?"

To my surprise, she smiled kindly. "Rachel, when you first came to us, you were so shy you scarcely answered when spoken to."

"Yes, ma'am, but I've studied hard. And I've learned to think things through clearly. You told me that if I read books, I would be able to do that."

A frown appeared on her brow.

"I know what I saw, and I'm not afraid to tell, Mrs. Adams. It's the reason I've studied so hard. So people would listen to me when I spoke. Like they listen to you. And they will listen now, because I've something to say and I know how to say it."

"Oh, dear." She looked ahead of her on the street as if to find some way out of her dilemma. Then she sighed again.

"Will you ask Mr. Adams to let me testify?"

"I'll ask him to listen to you," she promised. "But you must ask him, Rachel. Although, I must warn you. I don't think he's going to like it."

Mrs. Adams's family came to visit the next day: her mother and father and her sister Mary. Mr.

239

Adams's brother Elihu brought them down in the family chaise. Tied on back, with sturdy rope, was my dowry chest. It was beautiful! Made of stout cedar, it had that clean, fresh new-wood smell about it. Elihu carried it into the house and upstairs to my room. I had always liked this youngest Adams brother. He was very handsome, but a plain man, a farmer.

"Thank you, Elihu," I said, "it's beautiful."

He smiled and nodded happily. "You've worked for it," he said. "You've earned it, right well."

I felt that to be the highest praise. I knelt in front of the chest after he left the room. I ran my hands over it lovingly. Then I laid my finished pillow slips, sheets, and towels inside. I had never had anything like this in my whole life. Never had a single piece of furniture belonged to me. I was so happy I could cry.

Mrs. Adams's family stayed the week. The house was full to overflowing, and Sukey and Luke and I were kept so busy I scarcely had time to think of anything. That week, on March eighth, the funeral was held for those who had died in the massacre. Between that and the company and Mr. Adams so busy in his office, I pondered that Mrs. Adams had forgotten to ask him to hear my request. But I was wrong. At the end of the week, when Mrs. Adams's family departed, Mr. Adams summoned me into his office. It was just after supper.

And Mrs. Adams had been right. He didn't like it. He didn't like it at all.

"So, you want to testify."

"Yes, sir. If you'll allow it."

"Come in, Rachel. Sit down."

I sat. His desk was piled high with papers. His law clerk, Johnathan Williams Austin, made ready to leave.

"Don't go yet, Johnathan," Mr. Adams said.

Austin sat down in a corner. He was very young and he wore spectacles and looked very studious.

"Why do you wish to testify, Rachel?" Mr. Adams asked.

I explained to him about Mr. Revere's sketch of the massacre and how it wasn't correct. And that I could tell people the truth.

He listened patiently. "How many people have given depositions, Johnathan?" he asked.

"Ninety-six, sir."

"Ninety-six people, including Johnathan," Mr. Adams said. "Johnathan is going to tell what he saw that night in King Street. His testimony, while honest, will hardly be worth the effort, or the court's time. How say you, Johnathan?"

"That I heard no word given to fire," he answered.

Mr. Adams nodded. "Did you hear any such thing?" he asked.

"Everyone was yelling," I said. "I heard the

word *fire,* but it may have been people who thought a fire had started."

"What else can you tell the court then, that would make it worth my while to put you on the stand, Rachel?"

Tears came to my eyes. For a moment I couldn't answer.

"I am being kind, Rachel," Mr. Adams went on. "The lawyers for the prosecution will not be as kind. I must determine if you have anything that can help us."

"The crowd was throwing snowballs and sticks at the soldiers. The crowd was provoking them."

"I have ninety-six other people who will say the same thing," he said.

I searched around in my mind. "I know Matthew," I said.

"Yes?" He was waiting.

"He wouldn't have killed anyone without provocation. He was lonely and tired of being ill-used. When he went to the ropeworks for work, Mr. Gray told him to clean his outhouse."

"And wasn't it Mr. Gray whom Matthew Kilroy shot?" he asked.

I nodded. There was a knot in my throat. I looked at my hands in my lap. "There's something else, Mr. Adams."

He nodded for me to go on. I ran my tongue

along my lips and looked at him beseechingly, then at Johnathan.

"You may leave us, Johnathan," he said. "I'll see you in the morning."

The young man bowed and left. Again I looked at Mr. Adams. "Matthew told me, when he went to get a job in the ropeworks, that he was looking for a fracas. Because he'd been tormented so. And I feel guilty about it, sir."

"You?"

"Yes, Mr. Adams. You see, I tried to befriend him. But he wanted . . . he wanted more than friendship. And I was determined not to give it. We argued. He said I drove him to fighting." I felt myself get all flustered at having to tell him this.

But his face remained without expression. "And what do you think will happen to Matthew if you give such testimony, Rachel? The jurors will think he was spoiling for a fight. And he found it that night in King Street."

"But, sir . . ."

He stood up. "We already have enough evidence to acquit Captain Preston six times over. And if he is acquitted, the townsfolk will demand the blood of the soldiers."

I was trembling. My knees were shaking under my skirt.

"What you have just told me will send Matthew

Kilroy to the gallows. I cannot allow you to testify. Or the jury will know him for the hothead he is."

"He isn't a hothead, sir. But mistreated and homesick and confused."

"Please, Rachel. I know you think I am being harsh. I am not. I am talking to you like a father, trying to drive some sense into your head. Matthew Kilroy has the reputation of a jack-tar. You would do well to have no more to do with him."

I stared. "You mean, I can't visit him in prison?"

"You have made a place for yourself here, Rachel," he said. He uttered the words softly. The candle sputtered on his desk. "If you value that place as nursemaid to our children, I would advise you not to visit Matthew Kilroy in prison."

"But he's so alone, sir. And dirty. And underfed. All they give him is gruel and salted meat. I would just bring him some food. As I've done before."

"He is a conniver, Rachel. He once robbed a woman of her good velvet ermine-trimmed cloak. He was made to give up his booty. He has preyed upon your innocence."

"That can't be true." Tears were coming down my face. "He's misunderstood, sir. And innocent of murder."

"I have taken to defend his life, Rachel. I shall argue that the soldiers had a right to kill in their own self-defense. I shall attempt to reduce the offense of killing to manslaughter. But Kilroy has the spirit of the Devil in him, child. He not only shot Gray, he stabbed a dead man with his bayonet."

I was sobbing. I wiped my tears with the corner of my apron. I had always admired Mr. Adams so, and the work he did in his office. And the way he could look inside his books and come up with an answer for a person's problems.

But he could not do it for me now. And if he could not, then what good were the books? What good was my learning? One might as well run with the mob. They got their way. Look at Sam Adams. He never read books. And there was talk that before the end of the month he would have the troops removed from Boston.

"Enough now," Mr. Adams said kindly. "I am weary of it. Go to bed, child. Again, let me remind you of the place you have earned for yourself in this household. And promise me you will stay away from the prison."

I bade him good night. But I did not promise.

Chapter Sixteen

THE DAY WAS WARM for March, but a dampness rose from the ground as the sun's rays melted the snow. There was no music this time, no fifes and drums. Only the steady thump, thump, thumping of marching feet as the remaining British troops left town.

It was the twenty-seventh of March. The sky was bright blue. The sun on our faces had a warmth I had almost forgotten.

I stood with Nabby and Johnnie and Jane on the sidelines. All around us, windows were opening in houses as the straight-faced men of the Fourteenth and Twenty-ninth regiments marched to Long Wharf where they would embark for Castle William.

Ladies in gay dresses leaned out of the windows, waving long bright ribbons and clapping. Schoolboys darted between the ranks of soldiers, jeering.

The soldiers were being escorted out of town by the Sons of Liberty. I saw Will Molineaux, Mackintosh, and Sam Adams in front of the line, proud in their tricorn hats, shouldering muskets.

The crowds lining the streets cheered as Sam Adams walked by. The men gave three "huzzahs" and threw their hats up in the air. Young girls broke out of the ranks of onlookers and rushed to embrace the Sons. Then all of Boston's church bells started to ring joyously.

"Huzzah! Huzzah!" little Johnnie chanted as they tramped by. "Good-bye, soldiers, good-bye!"

Vendors were making their way through the crowd, selling ices, hot bread, sausage, pastries. The whole scene had the air of a street fair about it.

"Well, that's over with," Jane said as the last of the troops passed in front of us. "It doesn't seem that long ago that they came, does it?"

"Less than two years," I said.

She flung back her head and breathed in the springlike air. "And how many lives have been changed?" she asked.

"Everyone's," I answered. "I know mine has."

"Come, let's get some ices."

I bought the children ices and we wandered into a churchyard, where we sat on a nearby bench. "Have you decided what you are going to do?" Jane asked.

I wiped Johnnie's mouth and waited until he and Nabby were out of earshot, hopping on some cobblestones, making a game of it.

"I'm going to feed him, Jane. I'm going to bring him food. I met Lucy Flucker the other day. She said her own sister is bringing food into prison for the soldiers. Because they aren't being fed properly."

"Loyalists," Jane said. "You're not a loyalist."

"Why does everything always have to do with politics?"

"Because this is Boston."

"Matthew is a friend. He may go to the gallows. I keep thinking, if I'd been nicer to him . . ."

"Now don't go down that path again," she chided.

"I have to, Jane. I keep going over and over it in my head. I wouldn't give Matthew my favors because I didn't want to end up like my mother. In circumstances, having to marry. I worked so hard to better myself. But I wanted to be his friend. Only he didn't understand that. And he got angry. I know he did what he did, in part, because he was angry with me, Jane. So now I have to be a friend to him to the end. Or I'll go daft. Especially if he goes to the gallows."

"So you're going to endanger your place and feed him, then."

"I don't see what one has to do with the other," I said. "Look at Mr. Adams. He's endangered *his* place by taking on the defense of the soldiers. Surely, he'll understand. I'm only doing what I think is right. Just like he is."

"It doesn't work that way," she said.

"Why?"

She leaned back on the bench and held her face up to the sun's warming rays. "Because he has other places to go, other things to be," she said. "And you don't, that's why. You don't have to do this for Matthew, Rachel. He's a soldier. He'll keep. They always do."

"I'm not doing it for Matthew," I said. "I'm doing it for myself. Why doesn't anyone understand?"

I thought about her words, and mine, that night as I stood in the kitchen wrapping some ham in cabbage leaves, some rolls in a napkin. I'd overheard Mr. Adams tell his wife earlier that the trial might be postponed until October.

I hadn't counted on that. It meant that if I started bringing food to Matthew now, in March, I would have to continue all summer and into the fall. How would I do that without being found out?

I would not go every day, I decided. I would go twice a week, once on my day off and one night

249

I would slip out of the house. Surely, as spring came, no one could fault me for taking a walk around the millpond at night, could they?

The house was quiet. Mrs. Adams had retired to her room with a cup of hot chocolate. The children were asleep. Mr. Adams was working in his office. I slipped out the back door, minding what Mrs. Adams had told me when I first took the job. That once the children were abed at night, my time was my own.

The Boston jail was a dank place on the sunniest of days. At night, with the light of tallow candles, it was positively sinister.

The jailer's keys jangled as he shuffled in the passages between the cells. All the prisoners looked to see who was coming. I wore my hood to cover my face. It hid my hair. I was careful to walk in the shadows. The place smelled. Of stale bodies and wet woolen coats, of rank vegetation, of burning beeswax, of sewage. There was the constant noise of water drip, drip, dripping and a scurrying on the floor of something around my feet. What? Mice? Rats?

As the outside door clanged shut behind me, a guard came forward. "What's in the basket?"

"Some bread and meat."

"I must needs see."

I removed the linen napkin. By lantern light he inspected the contents. Beyond his shoulder I noticed a woman seated on a bench, watching. She was dressed in the plain garb of a Quaker. The guard nodded. "Remove your cloak," he ordered. "I must determine if you are carrying weapons."

Before I had a chance to resist, the woman came forward. "Mr. Salem," she asked, "will thee never stop trying?" She smiled at me kindly. "Just set down thy basket," she whispered. As I did so, she ran her hands under my cloak, feeling my person. And I blushed, realizing what Mr. Salem had been about.

"Who has thee come to see?" she asked.

"Matthew Kilroy."

She nodded. "Make thy visit quick. This is not a good place for such a young girl."

I followed the guard past a cell where some soldiers were playing cards. They peered at me as I walked by.

"Dammy, did you see that?"

"Oh, my sweet aunt, another Quaker woman."

"She was no Quaker, that one. No more than my sweet Molly is a Quaker."

"I *smelled* that. Fresh bread. Who d'you suppose she's come to see?"

"I'm fair to fainting. It doesn't matter. It wasn't me."

"Some fellows have all the luck."

"It's Kilroy. Dammy, it's Kilroy! The jackanapes. Fresh bread for Kilroy. And she's handsome,

251

too. Damned handsome. Some fellows have all the luck."

"Any hag would look handsome to you right now, Montgomery."

"No, by God, she *was* handsome. And not of the lower classes, either. You can tell by how she carries herself."

Matthew looked up in disbelief as I stood in front of his cell. "Rachel?"

"I've some bread for you," I whispered. "And ham."

"It's a wonder you got past the guard safely. Was the Quaker woman there?"

"Yes."

"Don't ever come in here if she isn't. Old Salem has the morals of a leech. And he demands part of the booty visitors bring. Then he sells it to us. God, I'm hungry."

He ate ravenously of the bread and meat. "The water is stale," he said. "And things are floating in it. I never drank the water in Boston before and I won't drink it now. I spend all my money on rum. By heaven, Rachel, it's good to see you. Have you heard anything about the trial?"

"Mr. Adams said Hutchinson is going to have it put off until the autumn." He was thin and sallow. He'd lost weight. His hair was badly in need of grooming.

"Don't get too close to me," he warned, "I've got lice."

I stepped back. It would not do if I brought lice home to the children. "Oh, Matthew, what else can I bring you?"

He grinned. "Yourself. It's bonny of you to come, Rachel."

"I'm your friend," I said simply.

He lowered his eyes. "I mind now what that means."

"I had hoped you would."

"I've treated you ill, Rachel. I've been a lout."

"No. You just didn't understand."

"Well, I do now. Never did I expect to find friendship in this place. This Boston, it's a cold, unseemly place, Rachel. It's unnatural for a people to be so full of hatred as the people here are."

"They're a different kind of people, Matthew. They have burning wants."

"So do we all."

"No, Matthew. That's something else you don't understand. I didn't, when I first got here. They want what no people have ever wanted before. They want liberty."

He shrugged. "To do what?"

"I don't know. Since no people have ever had it, who knows what they could do with it?"

"Well, all I want is a washing. And to go to a clean bed and sleep without hearing rats scurrying at my feet. And to wake in clean sunshine without fear. And to have a full meal in my belly and do some work I like and have no one take what I've earned. Or say I'm beneath him."

"I think that's what they want, too, Matthew. I think that's what liberty is."

"That's all?" He was disbelieving.

"No, Matthew, that isn't all. There's more to it than that. I don't know if I can explain. But near as I can grasp it, it's the right to make up your own mind about things, to decide for yourself what course of action you are going to take. And then follow it. With no one sweeping up after you if you're wrong and no one taking the gains if you're right."

"My, that sounds plain and sweet."

I fell silent for a moment, pondering. "Yes," I said. And it came to me that's what liberty was, something plain and sweet. And it came to me too that I was practicing liberty, coming to visit Matthew.

Then wouldn't John Adams understand me? It was he who'd said that in a free country every man was entitled to legal counsel. He considered it a free country then. But was all this babble about freedom only for certain people?

"What is it, Rachel?" Matthew asked.

"Nothing. Is there anything else I can bring you next time?"

"You mean to visit again?"

"Of course."

"If you would, Rachel, and mind, I'm not asking you to. But if you would, I could do with a tallow candle. And a bit of paper and something to write with. If you could manage it. I'd like to write to my mum."

I couldn't speak for a moment. When I recovered myself, we said our proper good-byes. On the way out the Quaker woman smiled at me. "I'm here on Tuesdays and Thursdays," she told me. "From noon until nine."

I felt my spirits lift. And that decided me. Tuesdays were now my day off. It must be meant to be that I visit Matthew. I thanked her and left. *Paper and pen and tallow candles,* I thought. *Yes, I could manage that very nicely.*

"The massacre had to happen," Henry Knox was saying. "If it didn't happen, someone would have had to make it happen. Oh, I'm not saying those poor devil soldiers were wrong."

"What are you saying then, darling?" Lucy Flucker asked sweetly. She had just come through the door, looking lovely in a blue-sprigged muslin dress and light cloak.

We were seated at the table in Henry's back

room, sipping chocolate as we'd done so many times in the past.

"You look as fine as the May morning," he said, standing to greet her. He kissed her lightly on the cheek. "Come sit. I was saying that the soldiers never should have been sent here in the first place. And once they came nobody could stop the killings. It was like a force of nature."

"You sound as if you're having a revelation," Lucy teased.

"Dull and plodding people like me aren't given to revelations," he said. "I'm thinking of more pragmatic matters. Like how I miss the business the officers brought to my shop."

"Well, I have a revelation, then," Lucy announced.

We waited. She took off her cloak and set it aside. She was smiling. "John Hancock's *Haley* just arrived from England. And his Captain Scott brought news. The Townsend Acts have been repealed."

"Huzzah!" Henry turned from the hearth where he was reaching for the pot of chocolate. "We'll soon be drinking tea again."

"No tea." Lucy frowned. "Parliament has lifted the taxes on everything but the tea."

"The fools," Henry said. "It will only mean more smuggling. More trouble. New Englanders can't live without their tea. And they'll not pay the tax."

Lucy sat down and accepted the cup of chocolate Henry poured. "I'm weary of talk of taxes. Tell me, Rachel, isn't Mrs. Adams's new baby due soon?"

"Within a fortnight," I said.

"You'll be busy then, with three charges."

"The new baby won't be my responsibility for a while."

I saw Lucy and Henry exchange glances. "What is it?" I said. "Is something wrong? You're my friends. Tell me."

"All right," Lucy agreed. "You know that I don't get along with my sisters very well, don't you? That I've been warned by them of the misery that will be my lot if I marry my Henry?"

"I've heard tell," I said.

"Well, my sister Lavinia would do anything to hurt me. Especially now that the troops have been driven out of Boston. She knows you've been visiting Matthew Kilroy in jail. She could make trouble out of that for you. Just to get at me. Because we're friends."

I felt the blood pounding in my ears. Tears welled in my throat. "I've a right to go," I said staunchly. "It's on my own time."

Lucy was examining a break in one of her nails

as if her life depended upon it. "I know, dear, but you work for the Adamses. Your behavior must be above reproach."

"Lucy, do *you* think it isn't?"

"Of course not. But others are waiting for the opportunity to attack Mr. Adams. Don't you understand?"

"Apparently I'm dim-witted," I said, "because I don't."

"Mr. Adams is defending the soldiers," Henry put in. "And you are visiting them."

"Only Matthew. I'm only visiting Matthew. And just because he's in such poor condition. He spends what money he has on rum so he doesn't have to drink the dirty water. I've only brought him some tallow candles and soap for washing and paper to write with."

Neither of them said anything for a moment. "If people want to make a fuss out of that," I said, "let them."

"Some will," Henry said. "It won't look well for you, Rachel. Especially since the Adamses' children are in your charge. We just wanted to point that out to you."

I didn't answer for a moment. "There's so much I don't understand, Henry," I said.

"Tell me," he said. "Mayhap I can help you."

"Well, Mr. Adams is defending the soldiers

because he thinks it's the right thing to do. And I'm visiting Matthew for the same reason. Isn't that what this liberty thing is all about?"

He smiled at me sadly.

"Or is it just for certain people? For the highborn. Like education."

"You know what I told you about education, Rachel," he chided.

"And liberty? What say you to me then about liberty, Henry Knox?"

His answer came from somewhere deep inside him, a hesitant rumbling thing, like a hibernating bear he was afraid to waken. "I don't know what this liberty thing is all about, Rachel. None of us do, yet. I pray that if we ever achieve it, we will know how to control it. And not let it control us."

I leaned forward. "That's all you can say of it?"

"No. I can quote from Aristides. 'Neither walls, theatres, porches, nor senseless equipage make states, but men who are able to rely upon themselves.' "

"And women," I pushed.

"Yes, women," he allowed. "But even if we someday achieve this liberty we must still adhere to the rules of proper behavior and the law. Or we will run amok."

"Whose rules? The high-placed make them and can do whatever they please. Because they have money." I stood up and pushed back my chair. "Is that the way this liberty thing will work, then?"

"Rachel." Lucy reached out her hand to me. "We're your friends. We care for you. We're only trying to keep you from harm. It has naught to do with liberty or education. But with the way things are."

"You're both doing what you think is right by courting," I argued. "You're not minding anyone's rules."

"Methinks, Rachel," Henry said, "that you have a legal turn of mind. Or is it the result of living in the Adamses' household?"

"It's the result of reading. Books you suggested. You helped me to become educated. And to use my mind. Well, now that I have it, I shall use it. To think for myself, thank you."

Henry nodded, considering that.

"And as for liberty, you yourself told me that I was no longer a British American. But that I'd become a plain American, a true American. Didn't you?"

He held up his hands in a gesture of peace. "That I did, Rachel."

"Then I intend to act like one," I said. "If that's all right with everybody."

Henry smiled. "I also told you not to run around telling everyone how you felt about things just yet, Rachel. The time has not yet come to do that."

I glared at him. "It's come for me," I said.

They did not answer to that.

"I'm tired of people telling me what I can and can't do. I know what I'm about and I've learned to think for myself. And if you say now that I can't, then what you are telling me, Henry Knox, is that all my book learning is for nothing. And I've studied so hard! Am I now to act like the little moth I was when I first came here?"

"I'm just telling you to be prudent, Rachel, that's all," he advised gently.

I glared at them both. What were they saying? Of all the people I knew, I thought at least *they* would understand what I was about. I was trembling. "I must go," I said.

"Don't leave like this," Lucy entreated. "Come sit and have more chocolate."

"I don't want chocolate. I want tea. I'm sick to the teeth of chocolate," I said. And then I ran out.

I ran all the way home, crying. I'd hurt two of my best friends. How could I have done such? I felt so torn, so muddled inside. Was that what book learning did for you? And liberty? If so, then I'd been better off before I had acquired them.

Chapter Seventeen

OH, WHAT A CHILD I still was. A petulant and stubborn and willful child who was so filled up with my newfound learning and my simpleton ideas of liberty that I thought all I had to do was read a few books and rub shoulders with people of great ideas and the world would change for me.

That people would see me coming and step aside and say, "Look out, here comes Rachel Marsh. She reads books. She's found that she's not afraid to speak out. She's decided what she's about and she thinks the promise of this liberty, that some have already died for here in Boston, means that she can go about and do anything she wants, regardless of who gets hurt."

I had so much to learn. Not from books. It wasn't the kind of thing you could learn from books. It was about people. And it had to do with understanding that they could be miserly of spirit and heart. And want to spite you just for the sport of it. And that people could be blessed with every great gift the Lord had to give, or plagued with every misery, like Job. And they could never rise above what they were. But just go on, stuck like that, being people. Oh, they might have moments of brilliance or goodness, like John Adams or Henry Knox, but when push came to shove, why they were just afflicted souls, worrying the small matters to the bone, above the big ones.

It made me sore of heart just to think on it.

Mrs. Adams's new baby arrived on the twenty-ninth of May. It was a healthy baby boy. They named him Charles. Mrs. Adams was completely taken with him. And everyone was glad the birth had gone well.

Within the week, Sam Adams came to the house with a bottle of Madeira in hand and clapped Mr. Adams on the back and congratulated him for winning the election. John Adams said, "What election, I haven't run for anything."

I was sent to fetch glasses then, and I brought them into the parlor on a silver tray. "Why," Sam said, "the citizens of Boston met at Faneuil Hall and have elected you to represent Boston in the House of Representatives and the General Court."

John Adams seemed stunned. "The people hate

me," he said, "for defending the British soldiers."

"The people love you, Cousin," said Sam. "You beat Mr. Ruddock 536 votes to 418."

They went up the stairs with the Madeira and glasses to tell Abigail the good news. She had not yet come below stairs after the birth of her baby.

So John Adams had to travel to Cambridge then, where the Legislature met because acting Governor Hutchinson had exiled it from Boston a while back. Mr. Adams was away a lot and the trip took time because the ferries were slow going.

Then, when the Legislature had its summer recess, he decided to ride circuit again. He was taking cases in Falmouth, Newbury, Portsmouth, Salem, everywhere. To make money, I overheard him tell his wife.

The job as representative had no pay. And he had to earn money to keep them until Christmas.

Summer came, with its cool mornings and hot days, its street noises filtering in open windows, its bay breezes smelling of the sea and billowing the curtains, its long evenings and its dreamy haze. With Mrs. Adams completely taken with the baby and Mr. Adams riding circuit, no one gave me any grief when I went, one evening a week and one afternoon on my day off, to visit Matthew.

Always, the Quaker lady was there. Always, she stepped forward to search me before Mr. Salem could get his hands near my being. We became friends.

· Quakers were not held in high esteem in Boston. It was a town of three Congregational meeting houses. Bostonians had learned to live amiably with their Baptists, French Protestants, Irish Presbyterians, and members of the Church of England. They only tolerated the Quakers. And barely that.

I took immediately to Alice Pattishell, seeing in her a kindred spirit. Her ancestors had been led behind a cart and whipped all through New England, she told me, for their beliefs, back in Puritan times.

She now belonged to Quaker Meeting on the corner of Salter's Court. Her family was in Philadelphia, she said, where Quakers were thriving.

It was she who becalmed me after Matthew told me that Captain Preston was receiving unsigned letters, warning him that if he was pardoned, the people of Boston would tear down the walls of the jail.

"The people of Boston love to hear themselves talk," she said.

And it was she and others like her who came to relieve her on her days off, who had forced the guards to provide tubs of hot water for the soldiers to wash. And who had raised such a fuss that a barber was sent into the prison to cut their hair.

One day I came to find Matthew wearing clean and pressed small clothes. "Alice Pattishell did this herself," he told me.

She had also brushed and aired and mended his red coat, foraged blacking for his and the other soldiers' boots, and requisitioned them reading matter.

"Thank you for what you have done for Matthew," I told her one day on my way out.

"Thy coming here does as much," she allowed.

I smiled at her. The woman had a grace about her. A presence. She stood out like a gray vision, cool and unruffled by the madness that permeated Boston that summer. The blood lust of the people, crying for the hanging of the soldiers, did not bother her. To her there were no British or Americans, no Tories or Patriots. And the soldiers were only sad and badly treated lads a long way from home.

She asked me no questions about Matthew. She did not pry. One day Lavinia Flucker was in the jail the same time as I. We passed as I came in and she was going out.

Lavinia was as beautiful as her sister and more spoiled. "Hello, Rachel Marsh," she said. "I didn't expect to see *you* here. Of all people."

When she left, I was near tears. "I'm in trouble now," I told Alice as she searched me for weapons.

"Why?"

"She's going to tell my master I was here. He's

John Adams, you know. He won't like it. I'm looking for trouble coming here. I could lose my position."

"Is thee doing anyone harm by coming?" she
asked.

"No. But I'm nursemaid for the Adamses' children. And some say it isn't seemly I should be
visiting a murderer in prison."

She smiled. "Thee is practicing charity," she
said. "I couldn't think of a better nursemaid for
children."

I thanked her politely, then went on to say that
I doubted if the Adamses would see it that way.

She drew herself up and looked me square in
the eye. "If thee loses thy position for practicing
acts of charity, Rachel Marsh," she said, "come to
me. I know where thee can find another. Thee is
bounded. Am I right?"

"Yes."

She nodded. "The Adamses are good people.
But even good people can have their patience
strained. This position I know of pays."

Everyone in the Adams household had far too
much to think of that summer to question me about
visiting Matthew. For one thing we had to move
again. The landlord of the Cold Lane house decided
he wanted to live there himself.

So, while Mr. Adams was away, we moved back

to Brattle Square. A different house this time, across from Dr. Samuel Cooper's Meeting House. I missed the millpond, and Mrs. Adams was worried that once the trials started people would gather in disgruntled groups beneath their windows.

Everyone was especially busy setting things to rights. One day in late August, I came in from the backyard with baby Charles on my shoulder to find Lavinia Flucker in the parlor.

"Hello, Rachel," she said. "I've brought some pot cheese and fresh bread and cooked fruit for supper. I know how difficult it is, when you just move into a house."

I stood stock still, staring at her.

"How nice of you," Mrs. Adams beamed.

"Well, 'twas my mother who sent it. If that man's going to defend the British soldiers, she said, the least we can do is see that on the first night in their home, the supper table is laid properly."

"Do you two know each other?" Mrs. Adams asked me.

I did not answer. Lavinia did. "Oh, Rachel is friends with my sister Lucy. As for me, I only see Rachel when she visits the jail. My mama sends food there to the soldiers, too."

"Your mama is a good woman," Mrs. Adams murmured. And when she turned from the front door she looked at me in a puzzled manner. But she said nothing.

So, it was done then. My secret was out. Nothing was said by Mrs. Adams, of course. We proceeded right back to work, making the house to rights. I helped her hang curtains that evening. I bathed the children. Then we all sat down in the backyard to the supper brought by Lavinia Flucker.

September passed in a haze. I played with the children, read to them, and took them on picnics for it was still hot. Evenings I worked on my dowry.

My dowry chest was filled now, with pillow slips, sheets, towels, cloths for the table. Mrs. Adams had even taught me how to do crewelwork. I was doing a bed cover.

Evenings, I would take my linens out of the chest and handle them lovingly. Then fold them and put them back. I would examine my copper-bottomed pots, my skillet on legs, my wooden bowls, and pewter plates. I would spend hours dreaming over my beautiful things.

Except for hard specie, the silver coins or English pounds or Dutch rix-dollars Mr. Adams might give me, my dowry was near complete. I had no idea of the amount of hard specie he might offer. The matter had been agreed upon between John Adams and Uncle Eb. I was bound for five years. I had one year's service to complete.

At the end of September, Mr. Adams returned home to prepare for the trial of Captain Preston.

Fall came, with its bright blue skies, its brilliant colors, its warm days and chilly nights. I loved fall the best, with its smell of wood smoke and the first cold nights under the warm blankets. The vendors hawked warm bread and hot cider on Long Wharf, where even the cry of the gulls seemed different. I always felt the hint of promise in fall. As if something were about to happen in my life. Back in Braintree it would be harvesttime.

That fall something did happen, but not what I expected. One evening, I was lying in bed. I had just set down a book and blown out my candle. A full moon shown in the window, making the outside landscape like day.

I must have dozed. Then I woke to the sound of voices, carrying low yet clear through the house. John Adams was speaking.

"But you have said nothing to her of the matter?"

"I could not bring myself to do it. She is so good in her duties. And the children love her so."

"But I distinctly warned her against such a course of action. I find it difficult to believe she has flown in the face of my directives."

"Oh, John, she's a young girl. With a head full of romantic notions. At that age, wasn't I the same?"

"At that age you were most studious and grave and decorous, my dear."

"Could you vouch for what I was thinking?"

"You were thinking what an excellent catch I was."

"No doubt I was thinking how to convince my mother that you weren't the mere pettifogging country lawyer she thought you were."

"And have I proven otherwise?"

"You have, John. But this is no time for idle talk. We must think of Rachel. I'm afraid the fault's been ours. We should never have allowed her to start walking out with Matthew in the beginning. She was our responsibility. We are to blame, John, as well as she."

"You are right, my love. She was a young girl from Braintree, thrown into the turmoil of life in Boston. The temptations would be too much for one of sterner stuff."

I lay in bed, shivering. Oh, the shame of hearing them discussing me. Like I was some common serving wench who hadn't worked out.

". . . two issues involved here," Mr. Adams was saying. "Issue first is that she is meeting with a young man whose life I am defending. There are many who could make much of that. Issue two is that, as nursemaid for our children, her actions should be above reproach."

"I'm sure they are, John. She is just befriending him."

271

"Abby, my darling, you may be right. But it is how her actions *appear* to be that can be just as damaging. No, I am going to have to take a firm stand on this."

"What are you going to do, John?" Mrs. Adams sounded worried.

"In due time I shall speak with her. We agreed to leave Boston after the trials, didn't we?"

"Yes, John, I could not stand another winter here. And if you win the case we will not have many friends left."

"I shall win it," he said.

"How can you be so sure?"

"Preston's trial opens tomorrow. That case will be easy. The people want the heads of the soldiers. And if Preston is cleared of giving the order to fire, the soldiers will be more likely to be convicted."

"But what of the fate of the soldiers, then?"

"I shall try to prove their firing was in self-defense and therefore justifiable homicide. It will be difficult, but I can do it."

Silence for a moment or two. "And what of Rachel?"

"I shall not reproach her or make her feel in any way that she has failed. No doubt, the child does not know the wrong she has done. Don't forget, Abby, she didn't have the benefit of your upbringing, with a kind father, who also happened to be the richest clergyman in the province. And a mother who was a Quincy. No, I shall not lay blame. I shall tell her we are going back to Braintree. And that I am quite sure she won't want to be going with us. What's there for her? I shall tell her we will pay her the dowry money and find her another position."

Mrs. Adams said something then, murmured soft and low. I could not hear it. No doubt it was because I was sobbing quietly, into my pillow.

Next morning I did not want to go downstairs. My eyes were puffy from crying. But everyone was so occupied with the Preston case little mind was paid to me. And Abigail Adams was just as amiable as always.

I waited all day, sure that when Mr. Adams came home from court that night he would summon me. But he did not. He all but ignored me. Then, the next morning early, the British fleet in the harbor started firing its guns.

"Wachel, Wachel," Johnnie came racing into my room. "Mama says you may take us to the harbor today to see the celebwation."

"What celebration?"

"It's King George the Third's birthday," Nabby reported.

"No, children, it's the anniversary of his accession to the throne," their mother said.

"The guns will boom all day," Johnnie announced. "Will you take me? Will you?"

I knelt down and he hugged me. "Aren't you afraid of the guns?"

"No, Wachel," he said solemnly, "I not 'fwaid. Not if you take me."

Over his head, as he hugged me, I saw Mrs. Adams watching us. What was she thinking? I took the children to the harbor that morning and we stayed all day for the festivities. The weather was warm and bright, I bought them sweets to eat, and we enjoyed ourselves together. I had a feeling, going home, that it would be one of the last good days I would have with them.

I had become attached to the children and they to me. Little Nabby asked endless questions, clung to my skirts, and was full of energy. Little Johnnie's hand clasped mine. "My Wachel," he called me. "My fwiend." And his chubby arms would hug me tightly. As I brought them home that day, I was full of guilt and sorrow for what I had done. I had allowed myself to be pulled into the politics and the hatreds and the sordidness of Boston. I had forgotten my real purpose for coming here, my vow to myself.

I had betrayed the people who had been good

to me. And now I would lose the place I had worked so hard to get. Now, one day soon, I would be asked to leave. I would have to say good-bye to these dear children and never see them again.

I went home and cried in my room. I waited for Mr. Adams to summon me. Every night when I went to sleep I wondered why he had let another day go by without delivering his ultimatum.

Every morning when I awoke I went downstairs fully expecting it.

But it did not happen. The days passed as before. No one said anything unpleasant to me. I went to visit Matthew twice a week, as always. No one made any attempt to stop me.

I saw Jane once, on the street, but she was occupied with attending the trial. Henry Knox was testifying, she said. I did not go to see Henry or Lucy. Except for visits to Matthew, I stayed home. I needed to collect my thoughts, to husband my strength. The rhythms of the household had always done that for me and now I found comfort in their sameness. I desperately wanted sameness and order. I began to fancy, as October deepened and the fires were lighted each day in the hearth, that perhaps Mr. Adams had had a change of heart.

But no. He was just too occupied with Captain Preston's trial. It went on for a week and it was all anybody in Boston talked about or cared about.

John Adams came home every night, grim-faced and edgy. Mrs. Adams told me to keep the children out of his way and I did so, gladly.

I went to visit Matthew on the day that the jury was deciding Captain Preston's fate. Matthew was glum. "Word has gotten back to us," he said, "that Preston testified that he gave us no orders to fire and we must take the consequences."

"Oh, Matthew," I commiserated.

Just at that moment, the inner door of the jail clanged open. And Lavinia Flucker burst in. "Oh, have you heard? Oh, everyone, listen. The jury has reported its verdict! Not guilty!"

Matthew and the others groaned. "Preston has thrown us to the wolves," he said. "Now we are murderers because we fired without orders."

On the way out I found Lavinia Flucker waiting for me. She flashed me a smile. "Just on the premise that you may be looking for a new position one of these days," she said, "you should know that my parents are desperately seeking a new girl."

"And why should I be seeking a new position?"

"No reason. Except that everything is changing in Boston. Oh, a person can just feel it, walking the streets. Preston not guilty! You know, Rachel Marsh, this business is not over yet between the Crown and the people. The British will be back.

And when they come back, you'd do well to be employed in a good Tory household."

And with that she tossed her head and walked into the street.

It was the perfect time for Mr. Adams to call me to his office, because I was so upset over what Matthew had said that afternoon that I did not care about anything. Whatever happened to me, it couldn't be any worse than what would happen to Matthew.

Mr. Adams summoned me after supper that very evening.

The fire in the hearth burned brightly. From upstairs I could hear little Johnnie's feet pattering down the hall as his mama readied him for bed. It was my job to put him to bed and the denial of that duty hurt me sorely.

"Rachel." He smiled. "Come in and sit down."

So he was going to be nice. Oh, that would make it twice as difficult to bear. I sat woodenly in one of the chairs.

"Well, Rachel, you must have heard the verdict. Captain Preston was cleared this day."

"Yes sir, you have done yourself proud."

"It isn't over yet, of course. The most difficult part is to come. The burden is on the defense now, to prove the soldiers' acts were justifiable homicide."

"What does that mean, sir?"

"It means they won't hang, Rachel, if I have my way."

I felt flooded with relief. He *was* a good man. "Oh, I hope you can do it, sir," I said.

"I shall do my best, Rachel. But right now my concern is you. My wife and I are greatly concerned about you. After the trials, you see, we are going to move back to Braintree. It's only ten miles from Boston. I shall ride in every day, to do business. But my wife and I yearn for the simpler life back there."

I ran my tongue along my lips and waited. My temple was throbbing.

"We do not wish you to pine away in the backwoods of this province, however. So, after much consideration we have decided to release you from our agreement. I shall speak to your uncle and give you your dowry money and find a good paying position for you. Here in Boston. You've become accustomed to the town, you have friends here now, and you will certainly find no husband back in Braintree. What say you, Rachel?"

What say I?

I wanted to say so many things! I yearned to say them. That I did not want to leave their service.

That I had been happier with them than I'd ever been in my whole life. That I'd felt as if I'd had a home here. And I loved the children so. And who would fix Nabby's hair every morning? And be there for Johnnie when he came bursting into my room? Who would comfort him at night when he awoke with nightmares? And what would he think when he called for me and I did not come?

I said none of this, however.

What was done was done. I had not lived up to my part of the agreement by being the genteel nursemaid to their children. I had run with the rabble in the streets. I had not honored the position they gave me. I had consorted with one of the British soldiers, possibly compromising Mr. Adams. And if not that, then certainly bringing gossip to touch their house.

But more than all of that, John Adams did not wish even to speak of such matters to me. He wished to conduct this interview in as amiable a manner as possible. He wanted to spare me hurt. And he wanted no unpleasantness to exist between us.

I was not accustomed to such gentility. Uncle Eb and I had screamed at each other. My mother and Uncle Eb had fought like cat and dog.

And so it was that that evening I learned my most valuable lesson since coming to Boston.

The Adamses and their kind *were* different from me and my kind. It had to do with breeding. And family. I had heard Mr. Adams say once that Abigail's great-great-grandsire had been a founder of the province.

Surely, no amount of book reading on my part could make up for such a family background. So all I did was sit there and nod my head and say, "Yes, sir."

He was so relieved, poor man. He positively beamed. Then he went on to speak of money, hard specie money. Silver. And how the rest of my dowry would be completed. I nodded, but I was not listening. What I was doing was trying to figure out how I was going to get out of that room without bursting into tears and disgracing myself.

Chapter Eighteen

"*WILLIAM WEMMS, William M'Cauley, Matthew Kil-roy, Hugh Montgomery, James Hartegan, Hugh White, William Warren, and John Carrol.*"

Court Clerk Sam Winthrop's voice boomed and echoed in the high-ceilinged room on the second floor of the Town House. The names seemed to echo off the large, arched windows. Outside snow was falling. It was November twenty-seventh, the first day of the trial of the soldiers.

I had come because it was my day off. And because I was pulled here by a rope of feelings that I had woven over the last two years for Matthew.

I had not known until today how strong that rope was.

Outside the Town House the street was cluttered with carriages. People had come in to town from the far countryside around Boston. They filled the Council Chamber. They huddled, like peas in a pod, on its uncomfortable benches. They gathered on the stairs. They sat in carriages outside. They shivered on the Common. The taverns and inns were overflowing.

"... *not having the fear of God before their eyes, but being moved and seduced by the instigation of the devil and their own wicked hearts, did, on the fifth day of this instant March, with force and arms, feloniously, willfully and of their malice aforethought ...*" The clerk's voice boomed on like an avenging angel.

The soldiers had entered the room and were led to the bar. They all wore new red coats. Their dress boots came up to their knees and were burnished black. Their breeches were the snowiest of white. They wore their swords and gold braid on their hats. And each had been supplied with a white wig, tied in back with a black velvet ribbon.

I had been unable to find a seat, so I stood in back, on tiptoe. I caught a glimpse of Matthew as the soldiers filed in. His face was very white.

"Prisoners hold up your hands," the clerk said.

The soldiers did so. Then Winthrop read the charges, naming the dead.

Maverick, an apprentice lad of seventeen.

Sam Gray, the ropewalker.

Crispus Attucks, the mulatto.

James Caldwell, a sailor from a coasting vessel.

Patrick Carr, who had lived and suffered ten days after being shot.

"How plead you?" Winthrop asked.

One by one the soldiers said, "Not guilty."

"God send you a good deliverance," said the clerk.

The jurors were sworn in. "Good men and true," said the clerk, "stand together and harken to your evidence."

It was cold in the courtroom, though fires burned in hearths at each end. People huddled in their cloaks. I looked at the judges. They wore deep red cloaks and white wigs.

I became frightened. This place had all the solemnity of Sunday meeting and more. One of the judges looked like God himself. A clerk was sitting up front, scribbling notes.

Samuel Quincy, older brother of Josiah, opened for the Crown. And he intoned his words as if he were bringing tablets down from the mountain.

"The cause today," he said, "is perhaps the greatest that has yet come before a tribunal in this part of the British dominions, a cause grounded on the most melancholy event that has yet taken place on the continent of America."

Oh, dear God, I thought, I prayed. *Help us.*

I stayed all day. My feet hurt from standing, so I edged toward a window seat and sat on it. No one seemed to mind. From where I sat I could catch a glimpse of Matthew's face on occasion. This was the day for the prosecution to speak, I'd heard someone say. So all day Sam Quincy brought forth his witnesses for the prosecution. And almost all said the same thing:

"There came seven soldiers from the Main Guard, without any coats on, driving along, swearing and cursing and damning like wild creatures, saying, 'Damn 'em, we are seven . . . by Jesus.' "

The world had gone crazy, I decided. There was Sam Quincy, a Tory, prosecuting the soldiers. While his younger brother Josiah, a Patriot, would defend them.

"Let them come . . . damned Yankee boogers, slay them all." Sam Quincy's witnesses went on.

Another witness testified that "the morning after the riot, Private Kilroy's bayonet was thick with dried blood to three inches from the point."

Still another said Kilroy had told him he would never miss an opportunity to fire on the inhabitants.

Nathaniel Fosdick told of being stabbed by a bayonet thrust from one of the soldiers. He opened his shirt and showed his scar.

And so it went on. And on. I closed my eyes. The Council Chamber began to smell of wet wool and my head began to hurt. I leaned my head against the wall and almost dozed once or twice, then was pulled away by a loud voice.

It was Sam Quincy. "In the events of March

fifth, there was food indeed for the passions to feed on; murder was done *sedato animo*—in cold blood."

It was over for the day. What had happened? People were starting to get up and move. I pushed through the crowds, toward the front of the chamber, hoping to see Matthew before they took him away, hoping he would see me.

"Matthew!" I called. "Matthew."

He turned, saw me, and nodded grimly. "I can't come tomorrow," I mouthed.

He turned away. I was cold and hungry. It was five o'clock. Outside in the cold, the Brattle Street steeple bell rang. The judges left the room. At the long lawyer's table beneath the judges' bench I saw Mr. Adams. He was wearing his best black robe and his wig was freshly powdered. He gave me a brief nod, then went back to his work. His face was very grim and without a glimmer of hope.

The trial went on for over a week. I stayed home and took care of the children. Mrs. Adams went to court every day. Evenings she and her husband would bring young Josiah Quincy home with them. I had been told to feed the children early, which meant I would not be privy to what had gone on in court that day. But after the children were abed, John Adams and Josiah Quincy would retire to Mr. Adams's office and go over the day's proceedings. They would leave the office door open.

Mrs. Adams would sit in the parlor and do some fancy sewing. Then I would bring her tea. From the open door of the office, I would overhear things.

That a witness, Patrick Keeton, had testified how Attucks reached into a woodpile for two four-foot clubs, urged him to take one, then went, cursing and swearing at the soldiers.

That a man named Daniel Cornwall saw citizens throwing oyster shells and snowballs at the sentry at the Custom House door and yelling "Let's burn the sentry box."

That most likely, no witness would ever identify the tall man in the white wig and red cloak who had given his speech in Dock Square.

When I went into Mr. Adams's office late, with a tray of food for him and young Josiah, neither looked at me. All that week, as a matter of fact, neither Mr. nor Mrs. Adams spoke to me directly of the trial. I felt hurt sore about that. Surely they knew how worried I was about Matthew.

But I went about my duties, asking nothing, straining my ears to overhear tidbits of information.

Then, on Sunday evening, December second, John Adams came out of his office while I was serving Mrs. Adams her late evening tea.

"Abigail, Josiah and I have searched the law books for this line and we have found it."

She looked up from her sewing. "Read it to me, John."

I stood holding the teapot, about to pour, as he read:

"Instead of that hospitality that the soldier thought himself entitled to, scorn, contempt, and silent murmurs were his reception. Almost every countenance lowered with a discontented gloom and scarce an eye but flashed indignant fire.

"The soldier had his feelings, his sentiments, and his characteristic passions also . . . The law had taught him to think favorably of himself. Had taught him to consider himself as peculiarly appointed for the safeguard and defense of his country. How stinging was it to be stigmatized as the instrument of tyranny and oppression!"

"It's wonderful, John!" Abigail beamed up at him.

"Yes, yes, I shall use it in court tomorrow." He smiled at me then for the first time in weeks, before returning to his office.

I thought all night of what he had said. His words went round and round in my head, even as I drifted off to sleep in my room.

And, as near as I could figure it, those words described Matthew.

They were the words Matthew had tried to tell me so many times. I fell asleep that night, knowing three things as I had never known them before.

First, the people of Boston had been wrong the

way they treated the soldiers. That was becoming more and more clear to me.

Second, I was as much to blame as anyone who had thrown ice balls or oyster shells at them. I should have taken more time with Matthew. No, I needn't have offered him my favors. Every lady of breeding knew how to keep a young man's attentions while holding his passions at bay. Why hadn't I?

And third, it was as I had originally thought: John Adams could come up with an answer for anybody's problems when he looked in those books of his. And just because I hadn't kept my part of the bargain with him, and he was not going to keep me on, well, it did not diminish what the man could do when he looked into those books. And I had no right to think it did.

On Tuesday, the fourth, I went to court again. It was my day off. I went to hear John Adams tell the jurors that twelve American sailors with big clubs had attacked the British soldiers.

I went and heard him say that "It would be doing violence to every rule of law and evidence, as well as to common sense and the feelings of humanity, to infer from the blood on the bayonet, that it had been stabbed into the brains of Mr. Gray after he was dead, and that by Kilroy himself who had killed him."

And this from the man who had warned me

against Matthew. Who had called him a jack-tar.

I was starting to understand the process of the law. By turns, that day, I found myself elated and plunged into the depths of despair. Once I saw Matthew cover his face with both his hands. I heard John Adams close for the defense, drained, white-faced, mopping his brow. "Gentlemen, to your candor and justice I submit the prisoners and their cause."

Robert Treat Paine closed for the Crown. And everyone quit the chambers and went out into the cold. Tomorrow the jury would bring its verdict. I felt sick at heart. I would not be able to come. I had to work. I would not be able to see Matthew as he stood and was condemned to the gallows.

But I was wrong. That night as I brought Mrs. Adams her tea in the parlor, she looked up at me. "Rachel, I know how deeply you have become entrenched in this. If you think you have the courage to go tomorrow, I shall have Sukey look after the children."

"Oh, ma'am!" I could not believe my ears. Since the trial had been in session she had not discussed it with me. I had thought her considerations were only with her husband.

"Oh, I do not have the courage to go, ma'am," I said. "But I will go. I will be there. And I'll work through next week and not take my day. Oh yes, ma'am, thank you."

Chapter Nineteen

I SCARCELY SLEPT all night. When I did doze off I saw the judges in their red robes, saw the court clerk pointing a finger at me and saying, "*God send you a good deliverance!*"

I heard the clock downstairs strike three. Again I slept.

"*There came seven soldiers from the Main Guard, without any coats on, driving along, swearing and cursing and damning like wild creatures, saying, 'Damn 'em, we are seven.'*"

I awoke feeling sickly the next morning. I could not eat, though Mrs. Adams urged me to. Neither she nor Mr. Adams said much at breakfast. It was like a wake. Even the children were quiet.

I waited until Mr. and Mrs. Adams left, then I put on my cloak and walked to court alone. *There came seven soldiers*. And one of them was Matthew.

———

It seemed like all of Boston was crowded into that chamber and waiting on the stairway and in the courtyard outside.

This day the judges would have their say. Judge Edmund Trowbridge gave a long speech. It was all about riot and rebellion. He even threw the word *treason* in for good measure.

Then Judge Peter Oliver, looking for all the world like God on judgment day, began his rumblings. His dark eyes were round and accusing. His white wig shook when he spoke and for a moment it looked as if it would fall off.

"I never saw," he intoned, "greater malignity of heart expressed in any one piece, a malignity blacker than ever was expressed by the savages of the wilderness."

He was speaking of the people of Boston. Then he quoted General Gage, who had said that "the people of Boston proved to be the most vile set of beings in the whole of Creation."

Then he wrapped his crimson velvet robes around himself and added: "I wish to God the next trial I preside at could be in London. And would result in Sam Adams's head gracing the spikes of Tyburn gate."

The jury was ordered to withdraw and to remember what a terrible burden rested upon them. "If upon the whole," said Judge Peter Oliver, "ye are in any reasonable doubt of their guilt, ye must then, agreeable to the rule of law, declare them innocent."

Everyone waited. Some left for a breath of fresh air and came back to report that a crowd was assembled outside. That started whisperings. What if the soldiers were found not guilty? Would the crowd turn into an ugly mob?

" 'Twouldn't be right," said an older woman near me, "to find them guilty to appease the mob." She said it to me, wagging her head.

I smiled at her from my perch on the window seat. I had a good view from there. I could watch the soldiers, who barely moved on their benches. I tried to get Matthew's attention. He looked my way once, but gave no sign of recognition.

Every quarter hour the clerk would announce the time.

I decided to pray. My religion had never been a source of comfort to me, the reason being that I was Catholic like my 'Protestant-burning' French father. My mother had had me baptized Catholic by a priest whom, she once said, "took his life in his hands by riding circuit through New England's towns." My mother was Congregationalist, like the Adamses, like Uncle Eb. But my churchgoing had been a matter of duty more than faith. Since working for the Adamses I accompanied them to meeting on Sunday to care for the children.

Needless to say, I did not know if my God was Catholic or Congregationalist. But I knew one thing. The jurors were old-time Puritan. And that was not a good sign.

I knew that because I had overheard Mr. Adams tell Abigail that morning that the jury was going to follow its Puritan conscience. And he seemed worried about it.

I decided to pray Catholic that morning. So I said the Lord's Prayer, as my mother had taught me to do. I said it for Matthew and all the soldiers.

Someone said it was two and a half hours that the jury was out. To me it seemed like forever. Then again, it seemed only fifteen minutes.

When the jurors filed back in, John Adams left his wife and went to stand with the soldiers.

"Gentlemen of the jury," said Clerk Sam Winthrop. "Are you all agreed in your verdict?"

"Yes," they said in unison.

Nobody moved in that chamber. Nobody coughed or whispered. All of time seemed to stand still.

"William Wemms," Winthrop ordered, "hold up your hand."

Wemms did so.

"Gentlemen of the jury, look upon the prisoner. How say you of Wemms. Is he guilty of all or either of the felonies or murders whereof he stands indicted, or not guilty?"

"Not guilty," the jury foreman said.

A murmur went through the crowd.

And so it went, as Clerk Winthrop followed the procedure with each soldier.

"How say you of William M'Cauley?"

"Not guilty."

"How say you of James Hartegan?"

"Not guilty."

"How say you of Hugh White?"

"Not guilty."

I felt faint. Sweat was breaking out all over my body, and yet I was cold.

Warren and Carrol were also not guilty.

"How say you of Hugh Montgomery?"

"Not guilty of murder, but guilty of manslaughter."

My heart was beating so fast, I felt faint.

"How say you of Matthew Kilroy?"

I knew the answer before they said it.

"Not guilty of murder, but guilty of manslaughter."

A babbling murmur went up in the courtroom. People started to rise. Then Judge Oliver banged his gavel, demanding silence. In an instant John Adams was on his feet before the judge's bench. At the same time they were leading the six innocent soldiers out of the chamber.

Only Montgomery and Matthew Kilroy remained standing.

I slid off the window seat. John Adams was standing before the judges, his arms raised upward. "My two clients pray the benefit of clergy," he said loudly.

The hubbub in the courtroom subsided. Everyone sat back down and became quiet.

I felt sick. I felt bile rising in my throat. What did it mean? Why had the others been let go and Matthew and Montgomery been convicted? Would they now hang them?

"What's happening?" I turned to the elderly woman who had spoken to me earlier. I was shaking.

"What's happened? Child, they've thrown those two soldiers to the wolves. To satisfy the mob!" Her head shook vigorously. The ribbons on her bonnet shook with the effort. "Now they've gone for the branding iron," she said.

"The *what?*"

"The branding iron. They will be branded on their thumbs. It's a common law custom, which can save them from prison."

"But that's barbaric! Oh, Matthew!"

"It's better than prison. Come now, child, you shouldn't wait to see this. It's barbaric for all those people to watch." Then, just as she said those words, the sheriff brought in a brazier. Someone else brought the branding iron. Everyone in the room rose again and stood on tiptoe. Again Judge

Oliver rapped his gavel and the people sat down.

"No, no!" I could see the branding iron being put into the brazier of hot coals. Then I saw Matthew rise again and offer his thumb. I smelled the burning flesh. It stifled my nostrils. I heard a buzzing sound in my head.

"Matthew!" I cried out. I recollect nothing else then, because I fainted.

Someone was holding something under my nose. "There, missy, it's all over. Come on, get to your feet now." It was Clerk Winthrop. "The only one to faint," he said to the gray-haired woman who had been standing next to me.

They helped me to my feet. "Where is everyone?" I asked.

"Left for the day. The country fair is over," said Clerk Winthrop.

"The soldiers. Where are the soldiers?"

" 'Tis Kilroy she's asking after," said the gray-haired woman.

"In that antechamber off to the side, up front," Winthrop said. "Ye'd best hurry if you want to see him. They'll be conducting the soldiers, under guard, to the wharf for their own safety."

"The wharf?" I asked blankly.

"Aye, and then to Castle Island. Hurry now."

I ran, pushing my way through remaining knots of people, who stood talking, loathe to leave. The whole chamber smelled of burning flesh. I ran in the direction of the buzzing of voices.

In a large room off to the side were the soldiers. They were all standing around John Adams.

"Sir, we are in your debt," said one, "and we always shall be."

John Adams stood in their midst, sheaves of papers in hand.

"We'll always remember you, Mr. Adams," another said.

"God bless you, sir," from a third.

"How's the hands?" Mr. Adams was inquiring of Matthew and Montgomery. "I'm sorry this had to happen."

Matthew was sitting in a chair, nursing his hand. Montgomery was just staring straight ahead, tears in his eyes. "Oh, God," Matthew said, "it hurts like the fires of hell. Forgive me, Mr. Adams. I wanted to take it like a man. I know what you've saved us from. Oh, God, I'm so ashamed." He was crying.

"I've sent for a doctor." John Adams patted Matthew on the shoulder. "Dr. Warren will be here in a minute."

Then suddenly everyone saw me. All the soldiers stared at me as I entered the room. But it was the face of John Adams that I found myself looking into.

It was a long moment of staring. His eyes were,

at first, stern, and I thought, *He is going to order me out. In front of everyone. And he has every right to. But oh, what will I do?*

I have a right to be here! The words came to my lips. Did I dare say them outright to him? *You defended the soldiers, Mr. Adams, because you thought it the right thing to do. And I am here, because I think it is the right thing to do. Is not that what this liberty thing is all about?*

It seemed everyone was watching us. Then John Adams smiled and his eyes went kindly. "Let her through," he said. "She has come to see Matthew."

"This is my friend," Matthew said, introducing me to the others. "She's the lass I've told you about. She's the only true friend I've had in America."

I knew real pride when he said those words. The others murmured their approval. And I saw respect in their eyes. Then Dr. Warren came in, and I stood by while he dressed Matthew's hand and moved on to treat Montgomery.

As Matthew led me to one side of the room, John Adams came over to us. "I shall wait for you, Rachel," he said, before leaving. "My wife and I will escort you home. It's coming on to dark and I can't vouch for the mood of the people in the streets."

"Yes, Mr. Adams. I'll be along shortly."

He nodded. His eyes went from me to Matthew, then back to me again. "You'll have to say good-bye now, you know. They are escorting the soldiers this night to Castle William, the fort on Castle Island. And then home."

"Home?" I asked. "You mean England?"

"Yes," Mr. Adams said softly. "England. They will give you no more now than ten minutes." And he left the room.

I looked at Matthew. *Ten minutes.*

He looked at me. *England.*

And we couldn't even get away from the others to be alone!

Then I saw his misery, felt my own, and knew, though I could not say from whence the knowing came, that I would not make that ten minutes unhappy for him. I smiled. "You'll be going home," I said. "You're free now and no one will be calling you names anymore or throwing things at you."

"Come with me, Rachel," he said.

I stared up at him. Go with him? To England?

"Not now," he murmured. "But afterward. When you are finished working for the Adamses. Follow me to England. I would marry you, Rachel."

I took his hurt hand into my own. "No, Matthew. I couldn't do that. Neither could you. You're not ready to marry anyone just yet. And I . . .

though I care for you deeply, it isn't that kind of caring."

He scowled.

"My spirit does not quicken to you in that way, Matthew. You're grateful to me now. And you are hurt sore. And you are afflicted with loneliness."

Tears came into his eyes.

"When you get home you will forget me," I said.

His shoulders, under the bright red coat, slumped in misery.

I felt time pressing down on us, like a weight on my heart.

"Hear me now, Rachel Marsh," he said, "for there isn't time to argue. We've spent too much time arguing."

I nodded yes.

"I shall not forget you. I shall write to you from England."

"I would like that," I said.

"Mayhap you'll change your mind someday."

"Mayhap."

"I don't know what's going to happen between your country and mine. I've heard tell we'll never reconcile. But know this. Whatever happens, I'll always hold a special place in my heart for America. Because it has women like you."

I could not trust my voice. "I'm not what

women in America are about," I said. "I'm only an indentured servant."

"You are exactly what they are about," he said. "And if they have any sense in their heads they will soon learn that."

"But I'm always muddle-headed. And I never know what I'm about or sure what is the right thing to do."

He smiled. "You've done right, as far as I can see. I wasn't sensible of what a true friend was before I met you. And even after we met, when you tried to teach me, I was too much of a dunderhead to learn."

I could not speak. All the words in my mind formed a tight lump in my throat.

"You've taught me trust," he said. "Now that I've learned it, the road won't be so hard for me anymore."

"Oh, Matthew! That this should be! When all around us our countrymen are fighting each other."

"And will continue to do so, unless I miss my guess," he said glumly. "But as long as two people like us, who were at such odds, could learn to be friends, there's hope, isn't there, Rachel?"

The guards were coming into the room and calling out the soldiers' names. "Yes," I said.

"Kilroy!" the guard was calling. "You there!"

Matthew bent down, put his good hand on the

side of my face and kissed my lips, ever so gently. I closed my eyes. It was more than a kiss. It was a promise. Of what, I did not know. But I knew it was a promise full of hope.

"Thank you," he murmured. "I shall write to you, Rachel."

"Kilroy!" the guard yelled.

"I'm coming!" Matthew said. Then to me, "Where, Rachel, where shall I write?"

I could not think. "In care of John and Abigail Adams," I said, "of Braintree, Massachusetts."

He nodded, took my hand, and raised it to his lips and kissed it. "Until we meet again, Rachel," he said. Then he crossed the room and took his place in line with the rest.

I stood there as they marched out of the room. He was a soldier again, straight and tall. They had taught him to be a soldier. I understood then. They had taught him to kill. Which was why he had shot Gray, then stabbed him afterward.

He couldn't help what they had taught him. Why didn't the people understand that? Why did they hate him and the others so, just for doing and being what they had been taught?

But I had taught him something, too. And he would remember.

As he marched past me his eyes met mine and he smiled.

Their footsteps sounded in cadence on the

wooden floors. I watched their backs. His was so straight under the red woolen coat.

Matthew!

No, don't take him away yet. We didn't have time! There was so much to say. It isn't fair. Matthew, don't go!

He was gone. I turned to the wall and blew my nose in my apron. Then I turned around. The room was empty, as if he'd never been here at all.

I sat very still on one of the straight-backed cherry chairs in the Adamses' parlor. My eyes went over the familiar things: the marble-topped tables, so smooth; the graceful lines of the draperies; the tall clock ticking in the corner, never missing a beat.

Always I had looked to these delicate and graceful household furnishings to not only soften the edges of my world, but to hold it up at the same time. I had thought such trappings had made Abigail Adams the woman she was.

What a foolish child I had been to think such. I knew now that you could grow strong and straight inside even if you never had nine straight-backed cherry chairs in your parlor.

I understood now that you could be as soft as the silken draperies, shine like the copper candle holders, and have something tick quietly inside you and never miss a beat, even if you lived in a rude sod hut in the wilderness.

It had been a long time in the learning for me. And I was not sure I fathomed it all yet.

Behind the closed door of Mr. Adams's office I heard murmurings. I held my breath and waited. Miss Alice Pattishell was in there conferring with Mr. Adams.

Thanks to Lucy Flucker, Mr. Adams had agreed to meet with Miss Pattishell, who was, this very moment, trying to convince him that her Quaker sister in Philadelphia would do well by me if I were allowed to go into her employ.

Miss Pattishell's sister had a fine, three-story brick house, a husband, and three children. Her sister's husband was a physician, held in high esteem.

Quakers were held in high esteem in Philadelphia. Not considered heretics as they were here in Boston. And they would pay me well.

Mr. Adams would decide. My fate was in his hands. He had contacted Uncle Eb, who had given him full authority to make the decision.

As I sat there waiting, my heart was tearing in two. I did not want to leave Boston. I would miss my friends, Jane and Henry and Lucy. In the last week since the end of the trials I had gone to visit Henry Knox's shop, bringing a pie I had cooked as a peace offering.

As it turned out the peace offering was not necessary, although Henry and Lucy and I enjoyed it with hot chocolate in his back room as we had done so often in the past.

"Do you think I should go to Philadelphia?" I'd asked Henry.

"By all means," he'd answered. "What other avenue is open to you?"

"Working for Lucy's parents," I said. "Her sister insists they want me. Mr. Adams says it would be a fine opportunity."

"That is no opportunity," Lucy said instantly. "My sisters want a ladies' maid. They would treat you shabbily."

"Mr. Adams is considering it," I told her.

"Then I shall have to meet with him"—she smiled prettily—"and convince him that Philadelphia would be a new start for you. Away from the madness of Boston. This is a mad town, you know. It always has been, since Puritan times."

"She's right," Henry had intoned. "Boston always needs a cause to fight for. They've won this one. The troops are gone. But there will soon be another."

"My father thinks the Whig party is falling to pieces," Lucy said, "and the people are tired of sacrifice. And that Massachusetts will now be dependent, dutiful, and loyal to the Crown again. But I think him to be wrong."

"You think right, Love," Henry agreed. "For a while, things will settle down. But the seed of rebellion has been planted. And in due season it will bloom."

And so, true to her word, Lucy Flucker had asked for and won an audience with Mr. Adams. She convinced him to interview Miss Alice Pattishell.

So it was that I now sat on the straight-backed cherry chair in the parlor, waiting for news of my fate.

The door opened. Mr. Adams gestured that I should come in. Miss Pattishell smiled at me as I sat down.

"Well, Rachel, it is agreed. You shall go to Philadelphia," Mr. Adams said.

My heart was racing inside me like a rabbit pursued by a hound. "Thank you, sir."

"You will receive a fine wage and work in a commodious house for genteel people as a nursemaid to their children. This is a second chance for you, Rachel. Do make the best use of it."

I met his eyes. I knew what he was saying to me. *Don't get yourself mixed up with the rabble in the streets.*

But who was the rabble? And hadn't the rabble won their Cause here in Boston? Wasn't his own cousin Sam their leader? And hadn't he, John Adams himself, been elected as a representative from Boston to the Legislature, because the rabble—the people—liked him so? Hadn't he helped the Sons get out their newspaper and prepared legal papers for them on so many occasions?

It came to me that Mr. John Adams of Braintree and of Boston did not yet know that he, too, had become part of the rabble. That he had become a plain American. I wished I could be around the day he became sensible of it.

"Yes, sir," I said.

"Tonight will be your last night under our roof. I have given Miss Pattishell a fine letter of recommendation for you."

"Thank you, Mr. Adams."

"Your uncle Eb wishes to see you tomorrow morning before you meet Miss Pattishell at the wharf to begin your journey. I have paid your passage. And I will give you the specie part of your dowry tonight. Luke will help you get your things in the chaise and take you to the wharf."

I nodded. See Uncle Eb? Well, I supposed I could manage that. He couldn't hurt me anymore.

"Good day to you, Miss Pattishell," Mr. Adams said. "Rachel will show you out. Come back then, Rachel, there is one more thing we must discuss."

"I know how you love the children, Rachel," he said. He was standing in back of his desk, hands clasped behind him. "And the affection they have for you."

"I love them very much, sir," I said.

"Do you love them enough to spare them the agony of farewell?"

I could not believe what he was asking! Not say good-bye to the children?

"They will not understand your leaving, Rachel. They are too young. Good-byes will only hurt them. And you. If you agree, we will explain things to them. We think it best this way. If you will agree," he repeated.

My mind was in a whirl. It's cruel, I minded. Yet it was clean and tidy. How like John Adams, the lawyer. I thought I had learned all there was to learn in his house, but I hadn't. There was now to be one final lesson.

His eyes were on me, waiting for my reply. I should do this thing he asks, I told myself, though it will tear my heart in two. He has done everything to spare me hurt. Neither he nor his wife remonstrated with me about my running with the mob. They never told me that I had failed in my duties to them.

I had put such behavior down to their years of genteel breeding. After all, Mr. Adams's great grandfather had come to America in 1630. There had been plenty of time for genteel breeding in his family. Not to mention that his wife's ancestors had helped found the Province.

All the time I had wasted, pondering on how I, who had no breeding, could become like them. And now, here it was, given to me to know.

It had to do with sacrifice. With thinking of another's feelings before one's own. No matter the price demanded of the heart.

He was asking me to help protect his children. No, with his eyes, he was begging.

I drew myself up to stand as straight as I could. If you're going to have breeding, Rachel Marsh, I told myself, this is as good a place to start as any. And be gracious about it.

"Very well, sir. I'll not tell them good-bye. But may I leave them each a little gift, as a token of remembrance? Perhaps I could leave it on their beds in the morning, early, while they are still sleeping."

He seemed to breathe a sigh of relief. "That would be fine, Rachel, yes," he said. "And thank you."

But, I decided, I will go even further to show the Adamses that I, too, could act with breeding. It came to me, as I prepared for bed that night, what I must do.

I opened my dowry chest and took out my beautiful linens and laid them out on the woven rug beneath me.

I ran my hands over them, lovingly. How many hours I had labored doing the stitches on the hem of my bed sheets. How I had pricked my fingers, sewing the lace on the edges of the pillow slips. How many evenings I had strained my eyes, working by candlelight, embroidering the edges of the two fine linen tablecloths.

I picked up the bed cover worked in crewel. It had been a labor of love. The crewelwork was done in deep rich tones of crimson and blue, green and black. Mrs. Adams had helped me with the design. There were peacocks with colorful tails in each corner. Cabbage roses on the border.

Oh, how I had dreamed of placing that cover on my marriage bed someday.

Then I took my pots and skillets and household utensils out of the wooden chest where they were packed for shipping.

Eight pewter plates, there were. Eight mugs. Three wooden bowls. A skillet on legs. A large cast-iron pot and three smaller pots with copper bottoms.

All this, together with the small sack of hard silver that Mr. Adams had given me that evening, was my dowry. I had worked for it. It was the start of my household. I would not go penniless when I found a husband.

Carefully, I put the household utensils back in their wooden crate. With almost a mystical sense of purpose, I folded the linens and put them back in the dowry chest that Mr. Adams's brother had made for me. I closed the chest carefully, breathing in the fresh scent of cedar. I ran my hands, lovingly, over its smooth contours.

Then, by the light of one meager candle, I wrote the letter. It took a long time, because what I had to say must be said just right.

I drew on every strength I had. And once again was flooded with a sense of purpose to sustain me. When the letter was finished, I folded the paper carefully and placed it on top of my dowry chest. Then I went to bed.

In the morning I was up before first light. The clock downstairs had just struck five. I lit my one candle and dressed quickly in the cold, moving around silently so as not to make any noise.

I dressed in my second-best petticoat and short gown and chemise. I wore my go-to-market cloak. In my one piece of baggage, I had my go-to-meeting dress. And the old clothes I had worn when I first came here. I would have put them on, but I was mindful that I had to look respectable when I met my new employers. And they did not fit me right anymore.

All the other clothing Mrs. Adams had made for me I left laid out on the bed. Then, with my one piece of baggage, I took a last look around the room, blew out the candle, and crept down the hall to where the children were sleeping.

Carefully, I leaned over Johnnie and kissed his delicate face and left a small package of maple sugar next to his pillow. Then I turned to Nabby. Her dark hair fanned out over the pillow. At five, she was already very vain of it. I kissed her forehead and left on her pillow my very best silk ribbon, to use in her own hair. The baby, too young to miss me, was in his parents' room.

Then I left. Never in my whole life did I realize that a body could feel so low and still be able to do what was expected of them.

I closed the back door carefully and stepped out into the cold. A faint light was appearing in the east. There was also lantern light in the small barn at the end of the yard.

Luke, I thought. *He's up and about already and feeding the horse. If I walk very carefully, I can get off without being seen.* I was halfway across the yard to the side gate when he called me.

"Rachel?"

I stopped. He came across the frozen ground,

holding a lantern, peering at me. "Is it time already?"

"No, I'm early, Luke. I thought I'd walk."

"I've my instructions to take you in the chaise. Mr. Adams will skin me for letting you go off alone. Say, where are your things?"

"I have all my things. Right here. I showed him my one piece of baggage.

He looked at it, then at me. Up and down, he looked at me. Saw my second-best dress, my go-to-market cloak. Then he nodded. "So, you're leavin' like you came, is that it?"

"Yes, Luke. I have everything I need. And more."

"Have you now?"

"Yes."

"And where's the dowry chest then? And the crate of household items?"

"Upstairs."

"And your payment in hard money? Upstairs, too?"

"Yes."

He nodded approvingly. "Always did think you were an independent little piece."

"I'm trying to be, Luke."

I saw the gleam of appreciation in his eyes. "Good for you," he said.

I smiled at him. He'd sprouted up in the two

and a half years I'd known him. And I felt sad then
that I hadn't taken the time to know him better.

"So you won't let me escort you to your uncle's
then?"

"No, Luke. I want to go alone. The streets are
quiet now. I have some thinking to do. And my
friends, Henry Knox and Lucy and Jane, will come
to the warehouse later and fetch me to the wharf."

"Well"—and he held out his hand—"Godspeed then, Rachel Marsh. I'm proud to have known
you."

Tears came to my eyes as I took his hand.
"Thank you, Luke. Godspeed to you, too."

Boston's streets were still silent. Mist rolled in
off the harbor and my footsteps echoed. One by
one, as I passed the houses, I saw candles being
lighted in upper windows. I heard a dog bark, a
bell begin to toll. From the direction of the wharves
came the call of a butter-milk-and-eggs vendor.
Soon housewives would be opening their doors to
buy fresh fish, fruits, live poultry brought in carts
to their doors.

I walked quickly, lest my resolve weaken and
I should take to running back. For there was still
time to have a change of heart, to slip back into
the house and take the small bag of silver, tell Luke
I'd taken leave of my senses, to carry down my
things and get them into the chaise.

Within twenty minutes I was at the front door of Uncle Eb's warehouse.

"So, they have thrown you out, have they?"

Once again I stood in his small dark office, the cavernous, yawning mouth of the warehouse black behind me.

"They have not. I choose to leave and go on."

He laughed. "They threw you out. Put any fancy label you want on the going. They won't have you anymore, since you disgraced yourself with that soldier."

I did not reply. I had determined that I would not debate with him. He was having his breakfast, brought to him on a tray by one of his lackeys. Eggs and fish and tea.

Tea! The fragrance of it near drove me wild. My mouth watered. I had taken no nourishment before leaving.

"I told you it wasn't your home and they weren't your people, didn't I, girl?"

I did not reply.

"I told you they may buy you books, allow you to sit at their breakfast table, clothe you in frippery, but that didn't make them family. Didn't I say such?"

"Yes, you did," I said dully.

"Well then? Was I right?" He took a gulp of tea. "I told you they come from old and venerable and monied people. The kind who make their way

315

by stepping on the rest of us. You were a servant to them. No more."

"I had no desire to be more," I said calmly.

"Oh yes, you did. Don't lie to your old uncle Eb. I've known you since you were born. You had some fancy notions there for a while. Well, you have been disabused of them now, haven't you?"

I felt no obligation to answer.

He peered at me in the half-light. He frowned. "Is that how they sent you off into the world? In those clothes? Where's that good woolen cloak you were wearing last time we met? Where's that fancy short gown with the print straight from France?"

"I've taken nothing from them," I said.

"Eh? What's that you say? Taken nothing? Mr. Adams said they would dower you. Did he not keep his word?"

"He did. I had a whole linen dowry. And a dowry chest. And household items aplenty. And hard silver."

"Had? Had? What d'ye mean *had?* What happened to it all, girl?"

"I left it there."

"Left it there?" His face went red first, then purple. He coughed on a morsel of food. For a moment I thought he would choke to death in front of me. He took up his cup and gulped more tea, drank it, and wiped his mouth with his hand, still

gasping for air. "Left it there? What are you saying, girl? Explain yourself."

I did not know if I could. Surely I would never be able to explain it to anybody, probably not even myself at times when I lay on my bed in Philadelphia, alone and lonely.

Oh yes, Luke had understood. But Luke had not needed an explanation to understand. Anybody who needed an explanation would never understand, I decided. But I took a deep breath and plunged in, anyway.

"I left everything. All of it. And a note, thanking them for everything they had given me, but explaining that I had to leave it. So they would know what kind of person I was."

He stared at me, wild-eyed. "A crazed person, is what!" he said.

I went on. "No. I gave it much thought, Uncle Eb. You see, I disappointed the Adamses. By running with the rabble. If they can indeed be called rabble. And by walking out with Matthew and feeding him in jail. And yet they never placed blame on me."

"They threw you out, instead."

"I was a nursemaid to the children. As such my behavior should have been above reproach. They simply decided I should not go back to Braintree with them, that's all."

317

"Threw you out, fool girl," he said again. "Don't you have the sense to know it?"

"They never *let* me know it, Uncle Eb. Never let me feel such. Because they are people of honor and breeding."

"People of money, you mean."

"It's more than money. I don't know what it is. And ever since I went to work for them, I tried to ponder it. And how I could be like them. And so I decided, the only way to show them that I could be, was to not take my dowry. In the note I asked them to give my things to the next girl."

"Fool!" He slammed his fist down on the desk so that I almost jumped out of my skin. "Just like your mother!"

I smiled.

"No. Like your father. That Protestant-burning father, who ran off to get himself killed. For what? Did he ever know?"

"I think he knew, Uncle Eb."

"Fool! You earned that dowry. And you shall have it! You shall turn right around now and go back and get it! I shall go with you!" He started to get up.

"Sit down, Uncle Eb," I ordered quietly. "I will not go back. I don't need it. I can make it on my own." I said the words loud and plain and with such force that they echoed in the warehouse. He was taken aback by my strength of purpose. He sat back down.

"You worked so hard," he whispered. "You had a good place. And now you've lost it."

"No, Uncle Eb. I thought so, too, in the beginning. I thought my place was with the Adamses. But it isn't. Don't you understand? I've found that out."

"Then where *is* it? In Philadelphia with some overzealous Quakers? You've lost the best place you've ever had a shot at, girl."

I spoke plain again. "My place, Uncle Eb, is wherever I choose it to be. Because of what I have become."

"A dafter is what you've become."

"No, Uncle Eb. I have become a plain American. A true American. I know now what I am and what I'm about. I know how to make choices and speak up for myself. And I like that feeling. And for the first time in my life, I know I have found a place."

He growled at me. Like an old bear. He waved a disgruntled hand. "That's all over with now, that nonsense of liberty and rebellion," he said. "Boston's shops are filling up with merchandise from England again. I'm importing woolens and brocades and satins and velvets. The people want it. They want the king's favors."

"I don't," I said. "Because I have no king, Uncle

319

Eb. I don't *need* one. And lots of other people out there don't, either. More and more people every day feel as I do. We don't need anybody to do for us. We can do for ourselves. And that's the place I've found, Uncle Eb. That's why I left my dowry, too. The Adamses will understand when they read my note. And they will respect me for it."

"You can't wear respect. It doesn't keep you warm in the cold," he growled.

"It does me, Uncle Eb."

He glared at me. I could tell he was trying to figure out how daft I had become. And if I was worth the bother. He decided then. "Get out of my sight," he said. "Don't darken my door again. Begone with you."

I picked up my one piece of baggage. "Goodbye, Uncle Eb," I said.

He did not answer. I made my way out of the warehouse and through the front office. The sun was shining brightly now. It was going to be a good day for a voyage to Philadelphia.

"Rachel!"

I had difficulty adjusting my eyes to the brightness of the world outside. I stood there a moment, hearing someone call my name.

"Over here, Rachel." Then I saw the chaise. With Henry Knox driving and Lucy sitting right up there next to him, pert as can be. Then out of it jumped Jane. She ran toward me. "We've got sweet buns," she said, "and a jug of hot coffee. Come along."

Then she stopped and looked at me, took in my appearance, my absence of possessions, and her eyes narrowed and she broke into a grin. "You didn't," she said.

"Yes, I did, Jane."

She shrugged. "Well, it's your decision to make," she said. She handed me a sweet bun and I jumped into the chaise. She poured hot coffee out of the jug into mugs. And we ate and joked and laughed as we drove to the wharves. And neither Lucy nor Henry remarked on my appearance or my one scant portmanteau.

So it was as I thought then, I minded. I was right. Anybody who needed an explanation about what I'd done wouldn't understand. And then there were the people who understood right off, and who were of like mind and spirit. And who would never need an explanation.

And there would be more and more people like that every day, who didn't need anybody to do for them. But who would do for themselves. And I was one of them. I had found my proper place. I was sure of it.

Author's Note

THE BOSTON MASSACRE is a part of American history that has long been ignored in fiction, though most everyone has heard of it and claims interest.

When I started my research, I could not help likening the massacre to the Los Angeles riots in 1992. There were many similarities. And the country was breathlessly awaiting the verdict from the second trial of the police officers involved in the L.A. affair just as I was revising the manuscript.

Indeed, when I give school talks and tell young people the ingredients that led to the Boston Massacre and ask them what it reminds them of, they immediately respond, "The L.A. riots."

It is by drawing such lines between the past and the present that I hope to help young readers realize that some historic events happened because of the everyday feelings of the people involved, whose concerns and aspirations were not so very different from those of young readers today.

I hope to make them understand that "history" is not that far in the past—and that they can easily identify with it.

Once I discovered that I could present John Hancock not as the person who penned the largest signature on the Declaration of Independence but as the rich, altruistic young merchant determined not to let British Customs men on his ships and to risk his fortune by fighting the Townsend Acts, I was pulled into the drama of Boston in 1770.

There I found John Adams, a young lawyer from Braintree, Massachusetts, whose cousin Sam was a leader of the American rebellion. I found John's lovely and intelligent wife, Abigail, whose parlor was the meeting place for women far ahead of their time in their intellectual pursuits.

I found young Henry Knox, bookseller, who later became General Knox in General George Washington's rebel army. And I discovered the "mob" and learned that when the mob was out at night in Boston, terrible things could happen. And did happen.

In 1770 Boston was practically under mob rule. The mob was a multilayered group that included foremost citizens like the wealthy John Hancock and Dr. Joseph Warren (later killed in the battle of Bunker Hill), the silversmith and "betimes dentist" Paul Revere, the Sons of Liberty, and the unruly street urchins who were sometimes paid to harangue the British soldiers.

One of those street urchins was Chris Snider (or Snyder or Seider), who was shot by Tories during one of the mob's escapades, whose funeral was attended by hundreds, and whose death became the focal point for the anger of the Patriots.

As with many movements or rebellions or causes, there were those who were involved in the massacre for the violence of it, or to avenge personal grievances. And then there were those brought in to act as "antagonists."

From reading Hiller B. Zobel, whose work *The Boston Massacre* has projected him as the acknowledged authority on the event, I learned that Crispus Attucks was one of these, an agitator brought in from elsewhere to help move the mob to action.

This tradition in America of involving outsiders to push for action was apparently started in 1770. If not for the agitators in Boston at that time, we would have had no groundwork laid for the American Revolution.

Having been pulled into my story, I then had to choose my protagonist. Abigail Adams was married, a mother, and too old to be a heroine of a young adult novel. I searched the books and my mind. And then I found Rachel Marsh.

But first John Adams had to find her. What I

actually found was John Adams *looking* for Rachel, or someone like her, to help his wife in the house.

In *The Book of Abigail and John, Selected Letters of the Adams Family,* 1762–1784, John Adams pens a letter to Abigail:

> I have this Evening been to see the Girl. What Girl? Pray what Right have you to go after Girls? Why, my Dear, the Girl I mention to you, Miss Alice Brackett. But Miss has hitherto acted in the Character of an House-Keeper, and her noble aspiring Spirit had rather rise to be a Wife than descend to be a Maid.
>
> To be serious, however, she says her Uncle, whose House she keeps, cannot possibly spare her, these two Months, if then, and she has no Thoughts of leaving him till the Spring, when she intends for Boston to become a Mantua Maker.
>
> So that We are still to seek. Girls enough from fourteen to four and Twenty, are mentioned to me, but the Character of every Mothers Daughter of them is as yet problematicale to me. Hannah Crane (pray don't you want to have her, my Dear) has sent several Messages to my Mother, that she will live as cheap as any Girl in the

Country. She is stout and able and for what I know willing, but I fear not honest, for which Reason I presume you will think of her no more.

Another Girl, one Rachel Marsh, has been recommended to me as a clever Girl and a neat one and one that wants a Place . . .

And so it was that I found Rachel. The Adamses did take her on as an indentured servant, and she is referred to in several books and in Irving Stone's biographical novel of the Adamses, *Those Who Love*.

For the sake of story, I invented Rachel's background. I did pick up on the theme of her "wanting a Place." Indeed, it formed the core of Rachel's character in my book.

At a certain point in time, according to historical accounts, Rachel disappears from the Adamses'—actually, just when they move back to Braintree after the trial in which John Adams defends the British soldiers. I assume that in reality they gave her the promised dowry and she went on her way. But my Rachel refused the dowry for the sake of drama and story.

I have, as in all my historical novels, been as faithful to the history of the time as possible. John Adams was a young, ambitious lawyer in Boston in

1770, who took a chance on sacrificing his career to defend the British soldiers when no one else would do so, because, to paraphrase him, "We want to be a free people, and the first right of a free people is that of legal counsel."

The British soldiers who came to Boston in 1768 came as "peacekeepers." How often have we heard that term used in the same spirit in our own time? "To keep the peace"—isn't that why our army has often been sent to trouble spots? The American Revolution was the Vietnam War of the British army. From their arrival in fall of 1768 to the time of the massacre in March of 1770, the British soldiers were treated horribly by the populace of Boston. The Boston Massacre, it is said, had to happen, or someone would have invented it. It was as unavoidable, perhaps, as the L.A. riots, and as was true of the L.A. riots, no one actually knows whom to blame, who was responsible.

Matthew Kilroy was one of the British soldiers from the Twenty-ninth regiment who did sentry duty. I placed him in front of the Adamses' house, just as a sentry stood guard there every night and challenged all who entered. Kilroy was one of the soldiers who went to work at Gray's Ropewalk Works to make money. He was involved in fighting there and, ultimately, in the massacre.

Henry Knox was courting Lucy Flucker at the

time. She was the light of his life, though her family disapproved of him. Henry and Lucy met often in his bookstore. He married her, and they loved each other dearly and lived to a happy old age together.

A maid to Sarah Welsteed (who was sister to Lieutenant Governor Thomas Hutchinson) did spend the Sunday evening before the riot with some ropewalk brawlers. It was then that this nameless maid, whom I bring to life as Jane Washburn, overheard talk that there would be a fight on Monday evening between the townsfolk and the soldiers. This maid passed such news on to her mistress, but her mistress apparently did not pass the word on to her brother until it was too late to do anything about the situation.

The *Boston Gazette* was called the "weekly dung barge" by the Tories, and, yes, Paul Revere did exaggerate what happened at the massacre in his sketches for the *Gazette* to sensationalize. The two convicted soldiers did have their thumbs branded as punishment after the trial. This was a bizarre practice in English common law that was meted out in place of imprisonment.

I cite these historical facts to make an attempt to distinguish history from what I have made up. It is impossible here to point out every historical accuracy or put forth a tidy disclaimer for every bit of literary license. These examples, however, should give readers an idea how my writing mingles fact and fiction.

In *The Fifth of March,* I did not have to make up much. The events leading to the actual massacre, the drama and color of Boston at that time, the massacre itself, and the wonderful, real characters who populated the city, all lend themselves to the making of a novel.

But the book is still a novel. Fiction. It is my interpretation of the events that led up to and surrounded the massacre. There are many factual books readers can consult to pursue the truth. I hope to kindle the minds of readers, like the agitators kindled the flame of the American Revolution.

—Ann Rinaldi
May 1993

Bibliography

The books and maps I found most helpful when writing this novel are listed here, with my heartfelt thanks to the scholars and historians who researched, wrote, or rendered them.

MAPS

Boston, Massachusetts, in 1769, reproduced from an engraving in the collection of Ambassador and Mrs. J. William Middendorf II. Courtesy of the United States Department of the Interior, National Park Service, Boston National Historical Park, Charlestown Navy Yard, Boston.

Boston, Massachusetts, and Vicinity, 1775, reproduced from an engraving in the Cornell University Library. Courtesy of the United States Department of the Interior, National Park Service, Boston National Historical Park, Charlestown Navy Yard, Boston.

BOOKS

Bowen, Catherine Drinker. *John Adams and the American Revolution*. Boston: Little, Brown and Company, 1950.

Brooks, Noah. *Henry Knox: A Soldier of the Revolution*. New York: Da Capo Press, 1974.

Butterfield, L. H., Marc Friedlaender, and Mary Jo Kline. *The Book of Abigail and John: Selected Letters of the Adams Family, 1762–1784*. Cambridge, MA: Harvard University Press, 1975.

Forbes, Ester. *Paul Revere and the World He Lived In*. Boston: Houghton Mifflin Company, 1942.

Miller, Lillian B. *In the Minds and Hearts of the People: Prologue to the American Revolution: 1760–1774*. Greenwich, CT: New York Graphic Society, 1974.

Stone, Irving. *Those Who Love: A Biographical Novel of Abigail and John Adams*. New York: Doubleday & Company, 1965.

Whitehill, Walter Muir. *Boston: A Topographical History*. Cambridge, MA: The Belknap Press of Harvard University Press, 1959.

Zobel, Hiller B. *The Boston Massacre*. New York: W.W. Norton & Company, Inc., 1970.

GREAT EPISODES

Other titles now available:

JENNY OF THE TETONS
by Kristiana Gregory

THE LEGEND OF JIMMY SPOON
by Kristiana Gregory

GUNS FOR GENERAL WASHINGTON
by Seymour Reit

UNDERGROUND MAN
by Milton Meltzer

A RIDE INTO MORNING
The Story of Tempe Wick
by Ann Rinaldi

EARTHQUAKE AT DAWN
by Kristiana Gregory

THE PRIMROSE WAY
by Jackie French Koller

WHERE THE BROKEN HEART STILL BEATS
by Carolyn Meyer

A BREAK WITH CHARITY
A Story About the Salem Witch Trials
by Ann Rinaldi

*Look for exciting new titles to come in the
Great Episodes series of historical fiction.*